Karen,

I hope you enjoy
vicarious trip to Italy!
See you at a SinC meeting soon!
Maureen Klovers

Murder Under the Tuscan Sun

Also by Maureen Klovers:

The Secret Poison Garden (Rita Calabrese Mystery Series, #1)

A Secret in Thyme (Rita Calabrese Mystery Series, #2)

Murder in the Moonshine (Rita Calabrese Mystery Series, #3)

Of Masques and Murder (Rita Calabrese Mystery Series, #4)

Hagar's Last Dance (Jeanne Pelletier Mystery Series, #1)

Graveside Reunion (Jeanne Pelletier Mystery Series, #2)

In the Shadow of the Volcano: One Ex-Intelligence Official's Journey through Slums, Prisons, and Leper Colonies to the Heart of Latin America (memoir)

Murder Under the Tuscan Sun

Maureen Klovers

Chesapeake Books

Murder Under the Tuscan Sun is a work of fiction. Names, characters, places, and incidents are either the product of the author's imagination or are used fictitiously. Any resemblance to actual persons, living or dead, or to actual events is purely coincidental.

ISBN: 0999494163
ISBN-13: 9780999494165

Cover design by Ken Leeder

For my sister, Christelle, who brilliantly suggested that Rita solve her next murder in Italy

ITALIAN-ENGLISH GLOSSARY

(Note: Only terms that are not immediately obvious from the text are included here. Approximate pronunciation shown in parentheses.)

Altra volta (Al-tra VOL-ta)–Again. Literally, another time.

Aperitivo (a-per-ee-TEE-vo)–The Italian equivalent of happy hour. Typically consists of a light, dry, alcoholic beverage such as prosecco or an Aperol spritz, accompanied by light salty snacks (olives, nuts, crostini) meant to whet the appetite for dinner later.

Arrabbiatissima (a-RAB-ee-a-TEE-see-ma) – Very, very angry. The 'issimo/issima' ending on Italian adjectives makes it superlative–and very fun to say!

Aspetti (as-PAY-tee) – Wait! This is the formal (i.e. polite) version of the command.

Bistecca alla fiorentina (bis-TAY-ka a-la fee-or-en-TEEN-a) – Literally "a Florentine steak." A T-bone steak that is char-grilled on the outside and very rare on the inside; a specialty of Tuscany and, in particular, Florence (hence the name).

Brindisi (brin-dee-zee) – Toast (i.e., propose a toast).

Bugiardo (boo-JAR-do)–Liar.

Buon giorno (BWON JOR-no) – Good day (a greeting).

Buona sera (BWON-a SARE-ah) – Good evening.

Cantucci (Can-TOO-chee) – Almond biscotti originally from Tuscany, traditionally served for dessert with a sweet *vin santo* (see below).

Caro/cara (CAR-o, CAR-a) – Dear (for a man if ending in -o, for a woman if ending in -a). A term of endearment.

Certo/certo che non! (CHAIR-toe, CHAIR-toe kay non) – Certainly/of course, certainly not!

Chiacchierando (key-ah-key-air-AN-do)—Chatting.

Commissario (co-mee-SAR-ee-oh)—Detective. An official Italian police rank - not a term used for amateur sleuths.

Che c'è? (Kay chay?) – What is it? What's wrong?

Dai! (DIE!) – Come on!

Ecco!—There it is! From the Latin "ecce," as in "ecce homo" ("there he is/behold the man").

Enoteca (eh-no-TAY-ka)—Wine bar. Plural is *enoteche*.

Figlia (FEEL-ya)—Daughter.

Indagine (in-DA-jee-nay)—Investigation.

Le voci corrono (lay VO-chee CORE-oh-no)—People gossip. Literally, the voices run (around and around, until everyone hears them!).

Lo so (lo SO)—I know (it).

Mangia! (MAHN-jee-ah) – Eat! (command)

Mi dispiace (Mee dis-pee-A-chay) – Sorry (literally, it displeases me).

Niente (nee-EN-tay)–Nothing.

Non ci credo (non chee CRAY-do)–I don't believe it.

Non ho capito (non oh ca-PEE-to)–I don't understand. Literally, I didn't understand. To Italians, this is always in the past tense since they didn't understand and they still don't!

Non ti preocupare (Non tee pray-o-coo-PAR-ay) – Don't worry.

Nonna (NO-na)/nonno (NO-no) – Grandma/Grandpa

Piccolo paese (PEE-co-lo pie-AY-zay)–Small town. Interestingly, *paese* can mean country (as in the country of Italy) or town, probably because of Italy's long history of city-states.

Poverino/poverina (Po-ver-EE-no/Po-ver-EE-na) – Poor (not low-income, but to be pitied).

Prima colazione (PREE-ma co-LATZ-ee-O-nee)–Breakfast.

Primo piatto (PREE-mo pee-A-toe)–First course. Literally, first plate.

Principessa (Prin-chee-PAY-sa) – Princess.

Ricordi (ree-COR-dee)–Remember.

Rifiuti (ree-fee-OO-tee)–Trash, refuse.

Salute (Sa-LOO-tay)–A toast to your health, literally just "health."

Sei d'accordo? (say dee-a-COR-do)—Do you agree? Literally, are you of agreement?

Spengi questo maledetto telefonino (SPAIN-yee QWEST-o MAL-ay-DET-to tel-ay-fo-NEE-no)—Turn off that darn phone. *Telefonino* literally means "little phone" but has come to mean "cell phone."

Spremuta d'arancia (spray-MOO-ta dar-AN-chee-aa)—Fresh-squeezed orange juice, often made with Sicilian blood oranges. The best you'll ever taste.

Stonzo (STRONTZ-o) – A not very nice word for a not very nice man.

Strega (STRAY-ga)—Witch. Usually not used in the literal sense but meaning a not very nice woman.

Subito subito (SOO-bee-to SOO-bee-to)—Right away. Repeating a word twice in Italian gives it extra emphasis.

Svegliati (SVEL-ya-tee)—Wake up!

Ti prendo (tee PREN-do)—I am coming to get you (pick you up).

Vedi/vedete (VAY-dee/vay-DAY-tay)—You see. Or, if a question, did you see? *Vedi* is the informal singular form, *vedete* is the plural form. *Vedete quello che abbiamo scoperto* means "see what we have found (discovered)."

Vieni (vee-EH-nee)—Come!

Vin santo (Vin SAN-to) – A sweet wine from Tuscany, traditionally served after dinner with *cantucci*. Literally, "holy wine."

ACKNOWLEDGMENTS

I don't know if it takes a village to raise a child, but it certainly takes a village to research and write a book!

Friends, family, and even very generous strangers pitched in with recipes, suggestions, and fascinating historical tidbits. My friend and fellow Italophile Barbara Brown dug up a recipe from a friend's long-gone patisserie to help me salvage a pear and almond tart recipe that went awry. (People often ask me at conferences whether I've had any kitchen disasters when creating the recipes for my book. The answer is, nearly always—most recipes require at least two or three attempts. This time, only my peaches with mascarpone and *pici* with pesto made the cut the first time!) Mandy Klovers, who is a fantastic baker (with a first-place ribbon in a pie-making contest to prove it!) and fortuitously my sister-in-law, generously provided her caramel apple coffeecake recipe which, after some tweaks, became the delicious blueberry sour cream coffeecake recipe you'll find at the end of the book.

My cousin, Julie Cline, determined that the perfect cat for a fastidious German archaeologist would be a Siamese, a suggestion I happily adopted. Pharmacist Luci Zahray, known to the mystery-writing community as "The Poison Lady," generously advised me on the toxicity of oleander.

Ken Leeder in the U.K. created my beautiful cover design, which very much puts me in mind of my own vacation at an *agriturismo* outside Volterra!

One of the highlights of researching this book was meeting the delightful Maureen Fant, a classical archaeologist turned Rome-based translator and food writer, and Liz Bartman, former head of the Archaeological Institute of America and the Etruscan Foundation. Together, they run Elifant Archaeo-Culinary Tours in Italy. Over a ninety-minute Zoom call, they most generously shared their knowledge of Tuscan ruins, customs, technology, and foodways, and prevented me from making some embarrassing mistakes. Maureen must have rattled off a hundred authentic Etruscan foods that I could incorporate into my recipes, and it was Liz who told me about the discovery of the world's only surviving Etruscan literary text—on an Egyptian mummy in Croatia! (For more on that story, see the historical note at the end of the book.)

Unbeknownst to her, Beth Elon provided culinary inspiration in the form of her book, *A Culinary Traveller in Tuscany: Exploring and Eating off the Beaten Path*. A cross between a guidebook to deepest rural Tuscany, a paean to hyperlocal cooking, and a compendium of authentic centuries-old recipes from *trattorie* in tiny, out-of-the-way hamlets, it's armchair reading at its best.

I also had fabulous manuscript editors: my mother, Mary Klovers; my sister, Christelle Klovers; and my fellow author, Eileen Haavik McIntire, creator of *The 90s Club* cozy mystery series.

My husband, Kevin Gormley, also served as an early reader, as well as a sous-chef, taste tester, and food photographer while I perfected the recipes for this book. He was particularly fond of the *pici* and the peaches with mascarpone, and his drool-worthy photo of the latter turned into my most popular Facebook post ever.

Perhaps more importantly, Kevin has always tolerated—and even nurtured—my Italophile tendencies. When I was pregnant with our daughter, Kathleen, he encouraged me to go to Rome for a two-week Italian course because, as he said, "it'll be much harder to travel later." While that's true, I have hope that Kathleen, now almost six, will soon blossom into a full-blown Italophile and bibliophile. She already enjoys baking and testing recipes, and she has started "writing books—just like mommy." And she's already asking when she will be old enough to go to Italy!

Even with all of this help, mistakes have undoubtedly crept in, and any and all mistakes are my own.

Chapter One

"These are our people," Rita Calabrese gushed to her husband Sal as she floated down the aisle of Alitalia flight 609, bound for Rome. "They're so fashionable, so elegant, so chic, so expressive!" She looked down at her purple cardigan, wrinkled slacks, and dowdy flats and frowned before remembering that she was sure to pick up the latest fashions in Milan. "And just listen to that sound! It's the sound"—she brought her fingers to her lips and kissed them—"of pure perfect Italian. It's like a symphony, *caro*!"

They had come to their seats now, and Sal was struggling to lift her enormous suitcase—floral like a bad seventies carpet—into the overhead compartment. At the word "symphony," he gave it one last push, grunted, and said, "Now, don't go getting any ideas, Rita—"

"*Lo so, caro.* I know—no symphonies, no art museums, nothing that smacks of art and culture of any kind. I will be touring the Uffizi on my own, smushed between a camera-wielding tour group and some art history students secretly titillated by *The Birth of Venus*."

Sal was not, as their daughter would say, "a culture vulture." That was a sore point with Rita, but not one that she wanted to dwell on at the moment, partly because she did not want to be interrupted in midflow and partly because it was their second honeymoon and she was determined to keep that honeymoon glow.

"How I wish they'd turn off that muzak," she huffed. "It muffles the musicality of the Italians *chiacchierando* all around us." She bent down and made her way to the window seat. "And they're so handsome, don't you think? So ageless, not a gray hair in sight." She self-consciously reached up and patted the top of her head, where normally there was a gray stripe down the center of her bushy jet-black hair, as if to reassure herself that she had touched up her roots. "Such elegant long noses. They look like Venetian doges—or Medicis. They're so, so—"

She plopped down and tried in vain to fasten her seatbelt, which had been cinched so tightly it might, just might, fit around her arm.

She sighed. "So thin," she concluded, her excitement ebbing a bit. "*Magrissimi*."

Beside her, Sal stretched his seatbelt to its widest point, buckled it, and crossed his muscular arms over his barrel chest. He turned to wink at her. "Well, I'm proud to be 'Merican," he said. Even though they were from New York's Hudson Valley—with accents to match—he attempted a Texas twang. "Yup," he said, patting his belly. "We're big people for a big land. Red meat-loving, football-watching, flag-waving..."

Rita patted him on the arm. "Yes, Sal, I know."

While Sal was of one hundred percent Italian stock, just like Rita, for some reason he was not nearly so much of an Italophile. It fell to Rita to keep the language, the traditions, and the food alive for their three grown children and, she hoped someday, their grandchildren.

Rita checked her phone. She had a message from their youngest, Vinnie, asking how to reheat her frozen lasagna. She had an enigmatic message from her overly dramatic and, in this case, probably jealous sister that her suave Italian boyfriend had just given her a tremendous "surprise." And Rita had five texts from Sam, her editor at the *Morris County Gazette*, who seemed determined to wring every bit of work out of Rita until the last possible moment:

Hear UR son starring in Legend of Acorn Hollow. Can we get exclusive?

SOS! Need recipe for Sunday food section. 10 ingredients or less, most people lazy like me.

Rumors of shake-up at senior center. U got an insider there?

Sentencing for killer of Jason Baker today. Since U caught him, got comment?

Dairy cow got drunk on local hooch, caused havoc on Main Street. U have dairy science contact?

Rita was about to respond that she had no idea her son was starring in a community theater production (and rather thought the director would live to regret it), type up her recipe for bruschetta, provide a seemingly-modest-but-not-really comment about her role in solving the Jason Baker case, and send her editor contact information for Sally Evans, a resident of the senior living facility who was as cantankerous as they came but had served with Julia Child as a WWII intelligence agent and was on Rita's speed dial, plus a tweedy, bow-legged professor from SUNY-Albany who had once confided in Rita that he loved dairy cows more than he loved his wife.

But then she heard "Rita!"

It was her husband's voice, and it had descended into that gruffly affectionate register which secretly thrilled her.

"*Spegni questo maledetto telefonino*," he said between gritted teeth.

Sal shot daggers at the offending *telefonino* clutched in her hand. When he spoke Italian, she knew he meant business.

"We are on our honeymoon," he said. "The one I should have taken you on forty years ago, except I had no money so you had to settle for Niagara Falls."

Rita smiled at the memory of the slightly musty honeymoon suite with a hideously fuchsia heart-shaped bed and a partially obstructed view of the falls. Sal had been so proud that he had been able to afford it.

"So you are not working. You are not running down leads for Sam, or calling your sources, or even telling our son"—he glanced over at her phone and frowned—"how to reheat his lasagna. He should be making his own meals, stop being such a mamma's boy."

Rita bristled in her seat. Learning to cook was all well and good, but her sons would always be good mamma's boys—if, that is, they knew what was good for them.

"And absolutely," he said, "no sleuthing. I don't care if you turn a corner in the Uffizi and see one crazed art lover bump off another and for some reason all the Japanese tour groups have left and you're the sole witness and the murderer drops his weapon and the sunlight streams though the windows illuminating a million incriminating fingerprints."

Rita stifled a laugh. It was never that easy.

"If that happens," he said, "you will not crawl over and slip the gun into your fanny pack, photograph the body, and go running to some Luca Zingaretti look-alike *commissario* with a smoldering expression and a six-pack of abs."

Luca Zingaretti was Rita's favorite Italian actor. He played the lantern-jawed, incorruptible Detective Montalbano who could always wrap up some devilishly complex, twisted murder in time for a shirtless run on the gorgeous white-sand beach behind his seaside villa in Sicily.

"No," Sal said. "You will say to the murderer, 'It's your lucky day. I'm on my second honeymoon with my hot hubby and too relaxed and blissed out to work. My only job is to ogle great works of art, romp through vineyards and olive groves, and glide along the canals of Venice.' Then you will step over the body and all of the blood running over the floor, finish exploring the museum, and then meet me at a little café by the Duomo for an espresso and some tiramisu."

He reached down, slid two novels out of her carry-on, and waved them in her face. "Reading about the adventures of Detectives Montalbano and Brunetti is as close as you will get to murder and mayhem on this trip."

What he said was both ridiculous and true. There was no way anyone would ever choose the Uffizi as the site of a murder, and no way she'd ever just walk away. But Italy did have a very low murder rate (what could one expect, Rita thought smugly, from such a civilized people?), and what violent crime there was tended to be far away from tourist zones.

But Rita did not want to give Sal the satisfaction of agreeing, and she rather suspected he wouldn't want that either. Their marriage thrived on a certain frisson of disagreement. Despite his grumbling, he liked her fiery and feisty, and for her part, while she liked to get her way, she wanted Sal to put up at least token resistance. Without that, there was no challenge, and where was the fun in that?

She unbuckled her seatbelt and stood up, nearly hitting her head.

"Where are you going?"

"As you said,"—she licked her lips—"I'm not working. I'm just a carefree girl of twenty-six again. And what would I do if I were twenty-six? Go see if that fit, fifty-ish man in first class—the one with the shaved head and dark suit—is actually Luca Zingaretti."

Chapter Two

Rita told a number of outrageous lies over the next few hours—all, of course, for the greater good. She flashed her press pass at the most glamorous stewardess and claimed to have an in-flight interview scheduled with Signor Zingaretti.

The flight attendant merely raised a perfectly arched eyebrow and said, "Signor Zingaretti does not wish to be disturbed while in flight."

Aha, Rita thought, her dark eyes gleaming, so he is in the first-class cabin.

She renewed her assault on the fortress that was first class an hour later, this time addressing herself to a middle-aged flight attendant with orange cat hairs on her collar and a slight bulge that hinted of a guilty late-night gelato habit. Rita told her she was a private investigator on the trail of an antiquities smuggler who she believed was traveling first class, and that she needed to make a positive I.D. before alerting authorities on the ground.

"*Mi dispiace*," the flight attendant said sweetly, looking truly apologetic. "But our policy is to only allow the carabinieri to carry out police actions—and only when we are in Italian airspace. And U.S. air marshals, of course, when we are in American airspace. Perhaps if you could convince one of them....?"

"Ah, yes, of course. I'll talk it over with one of the air marshals." Rita wagged her chin in the direction of Sal, who was snoring loudly, and the flight attendant frowned.

"Are they supposed to sleep on the job?" she asked. "And isn't he a little...old?"

"A special program." Rita winked. "For air marshals who want to come out of retirement for an occasional job. Kind of a boondoggle, you know? Flights to Europe and the Caribbean are very popular."

The stewardess frowned again and brushed a few orange hairs off her collar.

"And the sleeping," Rita said, "is cover. Deep, deep cover. It lulls the criminals into a sense of complacency. And then, just when they get comfortable, he springs into action."

Rita turned to go, but just then she heard a deep, slightly gravelly voice calling after her.

"*Signora*—"

Rita spun around and was gob-smacked to see the fit, fiftyish man from first class looking at her with that intense gaze that always set her heart aflutter when she watched Montalbano on TV.

"Zingaretti," he said, flashing a badge at her. "Commissario Zingaretti. What's this about an antiquities thief?"

Rita could not believe her ears. Could it really be Luca Zingaretti in the flesh? But why did he claim to be a detective—and, surely, if he was going to use his TV identity, he'd call himself Commissario Montalbano, right?

"You're taller than you look on TV," she babbled, "and your nose, well, I guess there's make-up involved, but you are just as *bellissimo*—"

He laughed—a gorgeous, deep, throaty laugh—and clasped her hand in his. "I think you have me confused with my cousin, Luca," he said warmly. "I am Commissario Matteo Zingaretti, and I am part of an elite *squadra* that specializes in art and antiquities theft."

He released her hand and winked at her, which only melted her heart further. "Sorry to disappoint you. Luca does base his portrayal of Commissario Montalbano on me, though. He spent a whole month shadowing me, learning to walk like me, talk like me, investigate a crime scene like me. He even shaved his head to look more like me. *Allora*"—he lowered his voice—"tell me what you know about the identity of this antiquities thief."

Rita turned bright red. "I—I don't. I'm afraid that was all a ruse to meet you—er, Luca, that is. I'm such a big fan and well...." She shrugged. "*Mi dispiace*. I didn't lie about being a detective, though. I may not be a licensed private eye or a police detective, but I have solved five murders to date—"

He looked at her in surprise. "Are you from New York City?"

"Acorn Hollow. A tiny town on the Hudson River."

"*Un piccolo paese*, you say." He wiggled his dramatic dark eyebrows at her. "America is a very dangerous country, no?" Then he broke into a smile. "So, if not to catch a thief, why are you travelling back to *bella* Italia? You are Italian, I presume."

Rita preened just a bit. She loved being mistaken for an Italian by an actual Italian. "A dual citizen, actually. My mother was Italian by birth."

"Ah—but you speak the language so beautifully."

She acknowledged the compliment with a smile. "My husband thought I was working too hard, between my job as a journalist and solving two poisonings and springing our son out of jail—a total misunderstanding, mind you—and getting my husband's completely shady cousin, the one who owns a dubiously legal vitamin shop in Jersey, back with his wife, who has cancer—"

Zingaretti's eyes were so wide open they looked like they would pop.

"Anyway," she said, "he surprised me with tickets to Italy. Two weeks of rest and relaxation. We're saving Florence, Venice, Rome, and Milan for the end of the trip and starting with a weeklong stay at an *agriturismo* in Tuscany. It's just outside Volterra and overlooks a vineyard and an olive grove and has the most delightful aquamarine pool—"

There was a smile starting to form on his thick, fleshy lips. "It wouldn't be Villa Belvista, would it?"

She stared at him. "How did you know?"

He threw his head back and guffawed, then seized her hand again and squeezed it. "Signora, your dream is about to come true."

"It is?"

"*Certo*! You will have a chance to meet my cousin Luca. He's headed there later this week for a wedding. The bride's family is very rich and quite the patron of the arts, so un *sacco* of actors and opera stars, plus politicians and Italy's leading industrialists, will be there.

Andrea Boccelli is even going to sing at the ceremony. I tried to secure an invitation myself, but I was not successful."

"But surely there must be some mistake. I can't see how my husband could get us a reservation if the *agriturismo* is booked for a wedding, especially of that size."

"What day are you leaving?"

"Friday."

"*Ecco*!" he said. "The wedding is Saturday evening. Nearly all the guests have their own estates in Tuscany, so they hardly need to stay at the *agriturismo*. Still, I'm sure Luca will pop in on Thursday or Friday to see everyone. And then you'll get your chance."

Rita could see it now—the front page of the *Morris County Gazette* dedicated to her interview with Luca Zingaretti, with a picture of him shirtless, lounging by the pool, a row of cypress trees snaking down the drive behind them, petering out into a ridgeline of hazy green hills.

"I'm sorry you won't be there," Rita said. "I'm sure it will be wonderful. And to hear Andrea Botticelli live in such a setting!"

She clapped her hands, at a loss for words.

"*Sì, sì*. It would be magical. But that's not why I wanted to go." He leaned towards her and lowered his voice. "I have reason to believe," he said, "that a real antiquities smuggler might be there."

Rita gasped. She knew she should turn around and run right back to her seat, that Sal had forbidden her sleuthing to go beyond trying to guess the identity of the murderer ahead of Commissario Montalbano in his fictional Sicilian idyll.

But a real Italian carabinieri—the inspiration for Luca Zingaretti's portrayal of Commissario Montalbano, no less—was confiding details of an actual investigation to her.

"Could you do me a favor?" he asked as if reading her thoughts. "Be my eyes and ears on the ground? No need to do anything dangerous of course, but just observe, talk to guests who'll be there early."

"Is there anyone in particular I should be paying attention to?"

He shrugged. "Both the bride and the groom are archaeologists. Luca tells me Alessandro, the groom, is straight as an arrow, although of course you never know. But his friends, well, perhaps they are not so scrupulous. Personally, I've always suspected Hans Clausnitzer, the pre-eminent German expert in Etruscan antiquities. He'll be there; in fact, he's the host—he owns the *agriturismo*. And then there's Tiffany Devereaux. I can't say she'd have a money motive, seeing how she's dripping with diamonds, but perhaps it's the challenge that excites her. All of the artifacts missing are from digs she financed. But, really, it could be anyone. No one is above suspicion."

Out of the corner of her eye, Rita saw Sal stand up, rub his eyes groggily, and glare in her direction. She moved to block Sal's view of Matteo Zingaretti.

"I must be getting back," she said apologetically, "but I'd love to help."

He pulled a pen and a business card out of his pocket, circled the phone number at the bottom, and handed it to her. "That's my *telefonino*," he said. "Call me anytime—day or night."

She palmed it carefully and then slid it into her pocket so that Sal wouldn't see it.

"And Rita," he said, his meltingly tender amber eyes boring into her, "*stai attenta*."

As she walked back to her seat, she shivered slightly. But whether it was because a carabinieri had just warned her to be careful, or because a gorgeous Italian man had just, as her daughter would say, "given her his digits," she couldn't quite say.

Chapter Three

Rita spent the whole train ride from Rome to Siena, and the bus ride from Siena to Volterra, and the bumpy taxi ride from the Volterra bus station reassuring Sal that the man in first class had been Commissario Matteo Zingaretti, not Luca; that he was much less glamorous than his famous cousin (she lied); and that no, she had not been flirting.

"Well then, what did you talk about?" he demanded, glowering at her beneath his big, bushy, salt-and-pepper eyebrows as they lurched past a field of sunflowers and turned onto a cypress-lined winding gravel road.

"Etruscan history and art," she said, feeling on solid ground. After all, she and Commissario Zingaretti had talked about how someone was *stealing* those things. "Speaking of which," she added, pointing at the honey-colored walled city receding into the distance behind them, "did you know Volterra was an Etruscan city before it was conquered by the Romans and later the Florentines? Its walls are medieval, but they incorporate parts of an earlier Etruscan wall."

Sal's expression softened and he shot her an admiring look. "That's my smart and cultured wife. It's like being with my own private tour guide. And speaking of private...."

He reached over and put a hand on her thigh.

"Sal," she giggled, "not in front of the taxi driver."

"Oh, this is Italy," Sal said equitably. "I'm sure they've seen everything."

They rounded a curve and went hurtling down a hill, flying past a grove of olive trees groaning with the fruits of the season on one side, and rows of gently sloping grape vines on the other. It was late September, and the leaves were already turning to russet. Rita rolled down the window and inhaled deeply. The slightly woody scent of hay mingled with pungent rosemary, and over them wafted the sweet smell of roses and bougainvillea.

"Oh, Sal!" Rita clapped her hands. "It's just like in the brochure. Better, even."

They turned onto another long gravel drive flanked by two rows of cypresses silhouetted against the golden sky, casting long thin shadows. This road was even rougher than the preceding one, and Rita clutched the door handle as they bounced violently up and down, her teeth chattering.

"Oh, it's so r-r-rustic," she managed to say.

"Good to get away from it all," Sal bellowed over the incessant crunching of the tires on gravel. "No work, no sleuthing, no family drama...."

Sal trailed off as the house came into view. It was a magnificent villa, its pink stucco façade accented by forest-green shutters and a red terracotta tile roof. A low, honey-colored limestone wall was rose-tinted in the warm glow of the late afternoon sun, a Siamese cat draped over it, basking in its warmth. In the center of the cobblestone entrance was a gleaming marble statue of a naked youth; with his tousled hair, washboard abs, and muscular calves, he looked like one of those Greek youths of antiquity. Beneath each window was a flowerbox bursting with red geraniums, and a series of shapely terracotta pots marched up the stone staircase, spilling fragrant, spiky rosemary and flowering lavender buds over and around the wrought-iron banister.

Rita felt as though she had never before seen a house in such complete harmony with its surroundings. "*Bellissimo*," she murmured. And then she added her favorite Italian word. "*Mozzafiato*." Breathtaking.

The taxi eased onto the cobblestones and came to an abrupt halt. Sal handed the driver a few euro notes, and they clambered out into the sunshine.

A beautiful girl of sixteen or seventeen, tall and lithe with bottle-blond flowing locks, was striding out of the reception area, an elegant middle-aged woman trailing behind her. Suddenly, the girl's face was transformed from pouty teenaged ennui to joyful exuberance. She stretched out her arms and seemed to be looking at something—or someone—over Rita's shoulder.

"Papa!" the girl shouted, breaking into a run.

The woman behind her did not share the younger woman's glee. Her expression was more enigmatic, something between apprehension and hope.

Rita spun around, expecting to see a joyful reunion.

Which, of course, she did.

But her eyes were immediately drawn elsewhere. She had already seen one dead-ringer today—for Luca Zingaretti—and now she saw another.

For herself—if that is, she had a fabulous makeover and looked at her own reflection in one of those magic mirrors that shaved off fifty pounds.

"Speak of the devil," Sal muttered beside her, just as her look-alike's mouth dropped open.

"Rose!"

"Rita!"

The twins stared at each other for a moment.

"What are you doing here?" Rita finally managed to say.

"I'm here with Paolo, of course," Rose said. "He invited me to his brother's wedding."

"That was the surprise you texted me about?"

Rose nodded.

Before Rita could say anything else, the teenaged girl broke in and said, "Oh—so you're papa's"—she wrinkled her adorable little nose in distaste—"friend."

The girl spoke perfect English, with just the slightest bit of an Italian accent.

"*Certo, certo*," Paolo said, kissing his daughter on both cheeks. While he was bent over her, Rita caught him shooting a warning look in Rose's direction. "I just thought I'd show her a little of Italy."

"Mamma and I," the girl said, "are staying in the Horta cottage." She turned to Rose, all smiles, although she wasn't fooling Rita. "And where are you staying, Rose? I hear the singles are delightful here—almost monastic in their simplicity."

"Actually," Rose began, "your father and I—"

"—are staying in separate cottages," Paolo broke in.

Rose glared at him and flushed.

"There was some mix-up at reception," he said, "and they gave us only one key, so we're just coming back to sort it out."

The daughter smiled, and it reminded Rita of the smile her two Bernese mountain dogs had right before they pounced on a baby rabbit.

"I do hope," she said sweetly to Rose, "your cottage will be just to your liking."

Of course, Rita thought, the girl very well knew that a cottage without Paolo in it would be very much *not* to Rose's liking.

"Well, that settles it," Paolo said. "I'm in the Feronia cottage, and we'll find something more suitable for my dear, er, friend Rose here."

Paolo slapped Rose on the back in an avuncular, hail-fellow-well-met kind of way, and Rose grimaced.

"Did you hear that, Mamma?" the girl squealed with delight. "Papa's in the Feronia cottage—that's right beside ours!"

And with that, she sashayed past them, towards the pool. With a long appraising glance at Rose, the elegant middle-aged woman strode behind her daughter.

"Paolo," she murmured.

"Chiara."

Rita noticed his eyes lingered on her form as she slipped past and retreated towards the pool.

"Well!" Sal clapped his hands. "It's a family reunion all around apparently. Shall we retire to the pool for drinks?"

Chapter Four

Rita could not remember a more uncomfortable hour in a more idyllic setting. Instead of reminiscing over old times and plotting out a week of wine tastings, cooking classes, and la dolce far niente, they hunkered down in the dappled light filtering through the purple bougainvillea, eyeing each other warily around the table as if engaged in some tense diplomatic standoff. As the silence grew more oppressive, the gentle lapping of aquamarine waters against the flagstone terrace began to sound like the roar of the ocean, and the call of a crow sounded like a call to arms.

Sure she could not stand another minute, Rita took a gulp of prosecco and decided to try out the one subject that should prove both the least likely to stir up family drama and the most likely to help Commissario Zingaretti with his investigation.

Turning to Paolo, she asked, "So, will there be many archaeologists at the wedding?"

"*Sì, sì.*" He shot her a look of pure gratitude and leaned towards her over the table. His movement was arrested, however, by his daughter, who was apparently named Olivia, and who had cleverly positioned herself between her parents and placed an arm possessively around each one. She meant it to look like childlike adulation, but, as Paolo had just realized, Olivia had them in an iron grip, however friendly it might seem.

He settled back in his chair and shot a wary sidelong glance at his daughter, who smiled sweetly.

"My brother, for one," he said, addressing Rita once more. "That would be Alessandro, the groom. And the bride, Giovanna."

Chiara blew a smoke ring and then stubbed out her cigarette. "I introduced them."

In three simple words, accompanied by a slightly sad, knowing smile, Chiara had said volumes, Rita thought. One, that the reason she was invited was not that she was the groom's ex-sister-in-law, but because she was the bride's friend. Two, that her own experience with marriage made it hard for her to believe that anyone would ever have their fairy-tale ending. And three, she was not happy about being here—or being reunited with her ex.

"And, of course," Olivia said while squeezing both her parents' shoulders, "both of my parents are archaeologists. They fell in love while excavating the Necropoli delle Pianacce."

Olivia was clearly ignoring the fact that her parents had fallen out of love, and the girl underscored this omission by grinning at Rose like a Cheshire cat.

"That," Chiara said, lighting another cigarette, "was a long time ago. A lifetime ago."

Rita noticed that Chiara watched the embers glow red for a rather long time before bringing the cigarette to her lips.

Paolo looked at his ex-wife thoughtfully for a moment, then turned back to Rita and said in a quite businesslike fashion, "Hans, our gracious host, is an archaeologist, too, of course."

He waved his hand in the direction of a tall, bronzed, silver-haired man who had just come out of the villa and was now striding towards them. He cradled the Siamese they had seen earlier in the crook of his arm. A Bernese Mountain dog trailed behind. Rita felt a lump rise up in her throat; she suddenly missed her own Bernese, Luciano and Cesare, very much.

"And Diana is an archaeologist too," Chiara said. "I did not introduce them."

"Oh?" Rita said. "Are they a couple too?"

Olivia smirked. "Hardly," she said in English in the perfect, clipped accent of a British aristocrat. Rita wondered if she'd been at an English boarding school. "They hate each other."

Chiara reproached her daughter with a tight, thin-lipped smile and a little shake of her head. "They are professionals rivals," she explained diplomatically. "Diana is the preeminent proponent of the theory that the Etruscans were of Anatolian origin. Anatolia was where Turkey is today. And Hans is the leading proponent of the theory that the Etruscan culture originated right here in Tuscany."

Sal frowned and popped an olive into his mouth. "Does it matter?"

"It does if you're an archaeologist."

Hans was bearing down on them now, his bronzed chest and washboard abs glistening in the sun. He was wearing a black Speedo and stood very straight, with an almost military bearing.

"*Buon giorno*!" His voice was loud, commanding, and he had a very strong German accent. Switching to English, he clapped Paolo heartily on the shoulder, and Paolo winced. "I trust everything is to your liking." He said it as a statement, almost an order and certainly not a question, as if he could not imagine that anything in his little fiefdom would not meet with universal approval. He was met by stony stares around the table, and so to compensate, Rita found herself enthusiastically blurting out, "Oh, yes! It's beautiful. So rustic—" Hans scowled. "Rustic" apparently was not the look he was going for.

"—but so comfortable," Rita hastened to add as she reached out to pat the Bernese and surreptitiously slip him a bit of prosciutto under the table. The dog was profoundly grateful, as demonstrated by his furiously wagging tail. "And the view is magnificent."

Seemingly mollified, Hans suddenly turned on his heels and loomed over Rose. "And who," he said, "is this charming creature?"

He seized Rose's hand, brought it to his lips, and kissed it forcefully, possessively.

Paolo frowned and tried to move closer to Rose, but Olivia's iron grip once again stopped him.

Rose glanced at Paolo, then at Hans. "Rose." Her dark eyes flashed. "Rose Mancini. I'm here as a guest of Paolo. He's my—"

"—friend," Olivia cut in. "She's Papa's friend. From America."

When Paolo failed to correct his daughter, Rose glowered at her erstwhile boyfriend before turning to smile coquettishly at Hans.

"Well," Hans said, "Rose is my guest now, too. After all, this is my villa." He clapped Paolo's shoulder, hard. "Isn't it marvelous how weddings bring everyone together? Why, before long we'll be co-authoring a paper agreeing that Etruscan civilization sprang from this magnificent landscape."

Chiara and Paolo glared up at him, Sal rolled his eyes, and Rose and Olivia looked amused. The Bernese nestled his head into Rita's lap.

To break the uncomfortable silence, Rita nodded towards the Siamese lodged in the crook of Hans' arm. The creature had the most unnerving eyes, ice-blue and penetrating just like her owner's. The stark contrast between her ebony face and snowy-white body only served to accentuate the blueness of her eyes further.

"And who is this charming creature?" Rita asked before realizing she had unwittingly just echoed Hans' earlier question regarding her sister.

"Artemis," he said proudly, stroking behind the cat's ears. Artemis purred loudly and arched her back slightly. She seemed to know she was being introduced and wanted to show off her figure to its best advantage.

"Greek and later Etruscan goddess of the hunt," Chiara said, stubbing out her cigarette. "The equivalent of the Roman goddess Diana."

"And she lives up to her name," Hans said proudly. "You won't find a mouse within two kilometers of the property."

Rita glanced past Hans and smiled fondly in the direction of the Bernese. In Rita's experience, dogs usually resembled their owners—or vice versa. But in this case, man and dog appeared spectacularly poorly matched, and the dog's body language—slinking behind, glancing longingly from their plates to his chiseled master and back—seemed to indicate that the dog was all too aware. "*E tuo cane?*"

"Wolf." Hans pronounced it in the German way as "volf."

He reached down and patted the dog's rather corpulent frame and slightly matted, dusty coat, which stood in stark contrast to Artemis' impeccably groomed coat.

"Unlike Artemis," Hans said severely, with a disapproving shake of his head, "Wolf does not live up to his name. He's not much of a guard dog, not even much of a truffle hunter. I leave that to Helga." Rita must have looked confused because he added, "The pig."

Hans went back to stroking Artemis' neck. "Enjoy your *aperitivo*." He winked. "I'll see you later, Rose."

Then he gently put Artemis down and dove into the pool, graceful as a swan.

Chapter Five

The next morning, Rita was already awake when the roosters began to crow; through the open window, she watched the sun peek tentatively over the horizon, suffusing a pale milky light over the hazy indigo mountains, illuminating the windswept hills and finally streaking through the French doors to their balcony, glinting on the exposed dark wood ceiling beams and casting an ever-changing display of light and shadow on the terracotta brick walls.

Rita stretched out, luxuriating in the silky-smooth Egyptian cotton sheets, and reached over a slumbering, snoring, blissfully dreaming Sal to check her watch.

It was five-thirty and her stomach was rumbling, but she knew there was no hope of breakfast at this hour.

She crept out of bed and tiptoed through the French door to the balcony. She felt the sun on her face, heard the happy chirping of birds, looked down on the brilliant turquoise waters of the pool. Last night, with its unsettling talk of professional rivalries and ill-fated romance, seemed far behind her. This was *bella Italia*, and she would not let anything dampen her spirits.

Rita tiptoed back to their room, changed into a fire-engine red one-piece swimsuit with strategically placed ruching and some seriously gut-slimming Spandex, and ambled over to the pool, her bare feet massaged by the weathered travertine terrace, still cool in the early morning light. Plopping into the crystalline waters, she found the water cool but refreshing and, as she glided across the pool, she tried to clear her mind of everything and just live in the present.

At first, she succeeded. But soon her thoughts wandered to Commissario Zingaretti's intense amber gaze, the business card she had secreted away in her suitcase, and her promise to be his eyes and ears on the ground.

Six archaeologists, she thought. Six people uniquely positioned to nick a funerary urn here, a delicate Etruscan necklace there, and to have the credibility needed to authenticate it for unscrupulous art collectors.

Whom had the detective said he suspected?

She thought of that warm, strong hand and those kind eyes and tried to remember his words. Commissario Zingaretti had mentioned someone who financed the expeditions, an American. The name was on the tip of her tongue. Tammy? Teri? No—Tiffany. That was it. She would have to be on the lookout for a Tiffany.

And he had mentioned Hans, too. Could he be an antiquities thief?

Her fleeting impression had been of someone power-hungry, aggressive, always looking to assert his dominance in any situation. An alpha male and an egotist. But while he would stop at nothing to get what he wanted, what he seemed to want most was professional respect.

Which made it rather unlikely he would risk his reputation by trafficking in antiquities.

Commissario Zingaretti hadn't mentioned Chiara by name, but perhaps she was in his sights as well. Rita found her mysterious, enigmatic, inscrutable. She seemed unperturbed by the presence of her ex-husband and his new girlfriend—yet she did nothing to rein in her daughter, who was so clearly scheming to bring her parents together.

Rita could very well imagine Chiara living a double life, the doting but slightly detached mother by day, wreathed in rings of smoke and melancholy, only to spring to life at night as an international criminal mastermind.

Rita plunged down deeper into the sparkling water, the sun warm on her back.

When she came up for air, there was a woman sitting at the pool's edge, a shapely milky-white leg trailing in the water.

Rita blinked and wiped the water from her eyes. The slightly blurry image crystallized into the most stunning middle-aged woman she had ever seen—a raven-haired, onyx-eyed temptress in a strapless, one-piece swimsuit that hugged her ample curves and was an even more lurid shade of red than Rita's.

"*Posso?*" said the goddess.

"*Certo.*" Rita moved over to make room for her, and the woman slid gracefully into the pool.

"Diana," the woman said. It sounded more like a regal pronouncement than an introduction.

"The huntress," Rita blurted out, remembering the impromptu mythology lesson from the night before. Strangely, she noted a certain resemblance between Diana and Artemis, one human, one feline, but both perfect. Diana's gaze, however, was much warmer, less unnerving.

"*Esatto!*" Diana exclaimed, clearly delighted. "I see you know your ancient history." She laughed. "I'm also the mother of the bride."

Rita could not imagine how a woman this glamorous had ever given birth, much less have a daughter old enough to be marrying Paolo's brother. But she checked her disbelief, extended her pruney fingers and shook Diana's slim, graceful hand. "Rita. *Piacere.*"

"*Piacere.*"

Diana tossed her dark mane and let out a fully, throaty laugh. Her voice and laugh matched her nineteen-fifties screen siren appearance. "Isn't Tuscany marvelous?" She spoke perfect standard Italian with a Roman accent. "I've travelled all over the world, but this is the place I always come back to." She smiled at Rita. "*È toscana?*"

Rita puffed up with pride. Now she was not only being mistaken for an Italian, but a native Tuscan no less.

She shook her head. "American, actually."

Diana looked at her sympathetically. "But of Italian heritage, right? And you speak the language so beautifully."

Rita had to smile. She'd spoken no more than ten words for the woman to come to this conclusion.

"I can see you are Italian," Diana said passionately. "You have a certain flair and expressiveness. You appreciate"—Diana flung her arms wide, as if to encompass the ever-brightening sky, the tall, spindly cypress trees, and the chattering birds—"all this. You have music and poetry in your soul. Yes, I can see all that. I'm very intuitive, you know."

Diana went on. "There's a reason Italians invented gelato and wood-fired pizza and opera and the whole concept of world empire. We are a people of extremes. We live in a land of fire-spewing volcanoes and ice-topped mountains. We love and we hate with the same passion. We never do anything halfway." She wrinkled her nose and smiled. "When I travel, I find the rest of the world seems so colorless, so boring. In Italy, anything can happen. It's never boring."

"Some people," Rita suddenly blurted out, "think I'm too emotional."

Diana shrugged her creamy white shoulders. "You're Italian."

They stood there a moment in companionable silence, the water lapping gently against them.

At last, Rita said, "If you think Italy is so wonderful—which it is, of course—why don't you think it could have been the source of Etruscan civilization?"

Diana looked at her quizzically, and Rita blushed. "Chiara told me about the rival theories yesterday."

"Ah—Chiara. Quite a brilliant colleague of mine. Yes, I believe the Etruscans are from Anatolia. Why? Because that's where the evidence leads. First, there are the writings of the ancient Greek historian Herodotus, who tells us they emigrated from Lydia, which is on the south coast of what is now Turkey, fleeing a famine. Then there's the DNA evidence; samples from the tiny Italian town of Murlo, where the people have lived in relative isolation, show that their nearest DNA matches are in what is now Palestine and Syria. And then there are the DNA studies of the cattle!"

Rita frowned. "The cows?"

"Yes! The famous Chianina cows that we use for *bistecca alla fiorentina*. They are like celebrities in Italy! Pity the Italian cook who uses any other kind of beef for *bistecca alla fiorentina*—they will be disgraced! Anyway, this supposedly most Tuscan breed, the soul of Tuscan gastronomy, is genetically far more closely related to cows in the Middle East than other breeds in Italy. And then there's the language: Etruscan is not Indo-European like Latin was, and there have been found inscriptions on the Greek Island of Lemnos, very near Turkey, that appear similar to Etruscan. Chiara translated them actually—she's the preeminent scholar of Etruscan linguistics."

By now, Rita's head was spinning. She wished she had a notebook nearby to jot this all down. It really would be a most interesting feature for the books and culture section of the *Morris County Gazette* Sunday edition: an exclusive interview with one of the world's leading experts in Etruscan archaeology. Her editor was always griping that the residents of Morris County were backwards country bumpkins, and that what passed for entertainment news was the announcement of the Morris County Player's upcoming season. But this—*this*—was culture. And a photo of Diana in her swimsuit would seal the deal, sure to attract male attention and help close the paper's frequently lamented "gender gap."

But then she forced these thoughts out of her mind. She had promised Sal no work, no sleuthing. She should at least keep *one* of those two promises.

"I can be passionate in my personal life," Diana said but I'm actually quite dispassionate in my work. I let the evidence lead me, not my emotions." She winked at Rita. "It's a nice little respite from the drama of everyday life, you might say."

"But Hans...."

"Hans–what?" Diana looked amused. "Hans can't stand coming in second in anything. He didn't want to be the archaeologist who merely wrote a paper supporting Dr. Diana Rossi's theory. No, he needed to be the leading proponent of some theory–*any* theory! And he's smart. A genius, really." She laughed. "There are plenty of Italian nationalists delighted to have some supposedly unbiased foreigner claim that the great Etruscan civilization sprang up right here on the Italian peninsula, home to the most creative, most civilized people on earth."

"Plus," Diana went on, "I've always suspected he did it out of spite. He was in love with me, you see, a long time ago. Or perhaps it was just lust." She shrugged. "But whatever it was, I turned him down."

Rita could only imagine the long line of would-be lovers knocking on Diana's door.

But then Diana said something that surprised her. "I only had eyes for my husband, Giorgio. He died three years ago of cancer." Her eyes clouded over, then she defiantly lifted her chin towards the now blazing sun.

"Well," she said, "it's up to us to go on living. *Sei sposata?*"

Rita noticed Diana had effortlessly, endearingly slipped into using the more familiar "*tu*" form with Rita.

Rita smiled. "Forty-one years this past June."

"*Sei fortunata.*"

Rita thought of Commissario Zingaretti's meltingly amber eyes, then Sal snoring like a freight train in their room. He might not be a gorgeous, suave Italian man, but he was hers.

"Yes," she agreed. "I am lucky."

Chapter Six

After several more laps in the pool, Diana invited Rita to do some yoga in the vineyards, but Rita's first and only sun salutation, years ago, had ended with Rita slumped on the floor, an egg-sized lump on her forehead. Uneager to repeat the experience, she demurred and instead slipped on her new black swim cover-up embroidered with little yellow daisies. It made her feel very chic. Then she wandered amongst the vines until she came to a walled orchard in a sheltered cove at the base of the hill.

She passed through the wrought-iron gate and plucked a lusciously ripe, golden-skinned pear off a tree. She was just biting into it, the sweet, sticky juices running down her chin, when she realized she was not alone: on a stone bench sat a bearded man with a bald pate. He had a bird perched on each shoulder and a basket of pears and blueberries on one side, a basket of bread and cheese on the other. And judging from the well-worn leather-bound volume he was reading, his Roman collar, and the simple wooden cross hanging from his neck, he was a priest.

He looked up and smiled at her. "Ah, you are the American," he said in Italian, "and, I hear, a very successful detective."

Rita frowned. She could not remember telling anyone that she was a sleuth, and she wanted to keep it that way. It would be hard to gather information for Commissario Zingaretti if they suspected what she was up to!

"How did you know?"

"Your sister told me."

Rita silently cursed herself for failing to take her twin aside to explain the situation.

His hazel eyes twinkled mischievously as he handed her a piece of coarse Tuscan bread—chewy and unsalted—and a hunk of crumbly pecorino cheese.

"And you are...?"

"Padre Domenico, Alessandro and Paolo's brother." He laughed again, and his belly—the only part of him where any weight had accumulated—shook. "You're surprised, no? Don't worry—you're not the only one. I'm the ugly brother. *Bruttissimo.* So I let the two of them go after the girls and I chose God."

"I'm not really a detective," Rita said, feeling as though it would be a grave sin to let a priest believe she was more accomplished than she was. "I'm just a..." She trailed off, searching for the word in Italian. The truth was that, as far as she knew, there was no such word.

"A what?"

"A regular citizen who solves crimes. I'm not a policewoman or a private investigator or anything like that."

His eyebrows shot up. "So you don't get paid to throw yourself in harm's way?"

She shook her head.

"You have no training? No access to fingerprinting equipment or forensic scientists? No police dogs? No gun?"

She shook her head no to every question.

He whistled. "You Americans are very brave. In Italy, we leave that to the professionals."

Rita thought of Commissario Zingaretti and blushed.

"You know," he said, "I think I would like to be one of those citizens who solves crimes." He popped a blueberry in his mouth. "After twenty-five years of hearing confessions, I know a lot about crime. First, they confess what they did, how they did it. Then a few weeks later, they're back in the confessional. Why? Because now they've committed some other crime to cover up the first crime—or to shut someone up."

"I didn't know there was so much crime in Italy."

"There's not really. But I've served in some dangerous neighborhoods. And now I'm the chaplain at Regina Coeli Prison in Rome—the one the Pope goes to every year on Holy Thursday to wash the prisoners' feet." He leaned back against the stone wall, basking in its warmth. "Yes," he said, seemingly unperturbed. "I've heard it all—murder, arson, human trafficking, armed robbery. Schemes to import black market cigarettes from Albania—you'd be surprised how lucrative that is! Plus, all the usual mafia stuff: protection rackets and taking a *pizzo* from every construction contract. And then the more creative only-in-Italy crimes: passing off wines made with grapes that are *not* sangiovese as Brunello di

Montalcino, art forgeries, smuggling out Roman and Etruscan artifacts."

Rita had been reaching for another hunk of cheese, but she stopped abruptly. Padre Domenico had an intimate knowledge of antiquities theft. He personally knew people involved in the trade. He'd heard details of their subterfuge.

Did that make him a good informant? A potential ally? A crime-fighting sidekick? Or a suspect?

She had to admit that he'd be the perfect criminal. No one would suspect the unobtrusive jolly little man with the Roman collar. No one would think anything of him passing from one cell to another at Regina Coeli; it was the perfect cover for passing messages between inmates and family members and associates, who might also be in need of spiritual sustenance.

"Antiquities theft," she repeated, trying to sound casual as she bent down low, pretending to pick a few berries low to the ground. One of the first rules of sleuthing, Rita had learned, was to know your limits. And one of Rita's limitations was that she was no actress; at times such as these, it was imperative to keep her face hidden. "I would think that's hard to get away with. There are only so many antiquities collectors, and they don't seem the type to mingle with the criminal element. And then if you're a collector, you want to show it off, but what do you do if your friends ask how you got that Etruscan urn in your living room?"

"Oh, never underestimate the criminal element! They've got a way around everything. One inmate I know actually painted over real antiquities and wrote 'FAKE' on the back; he convinced customs that they were exporting replicas that would be sold and marketed as such. Then his associate in Britain just stripped off the paint and sold them as the genuine article—which, of course, they were."

"But didn't they question its provenance?"

"No—people don't tend to ask questions they don't want the answers to."

"But aren't they afraid of getting caught?"

"And charged with what? If questioned, they'll just say that the seller assured them they were legitimately obtained. See, the dirty little secret in the art world is that you need an export license to get artifacts out of the country, but once they are in the destination country, antiquities dealers have no obligation to request the export license or any other documentation."

"So once you get into the country with rich buyers, you're home free."

"Usually. It's only an issue if it's a really famous object that an art museum or other institution has reported stolen."

Rita's mind was whirring now. "But if someone just stumbled upon an ancient jewelry hoard or a statue and dug it up, no one would ever know it was missing."

"Precisely. So who makes the best thief? An amateur archaeologist with connections to the underworld."

"Or a professional archaeologist."

"Like Hans or Diana or Chiara or my brothers?"

"Oh, I wasn't suggesting—"

"Of course you weren't. But as a hypothetical," he said with a wink, "wouldn't Hans make the perfect smuggler? He owns a property in an area rich in archaeological finds, he knows what to look for and where to find it, he runs an import-export business—"

"He does?"

"Oh, yes. Olive oil and wine. He's sending cases abroad every week. It'd be the easiest thing in the world to slide some coins or jewelry at the bottom of the case. Plus, he's got contacts all over the world. He knows lots of antiquities dealers who'd be salivating to get their hands on Etruscan antiquities."

He popped one more blueberry in his mouth and stood up.

"I'm not serious, you know," he said. "Hans cares about preserving our cultural heritage. He wouldn't steal it. And neither would anyone else here."

They headed towards the gate, leaving the blueberry patch behind them.

"If there were a crime to occur here," he said, "it wouldn't be antiquities theft. It would be a crime of passion." With a shudder, his jolly countenance suddenly turned grim. "That's what I'm worried about."

Rita stopped dead in her tracks and stared at him. She thought about the stony stares that had greeted Hans. She thought of Olivia's antipathy towards Rose.

"But surely you don't think...?"

He attempted a laugh. "Oh, don't mind me. I've probably spent too much time with arsonists, drug traffickers, mafia bosses, and murderers. My imagination's probably running wild. But the tension is palpable; it makes me nervous. I was invited because I'm Alessandro's brother, of course, and also to perform the ceremony, but I suspect the main reason I'm here is to keep the peace."

"Blessed be the peacekeepers," Rita quipped.

But he did not return her smile. Instead, he regarded her solemnly, touched his wooden cross, and said, "Let's hope so."

Chapter Seven

Padre Domenico continued his ramble through the vineyards while Rita took their basket of blueberries to the kitchen and presented them to a stout older woman who introduced herself in coarse, straight-from-the-country Italian as "Luisa, the best cook in Tuscany and don't you forget it."

Luisa leaned back against the counter, folded her massive flabby arms over her floral housedress, and fixed Rita with a stare that would have intimidated even the hardened criminals in Padre Domenico's care. She shot a contemptuous look at Rita's blueberries and then turned back to Rita, her nostrils flaring, her beady dark eyes flashing. "I've heard about you," she said, in the way someone might address a completely, hair-raisingly unsuitable match for one's teenaged daughter.

Rita tried to look unintimidated, blithe, and carefree. She suddenly feared that Padre Domenico's idle speculation was anything but. Maybe Hans really was an antiquities thief and Luisa's job as a cook was deep cover for her role as the linchpin in the smuggling ring. Maybe Luisa's husband was the one in Regina Coeli Prison crying on Padre Domenico's shoulders about his many sins, and Padre Domenico had just passed word to Luisa that Rita was asking too many questions—and that she claimed to be a sleuth from crime-ridden America.

Maybe Luisa was going to squeeze the life out of Rita with those massive arms and then pickle her in a barrel of wine, in between making fresh-squeezed *spremuta d'arancia* and setting the Nutella and homemade jams on the breakfast table.

Rita's eyes darted around the room, searching for a defensive weapon, but the only implement at hand was a rolling pin, and she feared that wouldn't make much of a dent in a woman as large as Luisa.

"Oh?" Rita said, her heart pounding in her chest. "What have you heard?"

"That you're an American," Luisa sneered, "who fancies herself a cook."

Luisa made it sound on par with being a pedophile. Her eyes narrowed, and her hands flew to her hips. "And I hear you think you can cook Italian food," she added venomously. "Everybody knows Americans can't cook Italian food."

Now it was Rita's turn to get mad. "*Certo che sì! Mia mamma era italiana–toscana!–e quindi….*"

Rita went on and on, tracing her mother's lineage from a small town in Tuscany not far from there although on the coast (to which Luisa darkly commented "Ah—where the fish-eaters live! They wouldn't know beef if a bull gored them in the stomach") and her father's descent from a sprawling clan in a remote mountain fastness in Sicily. Rita recounted the hours spent at her mother's and *nonna*'s sides learning to perfect Italian dishes.

"I make my own pasta," Rita said proudly.

Luisa crossed her arms over her chest. "Eggs or no eggs?"

It was a hotly contested debate in Italian cooking and one that betrayed one's regional allegiances. Northern Italians used egg pasta; poorer Southern Italians did without.

"Eggs," Rita said, her chin jutting out defiantly. The truth was more nuanced; she preferred egg noodles for lasagna, but used pasta without eggs for her other dishes.

Luisa pursed her lips. She was clearly disappointed that Rita had given the right answer. Then the gleam reappeared in Luisa's eyes. "Tell me how you make your pasta."

"Well," Rita began nervously, "I put some flour on my butcher block, crack the eggs into the center, then chip away at the sides of the well, and keep mixing until the flour and eggs are combined, adding water as needed. Then I knead the dough, put it in the refrigerator to rest a bit, roll it out, and then run it through my pasta maker—"

Luisa shook her head triumphantly. "*Vedi?*" she said, slipping into the informal "tu" form. But with her, unlike Diana, it was a mark not of friendship, but of condescension. "You are not a real Italian cook. Because every real Italian cook either cuts the pasta by hand or uses bronze dies to extrude their pasta. A real Italian cook *never* uses a pasta maker."

She shot Rita a malicious, gap-toothed grin. "Americans think they know Italian food," Luisa said.

"But they don't. They're barbarians who put pineapple on pizza, dump so much sauce on the pasta you can't even taste it, and drink wine out of a box."

Rita bristled. "I only eat wood-fired pizza made with *mozzarella di bufala*, my sauce is delicious, and I've never drunk boxed wine in my life."

That last bit was a lie, as she'd had boxed wine a few times in college, but Rita reckoned that didn't really count.

"It's strange," Luisa said. "Signor Clausnitzer told me your twin sister was *bellissima*. You must be fraternal twins."

"Actually," Rita said icily, "we're identical."

It was a sore point with Rita. The twin sisters shared a swarthy complexion, strong Italian features, and bright dark eyes, but that was about it. Child-free Rose with her wildly successful real estate practice and time to indulge in hot yoga and spin classes was svelte, toned, fashionably attired, and relatively unwrinkled, with expertly highlighted short blond hair. A lifetime of chasing after children and cooking had left Rita lumpy and bumpy. "Never trust a skinny cook," Sal always said, to which Rita added, "And never trust a wrinkle-free mother."

"Hmmmmph." Luisa said, sizing up Rita from head to toe and lingering on the especially unflattering middle parts. "Then time has been kinder to her than to you."

Rita's jaw clenched and she stood up ramrod-straight. "I challenge you," she said, "to a bake-off."

She said "bake-off" in English because she could think of no suitable Italian translation. She hoped that was one of the many English pop culture phrases that had wound their way into Italian.

"A what?"

"A—contest," Rita said, flustered. "To see who makes the best baked good for breakfast."

Rita clutched the blueberries tightly. They were no longer an offering to Luisa; they were now her prized ingredients.

Luisa, for her part, brandished her rolling pin. "I accept." Then she turned away and muttered, "*Questo será facile—facilissimo.*"

Rita found herself bristle. How dare Luisa demean her thus, to say beating her would be easy! But Rita also felt butterflies in her stomach, and not in a good way.

Rita feared she might have finally met her match.

Two minutes into her bake-off, Rita realized she was at a serious disadvantage. Luisa had commandeered nearly every kitchen implement and was busily crafting what looked like a killer apple *crostata.*

Rita had blueberries, a cake pan, and—when Luisa's back was turned—access to the larder, which contained stone-ground flour from the *agriturismo*'s own mill, coarse raw sugar (no American superfine sugar here), and other basic baking supplies. She also had access to a small refrigerator, which contained lots of unlabeled, homemade, and very pungent dairy products. Rita searched in vain for the sour cream necessary to make her much-loved blueberry sour cream coffeecake, but had to settle for what appeared to be homemade yogurt, rich and creamy, probably unpasteurized, and full of fat.

There were no measuring cups, and Luisa had confiscated the lone flour sifter. Rita thought of her sainted mother, the way she measured the ingredients by their feel on her palms, their heft and weight. She closed her eyes and tried to feel it too, the flour, soft like talcum powder, falling through her fingers. She tossed in the other dry ingredients, savoring the rich scent of Ceylon cinnamon and the powdery texture of snow-white Cervia sea salt. The salt smelled of the warm Adriatic from whence it had come, and she could see why it had been the official salt of popes for centuries. Hans certainly didn't skimp on quality ingredients.

She creamed the sugar, golden brown and gritty like wet sand, into a golden mound of fresh-churned butter. As she mixed the ingredients together, she hummed "*Nessun Dorma*" for confidence. Then she threw in several dollops of yogurt, filling the kitchen with its tangy aroma, added a few golden-brown eggs, split open a dark, shiny vanilla pod, and scraped the seeds into the batter. Soon, she had a thick, shiny batter that looked and smelled just right.

Hans' Bernese, the doleful Wolf, wandered into the kitchen. He cowered in a corner, casting a furtive glance in Luisa's direction, then a more hopeful look at Rita. When Luisa briefly stepped out of the kitchen, Rita snuck over to the refrigerator, rooted around until she found a leftover slab of *bistecca*, and then fed it to a very grateful Wolf.

Wolf settled down by her feet, and Rita began to relax. She started to sing aloud, "*Guardi le stelle che tremano. D'amore e di speranza...*"

She greased the pan, and poured in the batter. "*Tramontate, stelle! Tramontate, stelle...*"

Then Rita prepared the streusel topping, tossing butter, flour, and brown sugar into a bowl and mixing with a pastry blender. When she had a bowl full of thick, luscious chunks, she sprinkled these on top of the batter and crescendoed. "*Vincerò, vincerò...*"

Rita slid the coffeecake in the oven and slammed the door shut with a triumphant clang. Suddenly, she realized she was not the only one singing. She was in a duet with someone who sang off-key, someone rather like—

Rita looked up to see her twin silhouetted in the doorway.

Luisa looked up, too. "Ah—*la gemela bella.*"

The beautiful twin. Rose acknowledged Luisa's compliment with a little smile and crossed over to Rita's corner of the kitchen.

"So," her sister said in English, "what's this about you challenging good old Luisa here to a bake-off?"

"How do you know?"

"Oh, she ran out and told Hans and he told everyone else. Hans thinks it's hilarious. He doesn't think anyone can beat Luisa. He says she's the best cook in Tuscany."

"Yeah, that's what she says, too."

"Well, maybe she *was* the best cook in Tuscany—before you got here."

Rita felt a rush of affection for her sister. Sharp-tongued as Rose could be, Rose was always loyal.

"At least I hope so," Rose added, dipping her finger in the batter left in the bowl and nodding her approval. "I've got fifty euros riding on it. There's a pool going, you see."

"Who else bet on me?"

"At first no one else wanted to bet. But then Hans offered to bet his prized—what did he call it?—kouros. A Greek statue—you know, one of those perfect naked Greek youth with a six pack. The one that looks over the fountain in front."

Rita's mouth fell open. It was the centerpiece of the charming cobblestone courtyard. She couldn't imagine someone carting that away over a rash kitchen bet.

"Crazy," Rose said, "I know. Apparently, it was a gift from some antiquities dealer he knows in Switzerland. So then Diana took his bet," Rose went on, "and offered up a painting by Caravaggio from her castle."

Rita felt very much as though she'd fallen through the looking glass into an alternate world of wealth, privilege, and intrigue. How many famed—and extremely glamorous—archaeologists lived in castles?

"Apparently," Rose said, "Diana hates Hans. So, naturally, she took the bet. And she lives in a castle in Piedmont because she's descended from the royal family of Piedmont. They were deposed, of course, when Italy was founded, but they got to keep their castles and their art. And she's collected even more art on her own. She's a big-time art dealer; she's got galleries in Venice, Basel, and Paris."

Rita's eyebrows shot up. So Diana was not only an archaeologist who could authenticate antiquities for unscrupulous collectors; she was the owner of a gallery that could provide the perfect cover for black-market art deals.

"And before I knew it," Rose said, "nearly everyone was piling on the bet. Giovanna, the bride, bet on Luisa, but then she would as Hans' little protégé. Alessandro, the groom, bet on you. Paolo bet on you—he had to, if he knew what was good for him."

Rita poured a slurry of thick cream into a bowl, scooped out the seeds from a vanilla bean, and began to beat it by hand. There was nothing that couldn't be made more delicious by a side of freshly whipped cream.

"Tiffany backed Luisa. She said Hans was the most competitive person she'd ever met, and if he said his cook was the best, she must be."

Rita's ears perked up. This must be the Tiffany that Commissario Zingaretti had mentioned.

No one else would have noticed Rita's change in expression. But Rose did. That was the downside of having shared a womb—it was like there was an invisible thread connecting them, and it tugged at the most inconvenient times.

"What is it?"

The two sisters shot a furtive glance at Luisa, who was busy arranging little crystal bowls of homemade preserves and Nutella on silver breakfast trays. Despite the fact that Luisa most likely did not speak a word of English, Rita lowered her voice to just above a whisper.

"On the plane, I met an Italian detective specializing in antiquities theft. Luca Zingaretti's cousin."

Rose whistled softly. She too swooned over Luca Zingaretti and his shirtless runs on the beach as Commissario Montalbano.

"He found out," Rita said, "that I was going to be here, and he knew all about the wedding party. And he suspects someone here is trafficking in Etruscan antiquities."

"And he wants you to—what? Catch someone red-handed and perform a citizens' arrest? I don't think you can do that in Italy."

"Nothing so dramatic. Just be his eyes and ears on the ground. Call him if I see anything suspicious."

"You have his phone number?"

Rita blushed but said nothing.

Rose said, "Does Sal know?"

"No," Rita said as the timer went off and she retrieved her cake. It was a perfect golden brown. "And he won't find out. Because you won't tell him. Speaking of my husband, how much did he bet on me?"

"Twenty euros."

"Only twenty!"

"You know your husband's not much of a gambler."

"Still—twenty!"

Rita handed the bowl of whipped cream to Rose and grabbed the cake with a towel since Italians apparently did not believe in oven mitts. She motioned for Rose to follow her out onto the terrace.

"Did anyone not bet on the bake-off?" she asked.

Rose nodded and ticked off each person on her fingers. "Padre Domenico, naturally. And Monica—she's Giovanna's sister. She looks nothing like her. Kind of a meek, mousy thing. Her mother's got her on a pretty tight leash, so she probably doesn't have anything of her own to wager. Running Bear—he's from Arizona. Tiffany calls him her assistant but"—Rose rolled her eyes—"I'd guess he has other duties as assigned. He's very young, very delicious. Probably hasn't got two cents to his name, either. And frigid Chiara, of course, who can't be bothered to do anything but smoke and stare off into the distance."

Rita detected more than a hint of jealousy in Rose's voice.

"And then, of course, Olivia, my little tormentor. She probably doesn't want to use up Daddy's allowance on a stupid bet." Rose tossed her hair. "I will not," she said, "let myself be beaten by a sixteen-year-old."

Rita smiled. She glided past her rival with a backward glance, tossing one last chunk of leftover *bistecca* for a most grateful Wolf. "And I," she said, "will not let myself be beaten by Luisa."

Chapter Eight

The mood was tense as the plates were passed around the terrace, each one with a small sliver of apple *crostata*, a small square of blueberry coffeecake, and a dollop of whipped cream, blindingly white in the sunshine.

"*No, grazie*," Chiara murmured, lighting up her umpteenth cigarette.

"I thought you'd quit," Padre Domenico said to his former sister-in-law. He tried to say it casually, but Rita saw the concern etched on his face.

"I thought I had, too."

Rita followed Chiara's gaze to Olivia, then Paolo, then back to Padre Domenico. Neither Olivia nor Paolo noticed. Padre Domenico squeezed Chiara's hand, gave her a wink, and then accepted a proffered plate with a smile. He diplomatically took a bite of coffeecake, then the *crostata*, and pronounced both delicious.

Olivia took a bite of Rita's coffeecake and wrinkled her nose in disgust. In English, she said, "This topping–it's very American. It just doesn't suit Italian tastes. It's too sweet. The texture is too rough." She shot a meaningful glance at her father, who paused with a forkful of crostata in mid-air. Olivia went on. "American cooking and Italian ingredients just don't go together. Just like, I'm afraid, Italians and"—she glanced pointedly at Rose—"Americans in general."

From another table, Rita heard a derisive snort. "You keep telling yourself that, toots," someone said in English. The voice was loud, brash, a little shrill, with a Texas twang and Texas-sized confidence to match. Rita turned to see a middle-aged woman with a platinum blond bouffant hair-do, skin suntanned nearly into leather, and very blue eyes. The woman wore a slightly startled expression, as if she'd had one too many face-lifts, which was ironic given that there was nothing surprised or uncertain about her tone of voice. She was enrobed in a gauzy, bejeweled wrap over a white bikini, and her hands dripped with gaudy diamond rings.

This had to be Tiffany Devereaux, the American who financed so many archaeological digs in Tuscany.

Tiffany winked. "But I'd wager your father's going to end up with Rose no matter what you do. She's good for him." She shot an appreciative glance at the bare-chested, bronzed young man in the pool lounger beside hers. Rita guessed this must be Running Bear. "Why put boundaries on love?" she said. "I say '*Vive la différence.*'"

Tiffany had an absolutely atrocious French accent, the worst Rita had ever heard.

"Oh, there I go again!" Tiffany said with a laugh. "That's French, isn't it? How do you say that in Italian?"

"*Viva la diversità,*" Alessandro said pleasantly, beaming. "And you're so right, Tiffany." He reached over to take his betrothed's hand, brought it to his lips, and kissed it tenderly. "Giovanna and I have our professional differences of opinions, but what is that compared to love? We were introduced by my sister-in-law, Chiara."

He acknowledged Chiara with a brief nod, and she tipped her cigarette towards him. Rita noticed he referred to Chiara as his sister-in-law, not ex-sister-in-law. Padre Domenico had been similarly friendly with Chiara. Clearly, for this family, it was as if Paolo and Chiara's divorce had never happened.

"She knew," Alessandro said, "we could see past our differences of professional opinion and we would—how do you say?"

Alessandro brought his hands together.

"Get on like a house on fire?" Tiffany suggested.

Alessandro looked perplexed. Clearly, he had never heard that expression. "Well, not like a house burning. No, that would not be good. But yes, with fire, with passion!"

Giovanna was smiling now too. She was a petite, olive-skinned, brown-eyed, copper-haired young woman who reminded Rita of a portrait she had seen of a Medici princess. She was not nearly as voluptuous as her mother or quite as striking, but there was something of Diana in her cupid-bow lips and pert little nose and she was beautiful nonetheless.

"*Un brindisi*," Padre Domenico said, raising his coffee cup to the happy couple. "To love and happy endings. Alessandro and Giovanna have set an excellent example for us all—putting aside petty differences in the spirit of friendship, cooperation, and yes, Christian love." He winked. "And other kinds of love."

There was a ripple of appreciative laughter. Sal elbowed Rita and whispered, "Kind of cheeky for a priest, isn't he?"

She shrugged. "He's Italian."

The others lifted their coffee cups, and there was a chorus of "*salute*" and "*cin cin.*"

But Hans could not let the newly amicable mood last long. "Well?" he demanded in English, presumably for his American guests' benefit. "Shouldn't we vote on who won the baking contest?" He looked at them severely. "Now, remember only those who did not bet can vote." He proceeded to call each name, as if he were calling roll at a military academy. "Monica?"

The mousy girl with the sad eyes and scabby fingers almost jumped out of her chair. "Me?"

She looked shocked to be asked her opinion about anything. Yes, Rita thought, Rose had Monica's number—she lived in perfect, beautiful Giovanna's shadow and was dominated by her mother.

"Oh." Monica glanced around nervously and then, looking at her mother, squeaked, "Luisa."

Pleased, Hans turned to someone he surely regarded as a safe vote. "Olivia?"

"Luisa, of course. She *is* the best cook in Tuscany."

"Padre Domenico?"

"Oh, they're both delicious, it's so hard to choose. But, if I must, well—Rita's. I do love blueberries."

Hans grimaced. "Well, there's no accounting for personal taste. Some of us just really love...blueberries. Running Bear?"

"Rita," he said without hesitation. Rita noticed that he answered without so much as a glance at his employer, and the fact that Tiffany had money riding on Rita's opponent seemed to have no effect upon him.

"So," Hans said with a tight-lipped smile, "it seems Chiara will be a tie breaker."

Chiara blew a smoke ring. "Oh, but I can't be," she said. "I haven't tasted either."

"Ah, but now you must." He thrust a plate into her left hand and, suddenly switching to Italian, said, "*Mangia*." It sounded more like a threat than an invitation.

Chiara placed her still smoking cigarette in an ashtray and took the teeniest bite of each. It was so quiet Rita could hear Chiara's fork slice though the cake. With a sinking heart, Rita realized she would lose. Chiara must hate Rose, and by extension that must mean she'd hate Rita. She and Hans might have a professional disagreement, but she doubted that could stir the emotions the way the appearance of her ex-husband could.

Chiara smiled into the sea of expectant faces. "Rita's," she said.

Rita gasped.

Sal elbowed her and crowed, "What do you know? I just won twenty euros."

Diana licked the whipped cream off her fork, pointed it at Hans, and said, "I'm going to love having your kouros in my garden."

Hans turned purple.

All kinds of side conversations resumed, as bets were settled and old acquaintances renewed. The bride and groom had arrived just that morning, so there was much catching up to do.

Rita felt light-headed, ecstatic about her win. Now there was no doubt she was an Italian cook—she'd beaten the best cook in Tuscany.

Tiffany rushed up to congratulate her. "Good for you, toots. You showed them a thing or two."

"I'm sorry you lost your bet."

"Oh, don't be. I've lost more than that in Vegas in half the time—and for a tenth the entertainment value. The look on Hans' face was priceless. I love stirring the pot, if you can't tell. It's the best entertainment money can buy. That's why I fund Hans' digs and Diana's. People think I do it because I'm seriously interested in archaeology, want to get to the bottom of the Italy vs. Anatolia debate. That's kind of true, but I also just love the drama of seeing those two go at it."

Tiffany elbowed Rita. "You want a real challenge?" she said. "Cook something for the Etruscan banquet we're having tonight."

"Banquet?"

"What? Didn't someone invite you? Well, never mind, I just did. You and your hubby can be my guests. No one can say no to that." She rubbed her fingers together and laughed. "My moolah opens doors. The party starts at seven, at the end of that track there, in a field where Hans and his team have uncovered several Etruscan tombs."

"There's an archaeological site on Hans' property?"

"Well, right next to it. Why do you think he bought the place? Trust me, hon, you don't want to miss this. Succulent roasted wild boar, copious amounts of wine, platters piled high with goat cheese and honey. Crazy Diana pretending to be an Etruscan priestess and reading entrails to divine Alessandro and Giovanna's future. And the stories getting wilder as the night goes on."

Rita licked her lips. Surely, there was no better way to get Commissario Zingaretti a lead than to attend a bacchanalia with a bunch of loose-lipped archaeologists.

Chapter Nine

Rita spent the rest of the morning lounging by the pool, although perhaps lounging wasn't really the right word for it, as she was hardly relaxed. She was frantically thumbing through giant scholarly tomes from Hans' library, searching for clues about what the ancient Etruscans ate and trying to devise an authentic dish to bring to the banquet.

The problem was that the whole point of these banquets was apparently to gorge on meat, the wilder and gamier the better. The Etruscans loved nothing better than to devour a whole flock of pheasants, followed by a spit-roasted wild boar or deer, washed down with copious amounts of wine.

"Drunken, bloodthirsty carnivores," Rita muttered. "That's why their civilization died out—they probably all died of rickets, scurvy, or cirrhosis of the liver."

Chiara, who was on the other side of the pool smoking away, looked up from the scholarly journal she was perusing and shot Rita an inquiring glance.

"Oh, I was just wondering what to make for tonight's banquet," Rita called out in a loud voice. "You wouldn't happen to know what the Etruscans ate, would you? Besides meat?"

Chiara stubbed out her cigarette, rose, and crossed over to where Rita was sitting. "Farro," she said. "It's an ancient grain, a little like rice, but nuttier and very delicious. We still eat it in Tuscany. Mint. Lots of wild herbs. Onions. Olives. Lots of olive oil. Goat cheese." Chiara laughed. "We don't know exactly how they combined all those foods, but we know they ate them because we've done chemical analyses of the contents of their amphora, those big ceramic containers they had. So we know what was in them. And then there are many other types of foods we can infer they had, at least in later periods, based on contemporaneous Roman writings: cucumbers, chickpeas and other pulses, chard and leeks, lots of wild mushrooms, apples, pears, peaches, quince, plums, pomegranates, carrots, celery, figs, and garlic. Dates, too—but they were imported and very expensive. And lots of herbs, both those familiar and unfamiliar to us—basil, marjoram, thyme and bay leaves—but also chervil, which is related to parsley, pennyroyal, which is part of the mint family, and myrtle. Myrtle may not be familiar to you, but it produces a fruit that is still used to flavor some Middle Eastern dishes, and in Italy we still use the flowers occasionally to garnish salads."

"Tomatoes?"

"*Certo che non!*" Chiara looked rather horrified. "The Romans didn't even have tomatoes. Tomatoes didn't arrive in Italy until the 1300s, probably from France."

Rita blanched. She did not like to think of the tomato—the glorious *pomodoro* which undergirded nearly all of Italian cuisine—as an import. She did not like to think of tomatoes as French.

"But," Chiara added in a conciliatory tone, "the ancient Etruscans may have had pasta. There's a mural in a funerary tomb that shows Etruscans carrying baskets of what some historians believe are breadsticks or crackers, but others believe to be the first depiction of *pici*, which is like a fat spaghetti and the most Tuscan of pastas. So, there is some continuity with the past."

Rita was intrigued. She had a vague memory of her mother making *pici*, but it wasn't one of the recipes that had been handed down. She started mentally scrolling through her recipe book, racking her brains for some sort of whole-grain salad bursting with fresh herbs and studded with goat cheese. Perhaps she could make a sort of Italian version of tabbouleh....

"Rita?"

She suddenly realized that Chiara was had been speaking to her, and she had paid absolutely no attention, enraptured as she was by visions of zippy, whole-grain salads. Rita cleared her throat, fixed her best "yes-I'm-really-listening-now" expression on her face, and squinted at Chiara in the blazing sun.

"I'm very pleased that Paolo has found your sister," Chiara said. To Rita's surprise, the cool, detached demeanor was gone. Chiara said it with some warmth, as if she actually meant it. "She's good for him."

"Your *figlia* doesn't seem to think so."

"Bah! Olivia's sixteen. What does she know about love? She thinks it's all googly eyes over gelato and a moonlight ride on a Vespa and stolen kisses in the park. She doesn't think about the day-to-day."

"But on that score, I'd rather think you have Rose beat. You and Paolo share a language, a culture, a country, a love of archaeology, and, most importantly, a daughter. That is the day-to-day: work, children, a lifetime of conversations."

"I disagree," Chiara said, although Rita noticed that some of her confidence was gone and her fingers shook slightly as if she were itching to light another cigarette. "What did Tiffany say? '*Viva la différence*'?"

Rita noticed that Chiara's French accent, unlike Tiffany's, was flawless.

"Actually," Chiara said, "I was hoping you might pass on some advice to your sister. Not attributed to me, of course, because then she wouldn't take it."

Rita tilted her head to the side. It wasn't quite a nod, because Rita did not want to commit to a course of action without knowing what the advice was...or without having time to mull over Chiara's motives. She found it hard to believe that Chiara wanted to help Rose woo her ex-husband. Rita wondered if this was all part of a clever misinformation campaign designed to sabotage Rose's chances with Paolo.

So Rita limited herself to saying, "Go on."

"Paolo's two passions are his work and his daughter. Rose must try to show some interest in his work, and she needs to move here when his visiting professorship is up. He needs to be back on a dig, doing what he loves."

Rita sat straight up. She did not intend for her twin—her closest friend and confidant—to be snatched from under her. Sure, it would be fun to visit Rose and Paolo in Italy, but it would never be the same as having her sister in Acorn Hollow, where she belonged.

"And Rose wouldn't have to give up her work, either," Chiara said, as if she'd already worked out every detail. "There are loads of Americans looking to buy a villa in Tuscany, looking to play out their *Under the Tuscan Sun* fantasies."

Rita couldn't argue with that. Her book club had read *Under the Tuscan Sun* last year, and for months afterwards, the members had been sending each other photos of romantically crumbling Tuscan villas they had found online, each more beautiful and completely impractical than the last.

"So Rose could be their real estate agent," Chiara said. "It's perfect when you think about it. She speaks English and Italian, she understands the American psyche, their need for dishwashers and clothes dryers—all kinds of useless things!—and she's even a dual citizen!"

"And," Chiara added, "she must try not to alienate Olivia." Chiara held up a hand before Rita could protest. "*Lo so*—Olivia makes this almost impossible. She's scheming against Rose at every juncture, just like she does with every one of his girlfriends. But Paolo can't see it. So Rose just has to grin and bear it, make nice with Olivia. She'll be grown soon and off living her life."

Rita thought for a moment. "Why," she finally said, "are you telling me this?"

"Because I want Paolo to be happy."

"Why? Because you love him?"

Chiara did not answer the question directly. Instead, she tilted her head slightly and said, "If you love someone, set them free."

"From you?"

"If need be."

"Did Paolo ask to be set free? Did he want to be free?"

Chiara glanced in the direction of Paolo's cottage and then back at Rita. "No. But men never know what's good for them, do they?"

Rita couldn't argue with that.

Chapter Ten

Rita wandered through the kitchen garden, snipping a clump of parsley here, a dozen glossy basil and mint leaves there. She uprooted a few green onions, shook off the deep dark earth from their roots, and inhaled their pungent smell. Then she picked two long, emerald-green cucumbers and a clump of scarlet-hued radishes.

The sun was high in the sky now, turning her already tanned arms a deeper, richer shade of brown. She could almost imagine an Etruscan woman right here on this spot, harvesting the ingredients for her farro salad.

What would the woman have gathered? Rita tried to remember Chiara's words. Olives, she remembered, olive oil, and wine...but wine did not seem like an ingredient for a salad.

But if they had wine, they must have had red wine vinegar. Perhaps, she thought, they'd have made a vinaigrette, sweetened with the local acacia honey.

She passed behind the hedgerows that separated the garden from the rest of the fields and headed back towards the kitchen in the shadow of the estate's imposing stone warehouse.

The warehouse.

She stopped dead in her tracks, the priest's words reverberating in her head. *Olive oil and wine. He's sending cases abroad every week. It'd be the easiest thing in the world to slip something into the bottom of the case.*

Rita needed olive oil and red wine vinegar for her recipe. Now, there might be all she needed in the pantry...but there might not be.

Surely, it would not be unreasonable for her to take a little detour and nab a bottle or two for the pantry. It wasn't as though she were trespassing per se. She was a paying guest at a property billed as giving tourists "a peek into the authentic rural Tuscan lifestyle."

And what could give her better insight into this lifestyle than a quick "peek" into a case of olive oil and wine. If she *happened* to see an Etruscan artifact...well, she'd be doing the Italian government a favor. And then she could just give Commissario Zingaretti a quick call, say "case closed," and wash her hands of the whole affair, with Sal none the wiser. It would be almost like his ludicrous scenario in which she witnessed a murder in the Uffizi and then stepped over the body to go have an espresso in a little café by the Duomo.

She would be *almost* that uninvolved.

Rita moved closer to the sturdy edifice, slipping under the eaves and running her fingers along the weathered stones, surprisingly cool in the midday heat. As she reached the entrance, she cast a furtive glance about her before slipping through the half-door and entering the dark, forbidding cave of a room. It took a moment for her eyes to adjust to the light. She could make out a line of heavy oak barrels and a small Ushaped bottling area. She slid open the flap of a cardboard box, took out an elegant, long-necked bottle, and inspected the label. Villa Belvista, it said. She slid her hand under the box, along the smooth cardboard bottom, then picked up a few more bottles and did the same.

But there was nothing to be found.

Rita moved on to inspect the enormous rounds of pecorino cheese when she heard voices approaching. Her eyes darted frantically around the room. If she were a slip of a girl, like Olivia or Chiara, she might be able to squeeze between the two wine barrels and lurk, undetected, in their shadow.

But she was Rita of the child-bearing hips that would not squeeze, the arthritic ankles that would not crouch, and the bushy black hair that would not lie flat.

No, that would not do.

Out of the corner of her eye, she spied a dark corner with row upon row of prosciutto being air-dried until it could be shaved into wafer-thin, salty-sweet crimson slices and adorn a delectable tray of antipasti.

She dove headlong into the prosciutto. Inhaling deeply, she immediately began dreaming about wood-fired pizzas topped with prosciutto and arugula; slices of bright orange cantaloupe, sweet and ripe and soft as butter, draped with a salty layer of prosciutto; fettucine noodles drenched in a creamy Alfredo sauce studded with flecks of prosciutto and the season's first green peas....

"Ah," Hans said in his best clipped English as he and someone else crossed the threshold, "so you've come to get your pound of flesh."

"Not flesh," was the reply. "Not yet anyway. For the moment, fifty thousand euros will do."

The woman's English was excellent too, but the accent was not German. It had the musicality of Italian, and the beautiful rounded vowels.

Rita stood on her tiptoes and squinted between two enormous hunks of prosciutto. Frustratingly, she could not see the woman at all. But just for a second, she caught a glimpse of something else: a hand, curled over the window ledge, a glint of something thick and gold.

Rita was apparently not the only one spying.

And then, in a flash, it was gone.

Hans said, "Money can't buy you love, you know."

"No." The woman's nasty laugh echoed through the cavernous space. "But it can buy lots of things."

"You once wanted more from me than money."

"And look how that turned out."

"Better than you realize."

"What's that supposed to mean?"

"Oh, you'll find out soon enough. You're not the only one with secrets, my dear."

Chapter Eleven

The woman left, and Hans walked over to a large wooden work table in the center of the room, opened a laptop, typed something for a few minutes, and then shut it. Then he opened a second laptop, opened a spreadsheet, typed a few stokes, and shut it.

So he kept two laptops. Was one for legitimate business, and the other for...other activities? Not that she had managed to find any evidence of these other activities, of course, but Rita was confident that eventually she would. Then she heard footsteps, light and quick, approaching.

A lengthy conversation ensued. They spoke in a harsh, guttural tone, which had to be German.

But who was this second woman? Rita shifted slightly, trying to catch a glimpse of her between the sinuous curves of prosciutto, which swayed lightly as she moved.

But all she could make out was Hans' silhouette in the doorway. The woman was off to his left, just out of view.

"*Gut*," she heard, and "*danke*," but that was all she could understand; that was the extent of Rita's German.

It grew quiet again; Rita surmised that the woman had departed.

"*Frei*!" she heard Hans exclaim several times, pumping his fist with joy as he puttered excitedly about the warehouse for another fifteen minutes or so. Rita thought that meant "free," but what exactly that referred to, she could not guess.

Then Hans left, whistling. Rita waited fifteen minutes more, in case he returned, before making her escape. She squeezed back through the gauntlet of hanging prosciutto, tiptoed past crates of olive oil and wine, and then walked briskly from the warehouse towards the kitchen, her prized farro-salad ingredients in hand.

All the while, Rita's thoughts whirred. Hans kept two laptops. He ran an import-export business. His property backed onto an Etruscan archaeological site.

It was all circumstantial, hardly enough for Commissario Zingaretti to act upon. And then there was the pesky, inconvenient truth that she had not found any actual archaeological artifacts in the warehouse.

Rita's shoulders slumped as she stepped over the threshold and set her ingredients on the marble counter. The truth was she was no closer to cracking the case for Commissario Zingaretti.

Rita pulled down one of the hanging copper-bottomed pots, filled it with salted water, and set it on the stove to boil. Then she reached for a gleaming stainless-steel knife and began to julienne the cucumbers and radishes. As she turned her attention to pitting the olives—the coveted *frantoio* olives native to Tuscany, bright green with a purple-red blush—she marveled at how something so shiny and beautiful could harbor such a hard, ordinary pit within. Like Hans, she thought. Handsome and debonair on the outside, but harboring a secret so dark that it led to blackmail. She wondered if the cause of the blackmail related to the antiquities trafficking, or to something else entirely.

The water was boiling at a fevered pitch now. She tossed in the farro and turned down the heat, thinking all the while about transformation. How the farro would plump up into pearled little grains twice its original size, how grapes could become wine and then vinegar.

She remembered an obituary she'd read recently. It was for Charles Hill, the American-born star of Scotland Yard's Art Squad—the man who recovered Edvard Munch's "The Scream," plus masterworks by Vermeer and Goya. What fascinated her most was that his tool of the trade was not some high-tech gadget, but simply the art of transformation. This cultured, bespectacled man had adopted an alter ego as a dodgy art dealer clad in a bow tie, seersucker suit, and tasseled loafers. Later, he'd posed as a desperate, unscrupulous employee of the Getty Museum eager to recover their stolen masterpieces at any price, and an intermediary for Arab sheiks looking for the *pièce de résistance* for their seaside villa.

Rita was just hatching a plan to transform herself into a dodgy art dealer when Sal wandered in, his big nose hoovering up the aromas.

"Parsley?" he guessed when he had come no further than the doorway. "Basil and green onions—no, chives. I'm guessing some baby lamb chops on a bed of polenta…" He looked over her shoulder, and she turned in time to see his eyebrows furrow together and the corners of his big fleshy lips curl down. "Or," he said glumly, "a quinoa salad, beloved of health nuts everywhere."

"It's farro, *caro*, and it's not only nutritious, it's ancient."

"So's quinoa," he said, "but that doesn't make it tasty. You know, we're supposed to be on vacation. A relaxing, romantic vacation. But I've barely seen you. You spent most of the flight yakking about Etruscan history and art with Zingaretti." He said the *commissario*'s name with a slight growl and an inflection that cried out for air quotes. "Then you were up at dawn to swim and pick pears. Before we'd even finished breakfast, you'd entered a bake-off and now you're making glorified birdseed."

Sal reached up and started massaging her shoulders. "So, what do you say that we just toss this salad together, leave it to marinate, and go and enjoy a relaxing spin through *bella* Toscana together?" He waved a scrap of paper with his atrocious block-print handwriting all over it. "I worked with Hans to devise the perfect little itinerary: a *coppetta* at this gelateria in San Gimignano that won the World Gelato Championship, a tour and tasting at the *fattoria* that makes your favorite imported *caciocavallo* cheese, and then—given your sudden interest in all things Etruscan—a stop at a few Etruscan sites, including the *vie cave*, this mysterious network of underground passages. Then we'll cap it off with a *passegiata* on the *lungomare* as the sun sets over the Mediterranean in your great-great-grandmother's fishing village, followed by a seaside dinner at a little gem of a place that specializes in *cacciucco* made with that afternoon's fresh catch, homemade limoncello, and award-winning tiramisu."

Rita was truly touched. Sal had put so much thought into devising an itinerary just for her. He'd even remembered the name of her family's ancestral fishing village.

But she felt the siren song of Volterra's art dealers, sure that at least one of them was in league with the trafficker in their midst.

"That sounds wonderful, *caro*," Rita exclaimed, "but perhaps Wednesday would be a better day."

Sal's face fell.

"Only," she said quickly, "because then we'd have the whole day ahead of us. And the weather's supposed to be just ideal on Wednesday—cooler, seventy for a high, not a cloud in the sky."

"So, what are you going to do all day?" He glowered at her as she whisked together the dressing, combined it with the vegetables and farro, and put the mixture in the refrigerator. "Slave away in the kitchen?"

"No." They strolled towards the door. "I was thinking of going to Volterra for a bit of shopping, maybe some gelato."

"Sounds good to me."

She stopped dead in her tracks. "Oh—you're coming?"

He grunted. "I would have gone for 'Oh, how delighted I am that my evolved, sensitive hubby wants to spend time with me so much that he's willing to carry my bags like a pack horse and fork over his—"

"Our," Rita corrected him.

"—credit card like he's Daddy Warbucks. But yeah, I'm coming." He took her arm gallantly as they stepped over the threshold. "And forget calling a taxi, *principessa*." He thumped the seat of a cherry-red Vespa, and Rita gulped. "Your chariot awaits."

The cypress trees lining the road flew past at dizzying speed, the hay- and rosemary-scented wind buffeting Rita's face, sending her hair skyward like a giant cyclone.

"Are you sure you know what you're doing?" Rita shouted as they veered onto the smooth asphalt of the highway, weaving in front of a Maserati, then a snub-nosed little white delivery van.

"Relax," Sal said. "I was practically part of a motorcycle gang, remember?"

Rita did not remember that, and it did not make her feel any better. "Practically? What does that mean? You applied to be in Hell's Angels and they rejected you for flat feet?"

"Don't be ridiculous. With Joey Schiaparelli and Tony Fattone."

"They were in a gang?"

Sal shrugged. "Well, they rode motorcycles and drank down by the railroad tracks and graffitied half the town. And Joey did a couple of years of hard time for a burglary a few years after that."

Rita could hear the chagrin creeping into his voice. Even he realized what a pale imitation of a motorcycle gang this was. Rita bit her lip to keep from laughing.

"And they let me ride sometimes," he finished lamely.

The road arched up and around the volcanic rock, dark and foreboding, upon which Volterra was perched. Higher and higher they climbed, until the natural fortress began to meld into the manmade one, the limestone ramparts, warm and buttery in the afternoon sun, shooting up from the rocks. The effect was of contrast but also continuity, as if the walls had somehow grown organically out of the rock, as if a new plant had grafted itself onto an ancient one. Above them loomed a skyline of low-slung, amber-colored buildings with sloping, red-tiled roofs, their beautiful facades pockmarked by the long narrow slits, black as coal, that passed for windows in medieval times. The long horizontal lines were punctuated here and there by a lone looming tower, crenellated and foreboding, and, near the center, the graceful dome of the cathedral.

The smooth ribbon of asphalt suddenly turned to cobblestones, and Rita received a bone-jarring jolt that made her hug Sal even more tightly. Sal steered them beneath the city gates and through the winding, cobbled lanes lined with all the hallmarks of modern commercialism: cafés where patrons struggled to be heard over the grinding and whirring of gleaming espresso machines; gelaterias proudly displaying artfully arranged heaps of *stracciatella*, pistachio, and hazelnut gelato; stylish *enoteche* offering charcuterie, cheese boards, and wine pairings; and alabaster workshops with the prices displayed in every currency imaginable.

Rita tapped Sal's shoulder and they screeched to a halt.

"Well," Rita said brightly, "I think I'll just pop in a few of these alabaster shops."

Sal looked suspicious. "I didn't know you were so interested in alabaster."

"Oh, well..." Rita ran her eyes over the waist-high alabaster jugs in the entryway. Their delicate milky-white forms seemed to glow from within. "They're so..." – she groped for the only adjective that came to mind – "translucent."

"They won't fit on the plane."

"I'll mail them."

"They'll break in the mail."

Rita set her jaw in a determined line. "I'm sure I'll think of something. Now why don't you just run along and have a nice wine tasting while I shop?"

Sal furrowed his brows. "You want me to drink and drive? On a Vespa? With you hanging on for dear life on the back?"

Rita frowned. When he put it that way, her suggestion did sound downright dangerous. But Rita could not shoo Sal off to the museum, as that smacked of far too much of culture for her culture-averse husband. He would laugh off her suggestion to wander around and admire the architecture; he would shrug off her recommendation to visit the Roman ruins by saying there were much better ruins awaiting them in Rome. A trip to a gelateria would be enticing, but he'd be even more suspicious if she didn't want to come along.

Squeezing her eyes shut, Rita tried to conjure up some way of bringing him along on her investigation without having him *realize* he was on an investigation.

"All right," Rita said with a smile, "but let's spice things up with some role-playing, shall we?"

Sal took a step backwards and tripped over the curb, nearly colliding with a dapper elderly gentleman in a three-piece suit. "Role-playing?" he croaked with a mix of hope and trepidation. "Like what? You're going to buy a French maid costume?"

"No." Rita slipped her arm in his and steered him towards the nearest alabaster shop. "I was thinking more like we could pretend to be filthy-rich, slightly shady Americans."

"Huh?"

"You're a"—Rita took in Sal's rumpled shirt, black Reeboks, and New York accent and frowned—"Rhode Island dockworker turned Oklahoma wildcatter turned oil tycoon."

Sal jiggled his ears as if to make sure he had heard right.

"And I'm your bored socialite wife turned art collector who's been busy furnishing our ten thousand square foot 'cottage' in the Ozarks, which is a replica of the Parthenon, only with flat-screened TVs and ATVs out front."

Sal's jaw dropped as far as it would go. He looked at her as if she were stark raving mad. Under ordinary circumstances, that would have been a bad thing. But in the current situation, Rita chose to interpret it as a wholly positive sign. In the span of a few minutes, Sal had ricocheted from hope tinged with lust to bitter disappointment to bewilderment. But not once had he seemed to suspect she was sleuthing.

Chapter Twelve

By the ninth alabaster shop, Sal's eyes were glazed over and Rita's feet were aching. Both of their spirits were flagging, albeit for very different reasons. While Rita had perfected her mix of twangy, flat, nasal English and pidgin Italian delivered with breathless, wide-eyed enthusiasm for all things old and expensive, she was no closer to garnering clues about antiquities trafficking in the area.

"So these techniques," she said slowly and very loudly, the way she'd seen Americans speak English with Italians, "go back to the time of the Etruscans."

The salesman, a wiry little man with beady dark eyes and a balding pate, nodded vigorously. "Alabaster from under the earth in Castellina Marittima. Very soft. *Molto morbo*. Much more soft than marble. Hand carved. All top quality."

Like nearly all the salesmen she had encountered so far, he spoke only halting English and had an endearing habit of repeating himself in English and Italian, as if that would somehow help his foreign customers understand. She noticed that he rocked forward on his toes as he spoke, eager to make a sale. He would strike a hard bargain. Of this she was sure—she'd seen how he sized her up by scrutinizing her jewelry and her purse to see just how much she could afford. Luckily, Rita had insisted on changing before their Vespa ride and was wearing her best pearl necklace, a silk blouse, and well-tailored capri pants.

"But I don't want something that just looks old"—she stuck out her lip in what she hoped was a pout—"I want something that actually is old. *Molto, molto vecchio.* Like an Etruscan funerary urn with chariots and winged lions." She tried to think of the most gauche thing she could possibly say. "It would make a lovely umbrella stand for the foyer."

She looked at the salesman beseechingly. When he said nothing, she added, "And I'm willing to pay *molti soldi. Mio marito*"—here she jabbed a thumb in Sal's direction—"has *molti soldi.*"

The salesman glanced dubiously at Sal's battered Reeboks. Rita could tell what he was thinking.

"He's incognito," Rita said, lowering her voice. "He doesn't want the paparazzi following us. Or thieves. We left his gold Rolex at the hotel."

"Paparazzi? He's famous?"

"Oh, yes...he's the Bill Gates of Oklahoma."

Sal's eyes bulged out and he coughed loudly upon hearing this appellation, but the salesman just beckoned for her to follow him further into the depths of his workshop. He raised his index finger to just below his right eye, pulled it down, exposing his lower eyelid, and titled his head. It was the classic *occhio* sign that could mean "be careful," "watch out," or even "I'm watching you." In a low voice, he said, "No talk to anyone. Secret –*clandestino, capisce?*"

He rubbed his thumb and forefinger together in the universal sign for money. "It cost you *moltissimi soldi.*"

Rita nodded eagerly.

"I know a man," he said slowly. "You tell me what you want, he can get."

"Roman?"

"Better." He winked at her. "*Etrusco.*"

Rita squealed with delight, the way Tiffany always did, and he put a finger to his lips. She solemnly pantomimed zipping shut her lips and throwing away the key.

"And when," she said, "can I meet this man? Is he Italian? An archaeologist?"

He shook his head. "*Arabe o indiano. Archeologo? Non lo so. Neanche so come si chiama.*" When she remembered to look confused by his Italian, he barked, "No name."

"So how do you get in touch with him?" Rita pantomimed calling on the phone.

"Have number," he said.

Rita knew that she couldn't ask anything more without raising suspicion, so she made arrangements for the salesman to confirm the availability of a few particular items, the price, and the delivery date with the mysterious Arab or Indian man and said she would return in a few days.

Then she and Sal repaired to a gelateria on the cobblestone piazza. Rita ordered a *grande copetta* overflowing with the deepest, darkest *cioccolato fondente* she'd ever eaten, a marvelously tangy *sorbetto di limone*, and a delicately perfumed saffron and rosewater gelato studded with toasted pine nuts. Sal ordered *stracciatella*, *caffé*, and *gianduia*, the classic and universally beloved mixture of milk chocolate and hazelnuts.

They sat in a shady corner of the piazza, happily slurping their rapidly melting gelato and watching a group of *sbandieratori* toss and twirl their flags with synchronized precision to the beat of a drum. All of the performers, from the flag throwers to the drummers to the trumpeters, were in the brightly-colored medieval garb of court jesters.

While Rita and Sal's gelato dwindled, the *sbandieratori* organized themselves into two lines, the drummers ahead of them, the trumpeters behind. Townspeople began to flood the square; twilight began to descend.

Sal stretched out his legs and yawned contentedly. "So far today, we've enjoyed a hair-raising Vespa ride, pretended to be filthy rich, and eaten a ridiculous amount of gelato. Why not join a parade?"

Rita started to demur. "We need to get back to the villa for the banquet tonight..."

But then something caught her eye: a bobbing head of silver hair attached to a tall body. She shifted her body and strained to see across the piazza. The man walked quickly and with purpose; he had an almost military bearing. No Italian would walk that way.

It was Hans, she was sure of it—and he was walking down the narrow lane that led off the piazza, the lane, if she was not mistaken, that the parade route was about to follow.

"On second thought," Rita said, "it does sound fun, and it shouldn't take too long."

She tossed the sticky remains of her gelato in a trash can and raced towards the parade.

Sal followed her across the piazza as she half-walked, half-ran in the direction that Hans had gone. Instead of joining the procession behind the performers, she rushed in between the *sbandieratori*, ducking each time they launched a flag at one another. Craning her neck, Rita glimpsed Hans standing on a stone step in front of an arched doorway. He was speaking to a middle-aged woman with blonde hair and a chubby little man with a receding hairline. Rita was disappointed that neither seemed to fit the description of an Arab or Indian man.

"Hey," Sal said as a flag came flying particularly close to his face. "That one almost took my nose off. I really think we should move back–"

"Oh, Sal," Rita huffed, craning her neck to get a better glimpse of Hans in the distance. "Live a little. Pretend you're in a Fellini film."

"If I were in a Fellini film," he grunted, "I'd be frolicking in a fountain with a scantily clad Anita Ekberg."

Rita struggled to watch Hans through the ever-changing, dizzying display of colored silk flags shooting past them, up towards the ever-darkening sky, then sailing back down to be grasped, at the last second, by a teenaged *sbandieratore*.

For a moment, her view was totally obscured. Hans was eclipsed by a bright yellow flag emblazoned with a red lion. When the flag came crashing back towards earth, the doorway came back into view. But Hans, and the couple, were gone.

It probably meant nothing, she told herself. It was just a social call, maybe a quick meeting with one of his vendors, or a chance encounter with an old friend.

But all through the rest of the parade, the fireworks that followed, and the white-knuckle Vespa ride back, Rita wondered whether she had just witnessed a meeting between Hans and his fellow antiquities traffickers.

Chapter Thirteen

By the time Rita and Sal trudged down the dirt track with Rita's farro salad, it was after eight o'clock.

Sal reached for her hand. "Kind of romantic, isn't it? Just you, me, the stars"—he opened his arms to the sky, where the Milky Way spread above them—"miles of vineyards and olive groves...and my sister-in-law and a bunch of kooky archaeologists."

"It's not quite what you planned, is it, *caro*?"

"No, but that's all right." He put his arms around her and pulled her in to a kiss. "There's never a dull moment with you. Starting a new career at sixty-five, solving five murders....What will you do next?"

Rita felt her skin go suddenly clammy. This was the moment of truth. Now was the time to make a clean breast of it and tell her husband that their second honeymoon had become, for her, a working vacation.

"Sal, I—"

"*Non ti preocupare, cara*. I'm behind you all the way. But just for these two weeks, let's enjoy the peace and quiet. No drama, no murder, no family—well, except Rose."

Well, that settled it. Clearly, now was not the time to mention her latest assignment.

As they rounded the crest of a hill, a blazing campfire came into view, then a long, low table piled high with food and flanked by revelers reclining on cushions.

Sal muttered, "It reminds me of some Roman shindig. All that reclining on sofas and guzzling wine. What are they going to do next? Sacrifice a goat?" Suddenly, he stopped in his tracks. "What the–?"

Rita froze as well. She'd been warned by Tiffany, but even so the sight of Diana holding up a sheep's liver, blood dripping down her fingers, the flames fanning out behind her, sent shivers down her spine.

"She's divining the future," Rita whispered, moving closer to Sal and clutching his hand, "the way the ancient Etruscans did."

They watched, mesmerized, as Diana threw her milky white throat up to the sky and emitted an otherworldly groan, her eyelids fluttering. Then she caressed the glistening organ with her elegantly manicured fingers and inhaled deeply. "Before the cock crows at dawn," she intoned, "many dreams will be dashed. Many will be left bereft of hope, like a mariner thrust overboard into the wine-dark sea."

Rita frowned. The mannerisms and voice certainly put one in mind of an oracle, but the words were all wrong, an odd mash-up of Biblical allusions and Homerian legend.

Sal and Padre Domenico were apparently of the same opinion, because Sal whispered, "She's not even an original wacko," and Padre Domenico folded his arms across his chest and frowned; all this paganism was not to his liking. But everyone else seemed to be taken in. They were in the land of the true believers.

"Secrets shall be unearthed," Diana proclaimed, "and the ties that bind revealed. The dove of the East shall be united with the dove of the West, and the gods will smile on their union, bringing them wealth and prosperity."

Out of the corner of her eye, Rita saw Giovanna and Alessandro smile and squeeze their hands together. Sal must have seen it too, because he muttered, "They must be the doves, huh?"

It was a bit of stretch, given that they were both Italian. But Rita remembered Rose saying that Paolo's family was from a small fishing village on the Adriatic, so she supposed that was "the East." Diana had a Roman accent, so she surmised Giovanna had been reared in "the West."

Diana's neck now snapped down, and her head swung violently from side to side. Her eyelids began fluttering again. "The invader from the north..."

All eyes swiveled towards Hans.

"Yes?" Hans replied. There was not a hint of irony or mocking in his voice; clearly, he too was a true believer. "What about him?"

"He shall pass...through the final red door."

"When?" Hans cried.

"When...it is the gods' will."

Diana made this last pronouncement very slowly and solemnly. Then she went limp and fell silent. No one said a word; no one moved a muscle. At last, she raised her head, opened her eyes wide, and stared at those assembled, as if suddenly realizing she had an audience. Then Diana blinked a few times, smiled, and went to recline beside Giovanna, who patted her on the back warmly and said, "*Grazie, mamma.* I'm glad the gods are smiling on our union."

Tiffany spotted Rita and Sal and waved them over. "Ah—you came! Feast with us!"

Tiffany motioned for Running Bear to scoot over, and Rita and Sal settled into some cushions and found themselves staring right into the grotesque grin of an enormous boar, which was laid out on a silver platter and extended nearly the entire length of the table.

"Wasn't that a hoot?" Tiffany speared an enormous hunk of meat and thrust it in her mouth. "Better than a Chinese fortune cookie."

Rita set her bowl of farro salad on the table. It looked tiny and completely out of place next to the gleaming, glistening boar. "It's quite fortuitous that Giovanna and Alessandro got the blessing of the gods" - she put 'gods' in air quotes and crossed herself, feeling as if she were about to be smote by lightning—"right before their wedding."

Tiffany guffawed, and little pieces of pork spewed out of her pink-lacquered lips. "So much better than my daddy's toast at my third wedding. He said, 'Son, you just remember that I've got a Glock and two brothers in the sheriff's office. So you better treat my little girl right.'" Tiffany took a big gulp of wine, raised her glass aloft, and looked heavenward. "Which turned out to be a fortune in a way, because husband number three didn't treat me right and Daddy did fire a few rounds at him, although he missed like he always did when he was drunk, and he never did get charged with anything."

For once, Rita was at a loss for what to say. She took a gulp of wine and snuck a glance at Running Bear, who was turned away from Tiffany, but still in her clutches; Tiffany's fire engine-red nails, sharp like talons, rested possessively on his arm. He was deep in conversation with Rose about the wonders of Arizona's Red Rock country, but it seemed to Rita that both Running Bear and her sister were desperately trying to bring the objects of their affection–Paolo in Rita's case, and if she was not mistaken, Monica in Running Bear's case–into the conversation. Monica occasionally shyly interjected a question in halting English, and Rose kept attempting to bring Paolo into the conversation with a hint that they might journey to the archaeological sites of the Southwest–Mesa Verde, perhaps, or Canyon de Chelly.

But every time Paolo got too engrossed in the conversation, his daughter would interrupt with some pressing question about her father's first love, the Etruscans, or a brilliant idea of how her parents could collaborate on some obscure line of research.

What had Diana said? *Dreams will be dashed; many will be bereft of hope.* Rita wondered if that would include her sister.

Lowering her voice, Rita asked, "And what was all that about the red door?"

Tiffany smiled and wiggled her heavily penciled eyebrows. "Oh, it's an Etruscan thing. They put them in their tombs, see. Red doors through which the dead pass into eternity."

"So she foretold his death."

"I guess, but I mean, we're all gonna die someday. She didn't say when."

Rita's gaze roamed over the roasted boar, past the platters of goat cheese drizzled with honey, piles of figs, pyramids of unshelled nuts, and a few overflowing amphorae of wine and olive oil, to Hans, who was arguing some fine point of Etruscan history with Diana in a mix of Italian and English; Hans' English was far better than his Italian.

With each exchange, they moved a millimeter closer until their noses were almost touching. Hans seemed to have forgotten all about Diana's ominous pronouncement; he did not seem to be concerned about the prospect of passing through the red door of death anytime soon.

"You-hoo, Hans!" Tiffany's voice floated through the warm, humid air. When he still did not look up, she hooted, "Hey, intruder from the north!"

Now she had his attention.

Tiffany jerked a greasy thumb in Rita's direction. "Rita here wants to see the red door."

"Oh," Rita protested, "well, I–"

"Oh, shush. I'm sure Hans would love to show you his tomb."

Tiffany gestured expansively into the darkness. Somewhere beyond the bonfire was an Etruscan tomb with a red door of death.

"Of course." Hans stood up from the table with exaggerated gallantry as if he were struggling to stay upright, came around to the side of the table, and took Rita's hand. "If you'll just follow me."

Rita did not relish the prospect of being in an enclosed space with Hans, isolated from the rest of the group. In his current state of inebriation, he might confuse her with her twin and make a pass at her, or worse. Summoning her courage, Rita followed Hans, but not before lunging at her husband and dragging him way in mid-conversation.

"Hey, what's the big idea?" Sal muttered. "I was getting stock tips."

"From a priest?"

"Yeah. He ministers to inmates who've done time for insider trading."

"So you'll get the rest of the tips tomorrow. It's not like you're going to buy stocks at midnight, are you? And do you really want me to be alone with Hans?"

"No." Even though Rita couldn't see her husband's face, she could tell just from his tone of voice that he was wearing his trademark glare. "But–"

"I rest my case."

She elbowed Sal in the dark to indicate their conversation was over. Turning to Hans, she said brightly, "You were saying?"

Hans pulled out a pocket flashlight. "This is a cumulus tomb, very popular in the late Etruscan period when they were under Roman domination. It was carved out of tufa, the very soft, porous rock so common in Tuscany."

The light flit over a low curved façade of pockmarked stone blocks, beneath a turf-covered conical hill; nature had reclaimed the tomb. In the center, beneath a stone lintel, was a rectangular opening. Beyond it was a gaping black hole. Rita clenched Sal's hand harder.

They passed through the opening, and the orb of light rested on a magnificent fresco—revelers reclining on a long, low banquet table, guzzling wine and gorging themselves on wild game, much like the scene outside. Above them, two leopards faced off against one another. And then in the center, flanked by two horrible demons, black as night, with blood-red tongues and bloodshot eyes, was the red door. It wasn't solid red, as Rita had pictured it, but red and white striped, with a row of white dots down the center and across the middle, like a polka dot cross.

"The Etruscans," Hans said, "believed the dead would enter eternity through that door."

"And this tomb was just like this—empty?"

"Oh, no! It contained furniture, jewelry, pottery. Everything they thought they needed in the afterlife. And then the actual stone sarcophagus in which the body was placed. It had a marvelous hunting scene on it. It's all in the museum in Volterra, of course."

"Ah, well, that's a relief," Rita said. "Otherwise, it would be quite a magnet for tomb-raiders, antiquities smugglers, that kind of thing."

"Mmmmmmm." Hans made a noncommittal noise, and Rita wished she could see his face. Was he nervous, sweating, worried she would unearth his secret identity as a black-market antiquities trafficker, or merely pondering the wisdom of what she had said?

She felt Sal stiffen beside her, as if he sensed she was about to start sleuthing. "Shall we go back?" Sal said. "I don't know about you, but I could use a second helping of wild boar."

They emerged back into the moonlit night and walked towards the blazing bonfire and the revelry just beyond.

Rita turned to Hans. "It didn't bother you? Diana's prediction about you—at least, I assume the 'northern invader' is you—passing through the red door?"

"We must all pass through it someday," Hans replied in that clipped, emotionless Teutonic sort of way.

They came to a halt right behind Chiara, Olivia, Paolo, Rose, Monica, and Running Bear.

"It makes you think, though," Rita said. "About one's mortality. About getting one's affairs in order."

"Oh, my affairs are in order. Very, very good order."

"Papa," Olivia announced with childlike delight, turning to Paolo and clapping her hands, "I was telling mamma about your little problem—you know, the deciphering of that bizarre inscription—and she had the most brilliant idea!"

Chiara stubbed out her cigarette and looked at her daughter in amusement. "It's not brilliant, *cara*. The technique's been around for twenty years." She leaned forward and, in spite of her efforts to appear continually detached, there was a gleam in her eye. "But I was thinking...."

She launched into a complex explanation of various methodologies, and Paolo became animated. "*Geniale*! Perhaps, we could have lunch tomorrow together and I could bring you the fragment—"

"Paolo."

Rose's voice was sharp and commanding. Everyone stopped their conversation and looked up.

"You can't have lunch tomorrow with Chiara. We have plans to go into Volterra. You were going to give me a tour of the Etruscan museum."

"*È vero.*" He turned to his ex-wife again. "Well, perhaps breakfast then."

"Perhaps," Chiara said enigmatically as Rose reached over and put a hand on Paolo's knee.

Olivia jumped up and disappeared into the shadows. A moment later, Italian pop music blared. "Dance with me, Papa!" she cried, dragging him away from Rose. She started to lead him over towards the fire but then, as if having a sudden fit of inspiration, doubled back and implored her mother to join them. "*Per piacere*—it's so rare we're all together."

Chiara laughed and got up to join them, and the three of them danced together, backlit by the firelight, Paolo turning his daughter, then his ex-wife.

"They look well together, don't they?" Sal murmured. "Like they belong together."

Rita had to agree, but she wondered just why Chiara was so eager to push her ex-husband into Rose's arms. Something simply did not add up.

Her sister turned to Padre Domenico. "If I commit murder tonight, you'll absolve me, right?"

"Only if you're truly contrite," he said mildly, "which I very much doubt you would be." He clapped an avuncular hand on Rose's back. "What God has joined, let no man—or woman—put asunder."

As if on cue, Hans suddenly broke into their little circle. With a pointed glance at Chiara and Paolo, Hans held out a hand to Rose. "Shall we dance?"

"Might as well," Rose grumbled.

Then Sal took Rita's hand. Soon, they were kicking up their heels and singing "*Volare*" at the top of their lungs, their backsides warmed by the roaring fire.

"Now this," Sal murmured in her ear, "is living."

Sal spun Rita around, and she noticed that Running Bear had taken Monica by the hand and was leading her into their little dance circle. Chiara was shaking her head and seemed to be begging off another dance. She slipped out of her daughter's grasp and returned to the table, where she reached into her purse and extracted a golden vial that glinted in the firelight.

"So," Rita murmured, "she self-medicates with cigarettes and pills."

"What's that, *cara*?"

"Oh, nothing, *caro*," Rita said loudly into his ear. "I was just saying that Chiara's gone back to the table. This is Rose's chance."

"And there she goes."

They watched Rose break from Hans' grasp and head towards Paolo and Olivia. Rita and Sal danced on and on, amusing themselves by the constant struggle between Olivia and Rose for Paolo's attentions and by Hans' steady stream of dance partners: Giovanna, Tiffany, and even Diana.

"What do you know?" Sal chuckled. "Even Diana, who argues with him constantly and claims to hate him, is secretly in love with Hans. It's that Alpha Male thing." He turned her and laughed again. "Or maybe it's just beer—or, in this case—wine goggles. No one seems to be thinking clearly. I mean, Hans was speaking to Tiffany in German!"

Rita remembered Tiffany's atrocious French accent and laughed. The woman was certainly no linguist.

A moment later, the music suddenly cut out, and Rita heard odd snatches of shouted conversation that were clearly in mid-flow.

"On a white horse!" Diana was screeching, clearly recounting for the umpteenth time her plan to have Andrea Bocelli belt out his wedding aria from astride a white stallion.

"At two o'clock!" Rose was shouting in Paolo's ear.

Rita had a feeling her sister had been trying to arrange a secret assignation with Paolo. Well, it wasn't secret anymore.

"*Un brindisi*," Hans shouted, holding a wine glass aloft. His hand was unsteady and some of the wine sloshed over the side of the glass. His German accent was more pronounced than ever. Switching to English, he said, "To the happy couple. Giovanna, my darling protégé, may you be happy with Alessandro, who is determined to love everything and everyone—although most of all you."

Rita frowned, and she saw a few other furrowed brows around the fire. Hans' toast was skirting the line between tepid praise and a backhanded compliment.

"And Alessandro," he continued, slurring his words a bit, "may you realize just how fortunate you are in your choice of wife. Giovanna is brilliant and—what's more—on the right side of history. As you will discover soon enough, she was instrumental in uncovering our latest discovery—and that find is the basis for our upcoming paper in *Archaeology Today*, which will prove beyond a shadow of a doubt that the Etruscans originated right here in *bella Italia*." He raised his wine glass in Diana's direction. "And," Hans said, his voice dripping with derision, "we will prove that Dr. Diana Rossi is a beautiful fraud, a fake."

"*Stonzo*!" Diana roared, fists clenched, head thrown back defiantly. "*Bugiardo*!"

"Oh, no," Hans said, "I am no liar. I'm a lover of truth, of data—of evidence."

"Hans," Giovanna hissed, "you promised not to mention this before the wedding."

Alessandro turned to his bride. "You knew about this and didn't tell me...?"

Tears filled Giovanna's luminous brown eyes. "There just wasn't the right time. And it's only work, and you know Hans and I have been—"

But Alessandro just shook his head sadly and gently pushed her head off his shoulder. "And I'm the last to know."

"No!" Hans took a last gulp of wine and threw his glass into the fire. "You're among the very first! I'll be sending it to *Archaeology Today* tomorrow."

Gleefully, he danced a few steps of what almost passed for a jig, then grabbed a glass of wine from a stunned Alessandro and held it aloft. "To freedom! To truth! Be gone you vipers!"

It might have been the wine walking, but Rita sensed he was speaking to someone in particular. But was it his blackmailer or someone else entirely? She peered into the darkness, but try as she might, she couldn't tell who bore the brunt of Hans' ire.

Hans tossed this glass into the fire and then bowed dramatically. "And with that, I wish you a *buona notte*, ladies and gentlemen. I'll leave you to find your way back to the villa."

He stumbled out of the circle of light and lurched down the rutted track.

"What a jerk," Sal mumbled.

Diana and her acolytes—Alessandro, Paolo, and Chiara—closed ranks and began walking towards the house. Giovanna ran tearfully after them.

"Well," Tiffany said, nudging Rita, "didn't I tell you there'd be drama?"

Chapter Fourteen

Rita slept fitfully that night. That awful singed boar's snout loomed in her dreams, morphing into Diana and her dripping entrails and Hans' leering, exulting expression. Then the creature–a horrible tusked creature with Diana's raven-black hair and Hans' leering smile–plunged into an underwater cavern surrounded by a ring of fire.

Splash.

The creature plunged deep down into the water–

There was a shrill scream, angry shouting. Was this a dream? Rita rubbed her eyes and tried to will herself out of the nightmare and back into her warm, comfortable bed. The terracotta bricks slowly came into focus, then a wavy archway, finally the French door to the balcony. She fumbled for her glasses, slipped them on, and then peered at the clock. 2:04, it read.

She heard a clipped German voice shout, "You encouraged me!"

Her heart hammered in her chest. That was Hans' voice–it had to be.

But who was he talking to?

Rita tiptoed to the French doors. She slowly eased open the doors, crouched down, and peered through the balcony railing. Illuminated by the light of the full moon, Hans was flailing in the water, his silk pajamas billowing out behind him.

Her sister was standing by the side of the pool, dressed in a pale pink negligee, the moonlight glinting on her hair. "I did no such thing. I accepted your offer to dance—that's all. I'm here with Paolo, remember?"

"A lot of good that'll do you."

Rita watched as her sister crossed her arms over her chest and tilted her head slightly. She knew that look. It meant you'd made her mad, but there was some truth in what you'd said.

"Here," Hans said, "help me out. It's the least you can do."

Crossly, Rose bent down and offered him a hand. But instead of using it to pull himself *out* of the pool, he used it to pull her *in*. Towards him—and towards a sloppy, drunken, chlorine-scented kiss.

Rose shrieked, and Rita was just about to scream for help too, when Paolo suddenly appeared with a bottle of wine and two wine glasses. He stopped dead in his tracks. "*Altra volta? Non ci credo.*"

For a moment, he seemed torn between fight and flight. But just when it looked like he had decided to press on towards the inevitable confrontation, he suddenly spun on his heels and stumbled back down the hill, towards the row of cottages.

Rose struggled out of Hans' grasp. She swam frantically to the side of the pool, launched herself out of the pool, and chased after Paolo. They were soon both out of sight.

Rita ran back inside and slid on her flip-flops. She tossed the first article of clothing she saw—Sal's rumpled, tomato sauce-speckled Mets jersey—over her Bernese mountain dog-themed flannel pajamas. Then she flung open their door and ran across the moonlit terrace. During the day, she would not have noticed it, but now, in the deep stillness of night, each thwack of her plastic flip-flops on the travertine resounded in her ears. It sounded ominous, angry—and it matched her mood.

"Ah, Rita!" Hans lifted a waterlogged, pink pajama-clad arm and waved. "I rather fancied a swim," he said. "Care to join me?"

"No." Rita skidded to a stop by the water's edge. She glared at him, and her hands flew to her hips. "And you didn't fancy a swim. You fancied my sister—my very much attached, very uninterested sister. And you tried to get your grubby paws on her. So don't act all innocent with me."

Infuriatingly, in spite of what she had just said, he maintained a look of wounded innocence. "I admit that I might have gotten a little carried away, but..."

Hans trailed off. At first, Rita thought that he was finally at a loss for words, that even the great, silver-tongued Hans Clausnitzer could not conjure up a half-plausible excuse for his reprehensible behavior. But then she realized his gaze was not the vacant stare of someone plotting out his next move. No, his icy blue eyes—narrowed now, darting back and forth beneath furrowed brows—were fixated on something that lay in the middle distance just beyond Rita.

She spun around to face row upon row of vines. The delicate green leaves, which resembled maple leaves, only smaller and more feathery, were dotted with the early-morning dew; the carefully pruned vines, long and sinewy, spread out along invisible wires like tentacles, weighed down by enormous clusters of sweet grapes which glistened a deep royal blue in the moonlight.

At first, she saw and heard nothing to detract from this scene of ethereal, almost eerie beauty. But then she saw a flash of turquoise and, below that, a flesh-colored blur. Someone was running through the vines, two or three rows back. But was the person fleeing because he or she feared discovery, or was he or she running from something—or someone—else?

The blur passed over the ridge of the hill and dropped down out of sight.

Rita sighed. She could not see that it mattered much whether one of their party had observed her tense exchange with Hans, or his abhorrent behavior towards Rose. After all, she and Rose had no reason to be ashamed. If Hans was embarrassed, it served him right.

So Rita spun back around and demanded, "But what?

Hans pushed his torso up out of the pool and grasped the lip. "I wasn't—that is, I mean—"

"You're weren't what? Thinking? Acting like a gentleman? Considering anyone's feelings or needs but your own? Or all of the above?" Rita squatted by the pool and grabbed a fistful of his soaking wet pajama top with more force than she had thought she possessed. "I can see right through you, Hans Clausnitzer." Rita used her quiet, "scary mommy" voice, the one that had worked so well on her three children. She wished she knew Hans' middle name, because there was nothing like adding a middle name to show she meant business. "Other people may see a respected archaeologist, a wealthy villa owner, and a virile, suave, debonair European gentleman. But I see a man so small he has to tear other people down. A childless, probably impotent man who can't get a woman without forcing himself on her. A man who's got something to hide, who's under suspicion for trafficking in priceless stolen antiquities, who's being slowly bled dry by blackmail."

Hans uttered a strangled cry.

"Are you surprised?" Rita said. "Oh, yes—I know all that and much more. I'm a reporter. I'm a sleuth. I'm a *mother*. And I don't just have eyes on the back of my head." She tapped a finger just below her eye. "I've got laser vision into the soul."

This last remark was a bit of a stretch, as she'd occasionally miscalculated spectacularly when it came to picking out potential beaus for her perennially unlucky-in-love daughter, Gina. But while she occasionally was bamboozled by a charming rogue, the opposite was rarely true. If Rita took a strong dislike to someone, it nearly always turned out to be warranted. She could pick out the playground bully a mile away, not to mention the boy who'd knock up his Prom date and then skip town on a football scholarship and most of the louts, layabouts, alcoholics, and commitment-phobes.

But Hans did not appear to doubt the veracity of her claims, because he quailed and began to grovel. Really, Rita thought, I ought to do this more often. It gave her that rush she'd had when her children were young and malleable, when she actually had the means and opportunity to lay down the rules and enforce the consequences. Now, she had to resort to communicating with food—spiking their pasta sauce with the hottest Calabrian hot peppers here, shutting them out of a cannoli distribution there. Her options as a mother were now severely limited.

"Rita," Hans pleaded, "this is all a misunderstanding, I swear. Rose left me a note, see? If you don't believe me, check in my pocket."

Very slowly, like a suspect surrounded by the police, he reached into the front pocket of his pajamas, extracted a wet, pulpy mess, and handed it to Rita.

She peeled back the edges, opened the note, and stared at the wavy, tangled lines of blue ink, which ran down the page like a knot of varicose veins. There were no longer any words to decipher.

"Do you really expect me to believe that?" she scoffed. "It's illegible."

"I know, but I swear it said, 'Meet me at the pool at two o'clock. It's over between me and Paolo.'"

"My sister would never write that. Even if she and Paolo had broken up—which they haven't—she would never arrange to meet someone that very same night." Rita's whole arm was sore now; chiseled as he was, Hans was still heavy. She opened her fist with a flourish and let him sink back into the pool. "Besides, do you really expect me to believe you'd wear that"—she waved her hands at his billowing tunic—"to a rendezvous?"

Hans colored. "I'm European." His voice was cold, haughty, proud—but tinged with wounded masculinity. "Which means I have some pride in my appearance, feel secure enough as a man to wear pink, and"—he shot a pointed look at her attire—"don't feel the need to advertise my love for dogs on my pajamas."

Rita stood up. "You'd better be careful, Hans," she said. "With all of the enemies you have, I wouldn't be too surprised if you go through the red door of death sooner rather than later. And if someone here sends you there."

Without waiting for a response, Rita stalked off, past the vineyard, onto the cobblestone track, and over the ridgeline, where the little row of stone cottages came into view. She was surprised, then a little envious, to see a light on in the middle cottage—Chiara's and Olivia's. Perhaps, she thought, they are having a little mother-and-daughter talk, the kind she had all too infrequently with Gina.

Gina. Rita sighed. She hated to think of her daughter growing old all alone, with only her schnauzer to keep her company. Perhaps Rita could find Gina a nice husband here in Italy. After all, Rita was always struggling to find a nice Italian boy back in Acorn Hollow, particularly since Gina had already rejected all of the possible candidates ("all seven of them," as Gina would frequently complain. The truth was that, at thirty-six, Gina faced rather long odds; most of the marriageable men were, well, married.)

With a sinking heart, Rita realized she would not be finding Gina a husband here at Villa Belvista. The only single men were Padre Domenico (unavailable for obvious reasons); Hans, far too old and far too odious; and Running Bear, who already seemed to have his hands full with two women and, in any case, seemed to be of rather dubious character. Rita would never be able to countenance a son-in-law who'd been a kept man and, to that sin, she added deception. If he wanted out of his arrangement with Tiffany, he should have the courage to just tell her so.

But suddenly Rita brightened and, without even realizing it, began to whistle. The wedding! Surely, Rita could finagle an invitation to Alessandro and Giovanna's wedding and there would be loads of nice, single Italian boys there. After all, Alessandro was a nice boy (well, man, but really a thirty-five-year-old these days seemed like a boy to Rita!), and his brothers were quite pleasant as well. They must have nice friends and cousins. And Luca Zingaretti would be there...

Now, her heart was really pounding. On paper, he was too old for Gina, but he was in terrific shape, much better shape than most of the men Gina's age. But that would not do, either. Rita would break out in palpitations every time her son-in-law came to dinner...

She was so absorbed in her thoughts that she didn't notice she was just steps away from Paolo's cottage until she heard something between a moan and a sob and looked up to see her sister knocking disconsolately on the door of her lover's darkened abode.

"Are you all right?" Rita called out to her sister.

"All right?" Rose spun around. "How could I be all right? I've seen gorillas paw at each other more gently than that. And that Neanderthal actually acted surprised when I pushed him away. Like he couldn't believe it. Like he thought I was asking for it!"

Rita was silent for a moment, wondering if she should tell her sister about the note that Hans claimed to have received. She didn't know that she should trust Hans. Clearly, if he were such a trustworthy person, there would be nothing over which to blackmail him. But he seemed so genuine when he protested, and it was such an odd thing to lie about...

"Hans claimed he received a note from you," Rita said. "He said you wrote to meet you at the pool at two, that it was all over between you and Paolo."

"He—what?" Rose sputtered. "I never wrote any such—"

Then Rose stopped and stared at the cottage next door with a look of sheer murderous hate.

"Now, Rose, don't go jumping to conclusions..."

"It's her." Rose spat out the word "her" as if spitting venom out of a snakebite. She pointed an accusatory finger at Chiara's and Olivia's cottage, then shifted her finger slightly so it tracked Olivia's silhouette as she paced back and forth across the room, like a laser pointing the way for a heat-seeking missile. "The vile little b—"

Rita held up a hand. She could not abide swearing, even by her sister.

"Bundle of joy," Rose said sarcastically. "Her father thinks she can do no wrong, but I've got her number. She orchestrated this all, don't you see? Paolo didn't arrive until what—2:10?"

Rita nodded, not sure where this was going. It hardly seemed relevant.

"He's never late," Rose insisted. "That's one of his pet peeves."

"Really? That's not very Italian."

"No, but it's very Paolo. He says showing up on time is a sign of respect. And he's never been late for a single date. In fact, he's usually early—ridiculously early. But tonight, he showed up ten minutes late. We were supposed to meet at two."

"Maybe he overslept. Maybe—"

"No." Rose was shaking her head with such vehemence Rita worried she would pull a muscle. "I'll tell you what happened. That little, manipulative mastermind batted her eyes at her daddy and asked to see his watch on some pretext. When he was distracted, she changed the time. Then she wrote a note, pretending to be me, and slipped it under Hans' door. So that by the time Paolo showed up, Hans would be all over me and Paolo would get mad and leave. And," Rose muttered bitterly, "it worked. Her plan worked to perfection."

Rita was about to call Rose paranoid, but then she stopped herself. Olivia did hate Rose. It was all plausible—far-fetched, but still plausible. And personal experience had taught her to never underestimate the wiles of teenaged girls.

"Maybe," Rita finally said. "But don't go over there and give her a piece of her mind and don't retaliate. You'll lose Paolo for sure if you do that. Remember, to him, she's his precious, innocent little girl. Like you said, she can do no wrong."

Rose sighed in a way that told Rita she knew Rita was right.

"And what about Paolo," Rose said in small voice. "How do I fix this?"

"Just tell him what really happened."

"I can't."

"Of course you can."

"No, I *can't*. I've knocked and knocked and he's not here." Rose's glance flew to Olivia and Chiara's sweet little stone cottage. The light was still on. "You don't think...?"

The two sisters tiptoed over to the cottage and peered through the window. The shade was down, but they could clearly make out Olivia's trim hourglass figure, pacing back and forth, and the silhouette of Chiara's petite figure, hunched down on the bed. Rita frowned and revised her earlier assumptions. They might be having a tender tête-à-tête, but they could just as easily be having an argument or an intervention. But the women were not shouting; she couldn't make out any distinct words. Were they whispering, just talking quietly—so as not to disturb their slumbering neighbors—or was Chiara using her "scary mommy" voice?

Beside her, Rose sighed and shrugged. "Well, Paolo's not there."

Rita patted her sister on the arm. "He probably just took a walk in the vineyard to clear his head. Go to bed, sis. Trust me—all will be better in the morning."

Rose trudged back to her room. Rita, rubbing her eyes, walked back to the pool. Hans was gone now, the only visible sign of his presence a few puddles on the terrace.

She went back to her room, slipped into bed beside Sal, and lay awake, staring at the ceiling, trying to reassure herself that everything would be better in the morning. But just after dawn, there was a sudden, unnerving chorus of squawks, as if all of the birds had suddenly awoken from a nightmare.

And then the earth began to shake.

Chapter Fifteen

"It's an earthquake, Sal! Get up! *Svegliati! Dai!*"

Rita shook Sal vigorously and, when that didn't work, slapped him across the face.

"What?" One sleepy brown eye opened. "What'd I do?"

The gleaming coat of arms and crossed medieval swords that had been hanging on the wall behind their bed suddenly came crashing down, slicing into Sal's pillow an inch from his balding crown.

"Earthquake!" Sal bellowed, eyes wide with terror, as if Rita had not just said this.

He leapt out of bed, with Rita hard on his heels, and started dragging her towards the door. "There's no time," she gasped as spidery cracks in the walls sprang up and began to grow. Covering her head, she sprinted as fast as her thick ankles could carry her to the large brick arch that separated their bedroom from the sitting room, yanking him along with her. Plaster rained down from the ceiling. The floor beneath them shook; the walls seemed to be closing in around them.

"I love you, Rita!" Sal bellowed as their bed lurched into the air and came crashing down.

"I love you, Sal!"

"Some second honeymoon, huh? I mean, I know we said 'til death do us part, but I didn't think it would be so soon—or like this."

"I'm glad we had our little caboose," Rita chattered as the floor bounced up and down. By 'caboose,' she meant Vinnie, their late-in-life surprise who had caused every single gray hair on Rita's head.

"Me too."

"I'm glad I married you in spite of your mother."

"What's the matter with my mother?"

A chunk of ceiling fell into the bed, right where they'd been lying, and then a torrent of debris rained down. Rita could see a patch of blue sky over the opening.

"Oh—never mind my mother," Sal said. "I'm sorry about the time I broke your great-great-grandmother's prized ceramic Virgin Mary figurine and blamed it on Vinnie."

"You framed our *son*?"

"Hey, I'm not proud of it, okay? But he was five and I knew you'd forgive him faster. And we're still married so it worked." Another chunk of ceiling fell on Rita's suitcase. "Oh, and I have a secret bank account I use for betting at the horse track."

For a moment, Rita thought she had misheard. Sal hadn't grown up on a farm, and he'd never shown the slightest interest in horses, even when their daughter Gina had been in the throes of her My Little Pony phase. Rita had never seen him watch so much as a commercial for the Kentucky Derby, and the few times he'd accompanied her to Saratoga Springs on a shopping trip, he hadn't even snuck a glance at the race track. But his guilty look told her she'd heard him correctly, however incredible it seemed.

"Salvatore Francesco Calabrese," she thundered, drawing out each syllable, "you bet on horses–dumb, cloven-hooved animals!–and yet when given a chance to place a bet on the cooking prowess of your beloved, intelligent, talented wife–nineteen-time champion of the St. Vincent's pasta-making competition and seven-time winner of the Acorn Hollow pie-making contest–you bet a measly twenty dollars?"

She spat out each word, growing more and more incensed. Rita couldn't believe that she'd been so naïve. She blushed to think that just yesterday, she and Rose had rationalized Sal's paltry bet by saying he wasn't much of a gambler. How little Rita really knew her husband of forty-odd years!

"How much is in this secret account, Sal?"

"Oh, a little."

"How much, Sal?"

"Just a few hundred. Eight, to be exact."

Rita opened her mouth to say something, but the force of the shaking slammed it shut, which was probably just as well. She had a secret slush fund, too, so there was only so much she could say. Of course, hers was for much more noble purposes–bailing errant children and neighbors out of jail, for example.

"The account information," Sal said, "is taped to the bottom of my desk in the basement."

Rita was chagrined. In all her years of cleaning and snooping, this was one of her husband's hiding places that had apparently eluded her.

"Oh," Sal said, "and, while we're confessing, I used to, er, admire the female form when Emily Bachmann bent over. Sometimes I'd even drop things at work just so she'd have to pick them up."

This, at least, was not a revelation. Sal had admitted this in his sleep last year, and Rita had neatly solved the problem by arranging for Emily to get a job offer she couldn't refuse; Sal had been none the wiser.

The patch of blue sky got bigger.

Rita sighed. "Well, as long as it's confession time, I lied about my conversation with Commissario Zingaretti. He gave me a little assignment. He wants me to find out who in the wedding party is trafficking in stolen Etruscan antiquities."

"You—what?" Sal roared, glowering at her. He apparently had forgotten that they were supposed to be forgiving in their last few moments on earth.

"*Mi dispiace, cara, ma—*"

"You lied!"

"So did you."

"But my lie was years ago. Yours was two days ago."

"But what about your slush fund? How recently did you put money into it?"

"Last month. But at least I admit it. You still haven't fessed up about yours."

Rita's jaw dropped, then snapped shut. "You knew about that?"

The shaking suddenly stopped, and they eyed each other warily. Rita attempted a laugh. "Well, I guess we didn't die. We didn't need to confess after all."

Sal just folded his arms over his chest and grunted. Rita brushed plaster flakes out of her hair and off her nightgown.

"Well," she said lamely, "I told you now. Better late than never, right?"

But Sal was apparently not of the "better late than never" mindset, because he maintained a tight-lipped glower all through their search for survivors. They came across Rose first, who was straggling across what had been the terrace, picking her way through an apocalyptic, water-logged landscape of upended pool loungers and shards of broken terracotta roof tiles. She had a gash across her face, and her blond hair was matted and smeared with blood. Bits of plaster stuck to her pink negligee. A trickle of blood oozed down her left calf.

Rita sprinted across the terrace faster than she had ever thought possible and then pulled her sister into a tight embrace. "Oh, thank God you're all right!"

"I thought," Rose gasped, "I would die. Alone—all alone."

Rita felt the sobs racking Rose's chest and pulled her even closer. The was the first time she'd seen her sister cry since their father's funeral twenty-three years before. Normally, her sister was a rock, a pillar of strength who insisted she loved being the fun aunt, the eternally single bachelorette with a line of men out the door.

But when it mattered, she'd been alone.

They went in search of Paolo, picking their way carefully across the terrace, Sal following behind them.

Rose knocked on the heavy wooden door to Paolo's little stone cottage, timidly at first, then insistently, but there was no answer.

"He's trapped," Rose whimpered. "He must be. Oh, what if he's dead? What if—"

"Naw." Sal slid open the window and peeked inside. "He's not here. Look—see for yourself. There's not a pile of rubble big enough to conceal a body. His room wasn't hit too hard, actually."

Rose craned her neck over the sill. Relief, then confusion, washed over her features. She put her hands on her hips, and a little of the old Rose returned. "Well, if he's not here," she demanded, "then where is he?"

Rose stomped over to Chiara and Olivia's next-door cottage and rapped four times, rat-a-tat-tat, like machine-gun fire. Rita was quite sure that if Paolo did answer the door, he'd have a lot of explaining to do. When that failed to elicit a response and a quick peek through the window confirmed the room was also empty, Rose frowned. "A family reunion? At this hour?"

"Maybe," Rita said, "they wanted to get farther from the building in case there are aftershocks. Let's check the reception area by Hans' prized kouros."

"You mean the one soon to be possessed by Diana?" Sal said.

"It was a bet, fair and square."

"She bet on the right horse: you. Is that what you're saying?"

"One should never bet on horses, Sal," Rita said icily. "But wives? Always."

They rounded the corner of the row of cottages, and the villa, pale yellow in the early-morning sunlight, came into view. The cobblestones were all higgly-piggly, like pieces of a jigsaw puzzle that would need to be painstakingly put back together. The kouros still stood vigil over the fountain, but the marble youth had gone from model Olympian to para-athlete; his right arm had been sheared off above the elbow, the tip of his nose had fallen off, giving him the appearance of a snub-nosed frostbite victim, and a crack spread across his perfectly chiseled washboard abs.

"Huh," Sal grunted, shooting a contemptuous look at the marble youth. Almost reflexively, he sucked in his gut, which was spilling out over the waistband of his flannel special-order cannoli pajamas. "Not so perfect anymore, are we?"

They walked past the reception area and wound between the rows of olive trees, where they found Diana, her daughters, Alessandro, and Tiffany.

"Ah, you found us!" Diana trilled gayly, as if they were playing a game of hide-and-seek at a garden party. There was not a scratch on her, and Rita was disappointed to discover that even in the harsh morning light, with no make-up and little sleep, Diana looked as glamorous as ever. Or perhaps even more so—as her scarlet kimono, loosely tied in haste (or so she made it seem), kept threatening to come undone.

Rita caught Sal looking and elbowed him sharply. "Custody of the eyes, Sal." Rita muttered in a low voice through gritted teeth. "Custody of the eyes."

"Oh, yeah?" he muttered back in her ear. "Well, remember what Sister Helen also taught us: the Ten Commandments. Thou shalt not lie."

"I didn't lie," Rita insisted, dragging him away from the group until they were standing beneath an olive tree. "I didn't tell you that an Italian art crimes squad *didn't* ask for help with an investigation, did I?"

"Hah!" he said triumphantly. "Sister Mary Margaret, eighth grade. That's a sin of omission."

"Well, you committed a sin of omission, too, by not telling me about your secret slush fund."

"But you have one, too."

"But mine is only for a good cause. Sister Hildegard, seventh grade. It was acceptable for Jesus to break the Jewish Sabbath to heal people because he served the greater good."

Sal looked stumped for a moment. His fleshy lips twitched a few times, and his brows, thick as caterpillars, furrowed. Then his eyes suddenly brightened. "Is your Commisario Zingaretti married?"

Rita thought for a moment. She remembered the sculpted head, shaved smooth as a billiard ball, those meltingly tender amber eyes, the lantern jaw. Her heart started to beat faster. She tried to remember his hands, but for a moment all she could recall was the electric feeling she'd gotten when their fingers had touched, all too briefly, and he'd handed her his card.

"I'm not sure."

"Aha!"

Sal said it too loudly, and suddenly they could feel the stares of the group upon them.

"Keep it down," she hissed. "And what are you crowing about?"

"Sister Joan of Arc, seventh grade."

Rita involuntarily felt herself shoving her hands behind her back. Sister Joan had been terrifying, rather (she suspected) like her namesake. Sister Joan stalked the aisles with a ruler at the ready, primed to rap someone's knuckles at the slightest offense. She was also a big proponent of washing kids' mouths out with soap; Rita had endured it only once, but Sal had been a regular fixture by the wash basin. Rita had no doubt that Sister Joan would have been ready to be burned at the stake at a moment's notice, and never emit so much as a whimper. She would have made a drill sergeant cry.

"Commandment Ten!" Sal said triumphantly. "Thou shalt not covet another man's wife. And she said this applied to women too—thou shalt not covet another woman's husband. And she said it could be just in your mind, you know, like that idiot Carter. And she also said you shouldn't covet someone who *might* be married."

"How do you know 'I coveted'?"

"Please." He snorted. "I've seen how you drool when his cousin does one of his shirtless runs on the beach, right after wrapping up some wacky triple homicide. You drool worse than Luciano and Cesare watching me eat a cheesesteak."

"Fine." Rita's hands flew to her ample hips, and her dark eyes flashed. "I...admired his sculpted physique"—she glanced pointedly from Sal to the amputated kouros statue and back, which made Sal scowl—"and, more importantly, his exquisite gentlemanly manners, impressive knowledge of art and antiquities, and searing intelligence."

Sal harrumphed.

"And what about you?" Rita demanded. "I caught you admiring—one might say, coveting—Diana."

"Uh-uh-uh, Rita." Sal wagged a finger at her and grinned triumphantly. "She's a widow, so it doesn't count."

"Hey, you-hoo, lovebirds," –Rose's harsh voice, laced with sarcasm, floated over to them—"why don't you save your sweet nothings for later and help us look for the others?"

Rita was relieved for the interruption, as she was at a complete loss for how to respond. She'd run out of nuns to quote and lessons to cite—at least ones in her favor. How was it that Sal, never a great student, had actually paid attention in theology class and, even more irritatingly, beaten her at her own game?

Either he was getting smarter quickly, or she was slipping.

They rejoined the group, and Rose remarked, "Terrible as they are, isn't it wonderful how natural disasters can bring us together and make us realize what's really important?"

Rose glanced pointedly at Rita and Sal and then at Alessandro and Giovanna, who were huddled together. Apparently, the young lovebirds were back together.

"I say," Rose cooed, elbowing Rita, "isn't that wonderful?"

"Oh,*sì—meraviglioso*." Rita tried to look as pleased as she knew she should be although she was still smarting from being bested by Sal. Desperate to occupy her thoughts with something—anything—else, she cleared her throat and asked, "Was anyone hurt in the earthquake? Struck by falling debris?"

They shook their heads.

"Hell's bells," Tiffany hooted. "I've lived through a twister or two in my day. This was nothing."

The Italians looked rather confused—probably unsure of what a "twister" was or why there were bells in hell—but politely pretended it all made sense.

"And where is Running Bear?" Rita asked.

"Beats me, toots. He wasn't there when I woke up. He was probably taking a walk. He's an early riser, that one."

Luisa was bearing down on them now, clad in a frumpy floral housedress similar to the one she'd been wearing yesterday. Presumably, this was her work uniform, not her nightgown, although it was hard to tell. Her wrist on her right hand was crudely bandaged with rags as if she'd suffered a sprain—or worse. "My pears," she muttered, placing a bucket of fresh-picked but now bruised and battered pears at her feet. She looked more put out than anything else. "Signor Clausnitzer will not like this," she said archly, eyeing them as if this was all their fault. "He will not like this at all."

"This—what?" Sal blurted out, flabbergasted. "This earthquake?"

Luisa's eyes flashed, and she looked at Sal with a mixture of contempt and pity for his obtuseness. "*La prima colazione*," she said, "will be late today. Signor Clausnitzer will not be pleased."

"I think he'll forgive you just this once," Rose said. "Have you seen the others? Chiara, Paolo, and Olivia, for instance?"

"Paolo is no good for you," Luisa sniffed. "Signor Clausnitzer is much better."

"Not after the way he behaved last night."

"Oh?" Luisa's hands flew to her hips. "And how did you expect him to act after you were *faccendo la civetta* all night?"

"Making the owl?" Sal whispered in Rita's ear. "What's that supposed to mean?"

"Flirting," Rita whispered back. Sal's Italian was good, but some of the idiomatic expressions eluded him. "You know, cooing and strutting your stuff, just like an owl."

Luisa and Rose had raised their voices quite a bit by now, Rose heaping calumnies on Luisa's "sainted employer" and Luisa leaping to his defense. "*Signore, per piacere*," Rita interjected, "we need to find the others. Luisa, what about Chiara and Olivia? Did you see them?"

Luisa shrugged. "I saw Olivia go into the chapel."

Rita, Rose, and Sal ran towards the wisteria-covered rock chapel. "Olivia!" Rita shouted as she heaved open the massive oak door. Rose and Sal shouted too, Rose's slightly shrill call reverberating against the sturdy stone walls, Sal's call more of a bellow. "Olivia! Olivia!"

The walls and roof were remarkably intact, but the glorious golden altarpiece—a masterpiece from the fourteenth century—had crashed to the ground, and a huge crack rent the luminous frescos of the Madonna and child. The altar had tumbled on its side.

"*Qui, sono qui*," croaked a hoarse masculine voice.

Sal leapt over fallen beams and heaved the altar up a few inches. The sisters peered over his shoulders to see what—or whom—had been pinned underneath. She saw the Roman collar first, then the jolly little belly and the simple wooden cross.

"Padre Domenico!" Rita gasped.

His eye was nearly swollen shut, and blood was smeared all over his bald pate.

But Padre Domenico said, "Don't worry about me. Help"—he struggled to breathe—"help her."

Rita followed his agonized gaze to the corner of the chapel. A slim leg poked out from under an ornate gold picture frame. "Olivia!"

Chapter Sixteen

An hour and several aftershocks later, Padre Domenico and Olivia were resting comfortably in the shade, but they had not been able to locate her parents.

Alessandro was attending to his brother's injuries, while Olivia had her injured limb elevated on Diana's lap. Diana seemed perfectly content to be Olivia's footstool. Tiffany was seated nearby, popping olives into her mouth and admiring her jewelry glinting in the sun. Monica was picking at the grass, seemingly lost in thought, while Luisa continued to fume about her bruised pears.

Suddenly, Tiffany suddenly sprang up and pointed at a speck on the horizon. "Look! It's Running Bear!"

Running Bear was indeed sprinting towards them. When he got close, he stopped and gasped for breath. "We're cut off," he said, gesturing helplessly down the gravel drive. "Totally and completely."

Sal shrugged. "Sure, the phones don't work, but I can just walk–"

"No, that's just it. You can't. The earth has opened up, and there's now a crack twenty feet wide between us and the rest of civilization." Running Bear squinted towards the horizon. "Or what's left of it."

Rita's heart sank. Cell service was down; the road was out. She and Sal would be marooned here with no electricity, little opportunity to suss out a thief (Rita assumed that an earthquake would disrupt even criminal networks), no way to check in with her children, and no way to travel on to Rome and Venice. She sighed, thinking of the gondola trip she wouldn't take, the gelato she wouldn't devour, the Murano glass she wouldn't buy. "Well," she sighed, "I suppose the most important thing to do now is to organize ourselves into search parties and go find the others. Everyone, that is, except Olivia and Padre Domenico. They need to rest."

Diana and Luisa immediately volunteered to search Hans' living quarters. Running Bear and Tiffany offered to check the warehouse and other outbuildings. And Monica, Alessandro, and Giovanna volunteered to search the olive groves and orchard.

"I'll go with you," Sal said quickly to the latter trio. With his eyes, he telegraphed to Rita that he absolutely, definitively did not want to be her partner.

That left Rita and Rose, so the sisters volunteered to cover the vineyards that stretched behind the villa. They set off through the rows of russet-colored leaves, Hans' cat, Artemis, trailing behind them as if determined to join the search party for her favorite human. Rita noticed that the much-maligned Wolf chose to stay behind, nestled against the refrigerator.

As they crossed the vineyard, the fallen grapes squished beneath their feet, staining the soil a deep purplish red.

"Think of all this glorious *vino*," Rose groaned, "that Hans won't be able to make."

"You're assuming Hans is even alive."

Artemis hissed and flexed her claws. Rita wondered exactly what that meant. Did Artemis know Hans was dead, or was she angry that the two sisters were even contemplating the possibility he was dead?

"You think he's dead?"

"Do you really think Hans would pass up an opportunity to play the hero?"

Rose grunted. "Good point."

"Unless, of course, he's trapped like Padre Domenico and Olivia."

Rose popped a grape into her mouth and frowned. "Why was Olivia in the chapel anyway?"

"Praying, I expect."

"A sixteen-year-old girl at six o'clock in the morning? I don't have her pegged as the religious type. Something doesn't add up."

They rounded the top of the hill and were surprised to see Chiara trudging towards them, wending her way through a field of bent and broken sunflowers.

"*Buon giorno!*" she called, waving at them. "I thought I would just take a quiet, contemplative morning walk—how wrong I was! It turned out to be rather eventful. Is everyone all right?"

"More or less," Rita said. "I'm afraid your daughter has hurt her leg, but I think she'll be all right. She's in the olive grove a safe distance from the chapel. Frankly, one or two more aftershocks and it could collapse. Say, you haven't seen Hans or Paolo, have you?"

Chiara shook her head and hurried off in the direction of the chapel.

"Well, that's one disappearance solved," Rita said, "and two to go." She frowned, trying to imagine where two missing archaeologists might go. "Let's walk down to the ruins. I have a sixth sense Hans might have been drawn there to exult, to brood...I don't know."

They made their way down the dirt track. For the twin sisters, it was tough going, with rocks unearthed and the soil rearranged in a bumpier, lumpier pattern. But the terrain proved no obstacle for Artemis, who bounded ahead, then doubled back to urge them on. About a quarter of the way down the track, Rita nudged her sister and pointed to a silhouette way off to their right, tramping through a field of sunflowers. "Isn't that Paolo?"

Rose rubbed her eyes and squinted into the sun. The man was wearing dark clothing—pajamas, perhaps—and he was looking down at the ground.

"Paolo! Paolo!" Rose sounded almost like a giddy teenager as she called out to her younger lover. When he didn't look up, she cried all the louder and began to run towards him.

His head finally snapped up. He acknowledged them with a wave, then hurried off towards the row of cottages.

"Well, how do you like that!" Rose huffed. "I could have been killed in an earthquake, and all I get is a wave. Men!"

"I'm sure he's just disoriented and needs to lie down—"

"It's Chiara, isn't it?" Rose fumed. "And Olivia—she's poisoning his mind against me. And as for Hans, I could just wring his neck! Now Paolo must think I'm a flighty, two-timing vixen who'd throw him over for some pretentious windbag archaeologist."

"Paolo's an archaeologist," Rita reminded her sister.

"Yes, but that can be fixed."

Rita thought of her discussion with Chiara and frowned. Chiara was right—Paolo couldn't be happy without his work, even if Rose was his consolation prize.

"And," Rose was saying hotly, "Paolo's not pretentious or a windbag. And he's ever so much younger and more virile than Hans."

"Just how old *is* Paolo?" Rita judged his brother Alessandro to be no more than thirty-five, making her wonder if Paolo was even younger than she had thought.

"Fifty-two," Rose huffed. "But what's in a number?"

"A lot. You wouldn't date an eighty-two-year-old, would you?"

Rose glared at her, but said nothing.

They came to the clearing in front of the tombs, and Rita stopped to catch her breath. To Rita's annoyance, svelter, much fitter Rose—she of the hot yoga and Soul Cycle classes—was not even winded. Hans' Siamese came to a halt as well, wound her way between them, brushing up against their legs, seeming to nudge them towards the dark, forbidding entrance of the tomb that Hans had shown Rita—the one with the red door of death.

"I guess the Etruscans were quite the architects," Rita murmured. "Twenty-five hundred years and dozens—maybe hundreds—of earthquakes later, they tombs are still intact. At least, on the outside."

"Which is more than can be said for the hill behind it," Rose said. "Look." She pointed at the steep hillside behind the tomb, which now had a deep brown gouge in its verdant flank.

Artemis meowed, rubbed her ebony-furred face against Rose's ankle, and then darted into the tomb. Rose ducked beneath the lintel and disappeared into the darkness.

"I'll be there in a just a minute," Rita called out weakly, her voice swallowed up by the vastness of the landscape. "I just need to catch my breath."

She leaned against a rock, warm in the morning sun.

She basked in the sunshine for a few moments, her heartbeat slowly returning to normal. With a sigh, she steeled herself to enter the dank, dark tomb and turned towards the entrance.

But just as she turned, she caught a glimpse of a bright, shiny object—dazzling, almost blinding, in the sunlight—protruding from the sepia-toned deluge of earth and rock that had slid down the hill.

Rita crept closer, stumbled up the hillside, and stared.

It was a finger, a larger-than-life digit cast in bronze. She brushed the dirt gently away and another finger appeared, this one crooked. And when she poked and prodded further, she felt a smooth expanse of metal, slightly curved—the cupped palm of a hand.

Rita stumbled back down the hillside and flung herself into the tomb, once more out of breath.

"Rose!" she called, her voice echoing through the dark chamber. "I've found a man!"

She turned on her cell phone, illuminating the chamber with its eerie blue light. A large crack bisected the frescoed red door of death, zig-zagging its way through the polka dots. Her sister was standing next to all that remained of the alabaster pillar that had once graced the center of the chamber. Miraculously, the roof of the chamber was intact; perhaps the pillar had been more decorative than structural.

"I mean, of bronze," Rita said. "I think it's an Etruscan stat—"

"Yeah?" Rose sounded unimpressed. "Well, I found a man too. A real man."

Artemis looked at Rita, her eyes glowing in the darkness, and hissed. Rose stepped back, and Rita now saw that Artemis was winding her sinuous furry form over and around a large shape—a large *human* shape—that lay on the floor of the tomb.

"And," Rose said, "he's dead."

Chapter Seventeen

They stared at the prone figure, who was coated with a thin layer of dust. The two sisters managed to heave the section of the pillar that had fallen over the man's face just a few inches. Rita brushed aside the rubble from his face. Hans' blue eyes stared out at them, accusatory and icy.

"The last time I saw these eyes," Rose said with a shudder, "they were leering at me."

The pillar seemed to grow even heavier. Rita felt a trickle of sweat run down her brow; her fingers began to tremble from the exertion. This is why, she thought, most detectives were strapping young men, not middle-aged (and that was putting it kindly) dumpling-shaped women. With a grunt, Rita let go and Rose followed. The pillar came crashing down on poor Hans once more.

"Well," Rose said, "at last this time it didn't hurt."

Rita crouched next to the corpse. His left temple was encrusted in dried blood with little bits of rock, dirt, and even what appeared to be a delicate, sepia-toned fragment of dried leaf. She stepped gingerly over the body and examined the right side. A deep bruise spread from his high, pronounced cheekbones to his chiseled jaw, but there was no blood and nothing lodged in the wound.

It was both thrilling and disconcerting that she was now so accustomed to death—violent death—that she was able to examine a body so clinically, so methodically. Rita snapped photo after photo, carefully documenting the position of the body and each injury.

With the edge of her sleeve, Rita gently propped up each leg and took a quick glance at the skin under his pajamas. Blood had pooled on the left side of his body, but the right side looked almost as tan and healthy as when he was alive.

"Rita, this is hardly the time to act out your David Hasselhoff fantasies—"

"Fantasies!" Rita fumed. "I never watched *Baywatch* and, even if I had, David Hasselhoff never interested me in the least, nor did Hans—at least when he was alive. But as a corpse—well, he's quite interesting."

"Is he?" Rose frowned. "He looks like a typical corpse to me. Stiff as a board, that sort of thing." Rose snorted. "Not that the old goat wasn't stiff in life as well. Half the time, I expected him to break into a goosestep."

"Exactly—stiff as a board. Rigor mortis has already set in."

"So? That happens to all dead bodies."

"Yes, but beginning only two to six hours after death."

The light began to dawn in Rose's eyes. "But the earthquake," she murmured, checking her watch, "was only an hour and a half ago..."

"Exactly." Rita's eyes twinkled. "And look at the purplish blush on the left side of his body. That's called lividity, and the coloration is caused by the blood pooling in a particular area. So he was lying on his left side after death and then"—Rita gently brushed away the top layer of dirt between the tomb entrance and where Hans body lay, and smiled with grim satisfaction at the streaks she uncovered—"dragged into the tomb, rearranged face up, and the pillar set on top of him."

She scrolled through the apps on her phone until she found the temperature check. She held it close to Hans' forehead and hit the button. Ninety-one-point-six, it read.

"That's consistent," Rita said, "with the rigor mortis. Approximate time of death was maybe between two and four a.m."

Rose leaned down. She crooked her finger towards Hans' right hand. The fingers were tensed and curled; the tendons stood in high relief. "What's that in his hand?"

Rita inched closer, craned her neck, and peered through her bifocals. When she squinted, a single, tiny, gold link finally came into focus. "A fragment of a piece of jewelry, maybe."

Beside her, Rose shivered. "Belonging, perhaps, to our killer."

Forty-five minutes later, after a short detour to Rita's room to pick up some opera gloves, Rita and Rose were crouched in the shadow of one of the little stone cottages, checking to see if the coast was clear. "What ever happened," Rose muttered, "to stepping over the body and meeting Sal at a little café by the Duomo?"

"If I could simply call the carabinieri and alert them that there was a murder, I would," Rita lied. "But we're cut off from the rest of the world, remember? So it's up to us—"

"*Us?*"

"Hey, you were the one who found the body so, like it or not, you're involved." Rita turned businesslike. "Now, your first assignment is very simple. I'll search Chiara and Olivia's cottage—after all, you can't get caught snooping there—plus Paolo's cottage and Padre Domenico and Alessandro's room. You search the old gardener's cottage, where Diana, Giovanna, and Monica are staying, plus Tiffany and Running Bear's room."

Rose looked aghast. "We're going to just barge in and start rummaging through everyone's unmentionables?"

"That's standard police procedure, Rose."

"Not without a search warrant."

"Oh, this is Italy. They're not so particular here. Didn't you watch the Amanda Knox trial?"

"No." Rose had neither the time nor the inclination to watch true-crime drama on TV. "And in any case, we're not the police."

"A minor technicality," Rita assured her. "Now go."

And before her sister could protest any further, Rita had slipped into Olivia and Chiara's cottage. A ray of sunlight fell on one of the twin beds, illuminating the rumpled sheets, and Rita looked up to see a patch of blue sky. Strewn about were a few archaeology journals, an Italian version of *Cosmopolitan* (Olivia's, she guessed, as she could not imagine sad, cynical Chiara reading such drivel), a few flowery sundresses, and some equally tiny but more conservative blouses and long flowing trousers.

Rita searched in vain for Chiara's large leather handbag, the one that held those mysterious pills—Vicodin? Oxycontin? Xanax?—but it was nowhere to be found. She tried to remember if Chiara had been carrying the bag when they'd seen her crossing the field earlier. Rita thought not, which suggested Chiara had come back here to get her bag.

"It figures," Rita muttered. "The one thing she took with her was the bag with her pills and cigarettes."

Rita crossed the room, slid on her opera gloves, and started going through Olivia's personal effects, which were crammed into a pink sparkly suitcase, something more appropriate, Rita thought, for a girl of eight or nine. She found a family photo album, featuring adorable pictures of Olivia and her doting parents. There was a shot of them with skis in hand, the Matterhorn in the background; a photo of a gap-toothed, adorably awkward Olivia (my, how she'd changed!), flanked by her parents, with Mount Vesuvius in the background; and a picture of them frolicking with an adorable golden Labrador Retriever puppy in front of a field of sunflowers. What was most surprising about the photos was actually not Olivia's transformation from a gap-toothed, chubby-cheeked child to a tall, slim, sophisticated young woman.

It was Chiara's transformation.

In the photos, she looked happier and healthier, fifteen pounds heavier at least, with a pleasantly fuller face and wavy, unruly hair that looked nothing like her sleek dark chignon.

Rita carefully put the photo album back in its place. At the bottom of Olivia's suitcase, she found a few items of jewelry, including a locket inscribed with "PCO." Paolo, Chiara, and Olivia, she guessed.

And then she found a little perfume bottle.

Rita unscrewed the top of the bottle and took a whiff.

The scent was heavenly, vaguely reminiscent of apricots.

White oleander.

The flowers were beautiful and delicate. But every part of the plant, even water in which the flowers had been steeped, was deadly.

Rita's heart hammered in her chest, and a million questions raced through her mind. Had Hans been poisoned before the final fatal blow on the head? But she couldn't imagine what Olivia's motive would be; Hans was useful to her as a potential romantic partner for Rose.

Plus, the bottle was full. But then, she wondered, if Hans wasn't Olivia's intended victim....

Rose. The realization hit her hard. She gasped, and the vial slipped out of her hand. Rita lunged. She caught it just in time, a second before it would have been dashed to pieces and sent poison spreading all over the marble floor.

She held the vial in both hands, afraid of dropping it again and took a deep breath. It was against her every instinct to destroy evidence, but was it truly evidence if no crime—no poisoning, at least—had yet been committed? And could she live with herself if anything happened to her sister and she had failed to prevent it?

Rita set the vial of poison down on the dresser and rummaged in her purse for an empty bottle of sunscreen. Then she turned on her cell phone camera and, with her last tiny remaining bit of charge, filmed herself pouring the contents of the vial into the sunscreen bottle. Then she snapped the bottle firmly shut, placed it inside a Ziploc bag, and slid it back in her purse.

She took the vial into the bathroom, rinsed it at least ten times, filled it with water, and screwed it shut. She was about to shut the bathroom door and put the vial back where she had found it, when she spotted a satin, turquoise pant leg hanging over the shower door.

Rita ran a gloved finger over the hem, noting the slight green and brown stains. Turquoise, she thought, turquoise pajamas which had been dragged through the fecund Tuscan soil and the damp green grass.

She would bet anything that these were the pajamas of the person who had run along the vines last night, who had been privy to Hans' bad behavior and to her heated conversation with him.

She reached her hand up, gently pulled them down, and ran her gloved finger into the waistband to inspect the tag. Thirty-four, she read. Rita tried to recall the conversion chart she'd once seen of European and American sizes. She remembered that this was quite small. But how small? Glamorously thin like Olivia? Or too thin, like Chiara?

Rita put the pajamas back just as she had found them, left the bathroom, and tucked the vial back in Olivia's suitcase, all while riffling through it to see what size Olivia wore. She found a mix of thirty-four and thirty-six.

In Chiara's case, she found a mix of thirty-two and thirty-four.

"Inconclusive," Rita muttered, annoyed.

Crawling over to the window, Rita peeped one eyeball over the sash and breathed a sigh of relief. She was still alone. She crept outside and into Paolo's snug little stone cottage, where she found copious archaeology journals and a tuxedo crumpled on the floor. There was nothing of interest save a torn photo of Rose, eyes gouged out with a pen, which had landed under the desk. She could almost feel the hatred that had prompted such an act.

Who had done this?

Paolo, after discovering Rose and Hans in the pool—and misinterpreting what had passed between them? Rita remembered his expression—bewildered, disappointed—and his words. "*Non ci credo.*" I don't believe it. She found it hard to believe that Paolo, normally mild-mannered and fun-loving, would react so violently.

Then she thought of the poison she had just poured down the drain.

Could Olivia have snuck in and done this?

Yes, most definitely. That girl was like just like oleander: beautiful, but dangerous.

Rita stuffed the torn fragments of the photo in her purse. She tiptoed outside and sprinted over to Padre Domenico and Alessandro's room for a quick peek.

Finding nothing of interest, she crossed the terrace and slipped inside the gardener's cottage, where she'd just seen a flash of her sister's pink negligee in the upper window.

"Find anything?" she asked as she popped her head in the upstairs bedroom. Rose did not seem to be so much sleuthing as ogling the designer clothes strewn all over the floor.

"Hmmm?" Rose was running her hands over a robin's-egg blue cashmere sweater-dress. "Oh, only a half million dollars of high fashion. It's like being backstage during Paris Fashion Week." She wrinkled her nose. "Monica dresses like a nun, though. All blacks and browns and grays, some department store label. It's hard to believe Monica and Giovanna are sisters, huh?"

Rita looked at her reflection in the ornate gold mirror that was hanging askew on the wall, then back at Rose. She watched Rose do the same.

"But some people don't even realize we're sisters," Rita said, "and we're identical twins." She didn't like pondering the unfavorable comparison people were bound to draw between her and Rose, so she quickly said, "What did you find in Tiffany and Running Bear's room?"

"Not much other than, as my nephew would say, bling."

"Real?"

"Who knows? I'm not a jeweler. Anyway, her stuff was strewn all over, and he's a neat freak. There wasn't much in his suitcase—a few Speedos, shorts, T-shirts, flip-flops. A long strip of bandages, as if he were anticipating pulling a muscle. One tux—I'm guessing that's for the wedding. They're an odd couple, those two, but I did find something they have in common: a sentimental streak. She had a black-and-white photo of a little moon-faced girl in an old-fashioned white frilly dress. I turned it over, and all it said was 'Elke – 4.'"

"And in his wallet?"

"Two photos. One of an old man in war paint and a full headdress, very fierce-looking, just kind of staring intensely at the camera. And one of a young man in a U.S. army uniform with a buzz cut."

"Could the photos be of the same man, decades apart?"

"Can't say they looked that much alike, other than being Native American but, hey, people change. But the picture of the older man was definitely more recent. It was in color, good quality, not grainy. Then I came here and didn't discover much other than this fashion trove—oh, and the fact that Monica's a secret Bacci addict. You wouldn't believe how many wrappers I found!"

Bacci—literally "kisses"—were the chocolate hazelnut candies that proliferated around Italy at Christmastime, although clearly for Monica, Christmas came early.

"And Diana"—Rose's eyes twinkled—"reads trashy romance novels."

That was a surprise to Rita. She wouldn't think Diana would need to resort to romantic fiction when she could walk into just about any room and be swept off her feet by the best-looking man there. But she supposed it wasn't so much about gorgeous male specimens as the soul connection. And Diana did appear to miss her husband dreadfully.

"Well," Rita sighed, "I don't think any of that helps us solve this crime but"—she hesitated for a moment before pulling out the torn fragments from her purse—"these may help us prevent the next."

Rose frowned and brought a single fragment up to eye level for inspection. "What is that?"

"Your eye," Rita said matter-of-factly, "or rather, a photo of your left eye, gouged out."

"By whom?"

"By Olivia or Paolo."

"Surely not Paolo."

Rita sighed. "It was in his room, and he did see you with Hans last night."

"That was nothing!"

"Yes, but he didn't know that. And he ignored you when we saw him this morning." Rita suddenly plopped down on Diana's bed, hard, and said, "You do realize that he could have been walking back from the tomb where we found Hans."

"No—*no*."

"I'm just saying...he was coming from that direction, that's all."

And, Rita silently added, after the incident in the pool, he certainly had a motive to kill Hans. But partly to mollify Rose and partly because it was the truth, Rita said, "But I think you have more to fear from Olivia."

"What? You think she's going to lunge across our *primo piatto* today—maybe some lovely ravioli stuffed with spinach and ricotta—and gouge my eye out with a butter knife?"

"No, I think she's going to poison you with white oleander."

"*What?*"

"I found it in her suitcase."

"And you're going to just let her poison me?" Rose sputtered.

"Of course not," Rita huffed, neglecting to mention the white oleander was safely stowed away in Rita's sunscreen bottle. She wanted her sister on edge, alert. Rita needed her sister's eagle eyes more than ever. "But you can play dead, right?"

"Huh?"

"Never mind. We'll work on catching Olivia later. Now, it's time to break the news of Hans' death to everyone—including the murderer."

Chapter Eighteen

It took longer than Rita had expected to gather all of the guests into the Etruscan tomb that was now the resting place of Hans Clausnitzer. Olivia had to be transported in a wheelbarrow; Padre Domenico hobbled along slowly. And even the able-bodied among them were rendered momentarily speechless—and immobile—when they arrived at the spot where the gigantic bronze finger protruded out of the earth. The archaeologists oohed and aahed, practically salivating at the prospect of excavating the rest of the statue, and it was only with great effort that Rita finally coaxed them inside the tomb.

They were greeted by a sharp hiss. Artemis had stayed with the body and now sat, sphinx-like, guarding Hans fiercely.

"Well, I'd say he's deader than a doornail," Tiffany said. "Talk about karma and reaping what you sow and all that."

"Tiffany," Running Bear murmured, "show some respect for the dead."

"Diana predicted this," Chiara said. "What was that you said? 'The invader from the north will pass through the final red door'?"

Diana smiled indulgently. She did not look the slightest bit discomfited by a dead body. "Actually, I didn't predict it. The entrails did. I only interpreted for the gods."

"So the Etruscan gods"—Padre Domenico made air quotes, looked heavenward, and crossed himself, as if expecting to be smote dead at any moment—"preordained Hans' death? They wanted him dead?"

"It was their will, shall we say. It was his time."

"But you didn't," Padre Domenico said, "predict the earthquake. *Mi dispiace*—the 'gods' didn't predict the earthquake. Quite an oversight, no?"

"Perhaps I misinterpreted some of the signs. I'm only human, you know." Diana sighed. "Poor Hans."

A few others made sympathetic noises, but try as they might, they couldn't muster much sorrow for the recently departed.

Giovanna looked down the line of untroubled faces and stomped her feet like a petulant schoolgirl. "Hans was my mentor," Giovanna thundered, her eyes scanning the chamber and boring into each one of them. "He was my friend. He was my teacher. He was like a second father to me. And he was supposed to walk me down the aisle."

Monica reached over and squeezed Giovanna's hand.

Luisa spat on the earthen floor. "He was also a wonderful boss. You should all be ashamed of yourselves."

They were momentarily chastened into silence. Then Monica frowned and raised her hand. Rita sighed. What did Monica think this was? Kindergarten?

"Yes, Monica?"

Monica seemed to shrink before their gaze. She reminded Rita of a turtle retreating into its shell.

"Well," Monica began shyly, "I was just wondering, er, that is, was anyone else wondering...what Hans was doing out here?"

Rita decided now was not the time to reveal that the body had been moved.

Chiara shrugged. Rita would bet anything she was itching for a cigarette. "He was an archaeologist. We're a strange tribe, you know. These sites exert an almost mystical pull on us."

"Or maybe," Rose said, "he felt the need to dig in the middle of the night."

"In here?" Chiara was incredulous. "It would have been pitch black. Plus, it was excavated years ago. Everything's in the museum in Volterra."

Rose shrugged. "Maybe he thought they missed something."

"Well, if that's the case," Chiara said, "he'd have assembled a team. He'd have surveyed the site first so they could pinpoint exactly which one-foot square plot it came from."

"Not if he didn't plan on handing it over," Rose said. "Not if he were, say, an antiquities thief."

Rita started to cough. She didn't know if she should be pleased or annoyed that Rose was bringing this up. "*Scusate*," she murmured. "There's so much dust in here."

As Rita doubled over coughing, she cast a surreptitious glance around the room to see if anyone looked discomfited by the reference to antiquities theft, but no one looked particularly guilty.

She did notice, however, that Padre Domenico was looking from Hans to the ceiling and back again. The creases on his forehead grew more pronounced.

"*Che c'è, Padre?*" Rita asked softly.

Everyone turned to stare at the priest.

"I am no detective," he said, "or even a—what did you call it, Rita?—a citizen who solves crimes. But it would seem to me that this was no natural death. His injury is in the wrong place, his body looks laid out strangely, almost for a funeral. No"—he raised his eyes and looked at them, fear creeping into his features—"I'd say he was murdered."

At the word "murdered," Artemis yelped and there was a chorus of gasps that ricocheted around the chamber and came back to them in a macabre echo. Sal glowered at Rita as if it were somehow her fault that another murder case had fallen in her lap.

"And I'd say," Padre Domenico added, "that Rita was just waiting to see who would notice—or admit guilt."

"Guilt?" Giovanna gasped. "Why it couldn't be—"

He silenced her with a look. "That's the thing, my child. Not only could it be one of us, but it *had* to be."

The sun was high in the sky by the time they turned back to the house.

"I slept all night," Diana was saying, squeezing Rita's arm for emphasis. Even now, after being jolted awake by an earthquake, Diana looked calm, confident, and obscenely, unfairly beautiful. "The minute I crossed the threshold," she said, "I stepped right out of my clothes." Diana, Rita noticed, made no mention of actually stepping into pajamas. "I then fell right into bed and drifted off to sleep. I slept like a baby, I tell you, and I didn't wake up until I was so rudely awakened by the earthquake."

"Surely you must have gotten up to go to the bathroom."

"No."

"Or to put on more covers? It got rather chilly last night."

Diana shrugged. "I always sleep in the nude."

"Well, even if you didn't get out of bed, surely you must have awoken at some point because you heard something."

"Just an argument," Diana said, "between my daughter–Giovanna, that is–and Alessandro. A little lover's spat. Oh, how I miss those! The drama, the passion, the feeling that you can't live with this person, but you can't live without them either. The sense that you are fused together, destined to be together. It always made me feel like Madame Butterfly."

"Madame Butterfly died a horrible, tragic death."

"Yes–so she did." Apparently, this did nothing to dampen Diana's ardor for epic lover's fights. "But that's all I heard. A fight between two lovers–nothing to do with Hans' death."

"Oh, I wouldn't be too sure about that," Rita said. "After all, Alessandro felt betrayed by Giovanna precisely because of her professional partnership with Hans, that she would co-author a paper refuting Alessandro's life's work without dropping so much as a hint over the dining room table. Of course, what's even more unforgiveable, between you and me, is that Giovanna didn't even tell you, her own mother." Rita shook her head and clucked sympathetically. "Children can be so ungrateful. You wreck your figure for them"—she shot a surreptitious glance at Diana's flat stomach and winced—"at least, the mere mortals among us do. You suffer through the agony of childbirth, nurse them through chickenpox, and suffer through all of that teenage angst and this—this—is how they repay you, by shutting you out, denigrating your life's work."

Rita frowned, realizing she had inserted a few more autobiographical details than necessary. "And your other daughter, Monica—she was with you all night?"

"Oh, yes. She was there when I went to bed and there when we were jolted awake. *Mi dispiace*," Diana said with an air of finality that suggested she was taking her leave. "I wish I could be of more help, but I suspect this will never be solved. Only the gods know who killed Hans."

They had arrived at the terrace. Luisa clapped her hands peremptorily. "*Il pranzo*," she announced, "*será presto in un'ora*."

Rita could not believe her ears. Luisa had only the use of her left arm and yet she was promising to have lunch ready in an hour.

"Let me help," Rita said impulsively. "I don't want you to hurt yourself."

Luisa glanced down at her bandaged right arm, then back at Rita. There was distrust—and intense dislike—in her gaze. "Only," she said, "as my sous chef. You must do exactly as I say."

"Don't do it, sis," Rose murmured in Rita's ear. "Following directions is not your forte, and the last thing we need today is more bloodshed."

But Rita just stiffened her spine and smiled through gritted teeth. "*Certo*," she forced herself to say to Luisa. Then she followed Luisa through the portico and into the cavernous kitchen. Luisa might think she was getting a sous chef, but she was also getting an interrogator.

Chapter Nineteen

"We will make *pici*," Luisa declared, eyes blazing, as they stared down at the mound of semolina flour on the marble block, and the four tangerine-hued egg yolks that nestled in the center. Luisa sounded as though she were commanding Rita to go on some sort of suicide mission, which perhaps she was, since Rita was sure that no matter what she did, Luisa would not judge it a success.

"Rolled out by hand, not a pasta machine," Luisa tut-tutted, wagging a thick finger at Rita. "*Pici* is Signor Clausnitzer's favorite pasta."

"But Signor Clausnitzer is dead."

"Death," Luisa said severely, "is no reason to let our standards slip."

Under Luisa's watchful–wrathful–gaze, Rita chipped away at the sides of the well with a fork, sending a steady stream of flour, soft like talcum powder, swirling into the golden center. Luisa grumbled, "Too fast," so, just to annoy her, Rita sped up. When at last she had a golden ball of dough, Rita kneaded it a few times, then set it aside to rest. "Should we start the second course? What is it, by the way?"

"Meat, obviously." Luisa peered contemptuously down her long nose at Rita. "*Non c'è elettricità.* Whatever we don't eat will rot. And, no, we will not be using the stove—the gas line might be cracked. Everything will be cooked in the old way—in the wood-fired oven or over an open fire."

Luisa opened the darkened refrigerator and pulled out the most enormous slab of meat Rita had ever seen. With its thick bones and heavily marbled flesh, it left nothing to the imagination. A vegetarian like her daughter-in-law Susan would faint dead away.

Reaching up a flabby forearm, Luisa snatched a gleaming meat cleaver off the rack above. She placed the meat on the counter and brought down the cleaver with a decisive blow, slicing through the bone with a jarring thwack.

"That," she said, "is what I'd like to do to whoever killed Signor Clausnitzer."

"He was a good employer?"

"The best."

Rita uncovered the pasta dough, and Luisa handed her a rolling pin the size of a baseball bat. It had no handle. Rita rolled it thoughtfully over the dough, then ran her fingers over its worn ends, wondering if a blunt instrument like this could have been used to kill Hans.

"He was a prince," Luisa was saying. "A man without equal. A man of taste, a man of vision."

She roughly pried Rita's hands off of the rolling pin. "Not like that. What are you—some delicate American flower? Put some muscle into it. Use your forearms, like this."

Luisa demonstrated by placing her own massive forearm on the rolling pin and shifting her considerable body weight forward.

"I've only been making pasta like this for fifty years," Rita said testily.

"Then for fifty years you've been making it wrong." With two deft flicks of her left wrist, Luisa sprinkled each steak with a generous amount of coarse sea salt and then fresh-ground black pepper. Then she tossed each one onto the searing hot wood-fired grill, which answered back with an angry sizzle. "He's too generous for his own good, you know."

Rita noticed that Luisa spoke of Hans in the present tense.

"Hosting Giovanna's wedding," Luisa muttered, her beady eyes fixed on the roaring flames, "without accepting so much as a cent. Even agreeing to walk her down the aisle. He took her under his wing, he did. Felt sorry for her, I guess, what with her dead father and her flighty mother, who puts on a good show—all that deposed princess act—but hasn't two euros to scrape together."

"But she is royalty, isn't she?"

"Not anymore. So her ancestors killed someone else's ancestors a long time ago and ended up with a drafty castle. Big deal. My *nonno* used to own this estate and look where it got me."

Rita blinked. Surely, Luisa was joking. This coarse woman in a ratty housedress and orthopedic shoes was about as far from nobility as she could imagine.

Luisa stabbed one of the steaks with a giant fork and plopped it onto a silver platter. She laughed, but not in a merry way. "Don't believe it, do you? Well, Signor Clausnitzer knew, and that's what mattered. And now it's all back in the family again."

"What do you mean?"

"He left it to me." Luisa tapped a garish red rose that spread over the swell of her very ample chest. There was a crinkling sound, as if a crumpled slip of paper lay tucked inside Luisa's no doubt formidable brassiere. "In his will."

Rita could not quite believe her ears. She stood there for a moment, entranced by the flickering blue flames, serenaded by the bubbling of the giant vat of salted water over the hearth and the intermittent hiss of melting fat dripping in the fire.

"He left a will?" she repeated, dumbfounded. "And left everything to...you? He had no family?"

"No family," Luisa sniffed, "worth remembering. A sister that he didn't get on with. She's married to a Greek who's got a shipping company. He's as rich as Croesseus, that one. They live on a private island in Greece, and she couldn't be bothered to come here, so why should she inherit Villa Belvista? And an ex-wife in Frankfurt—or was it Berlin? Some awful, cold place. And she was a cold woman, too, from what Signor Clausnitzer says."

"And you've read the will already?"

"I haven't opened it," Luisa said tartly, "if that's what you're asking. But I know what's in it."

"He told you?"

Luisa nodded and took another steak off the fire. "Plus, I saw it with my own eyes. I wasn't an official witness, but I was standing there when he signed it."

"Who were the witnesses?"

"Village folk." Luisa's lips curled into a little smile. She tapped her chest again. "I thought we might read the will over dessert."

The *pici*, Rita had to admit was excellent, wonderfully springy and glutinous, thicker—and so much more satisfying—than spaghetti. It was dressed with a most unusual pesto of hard-boiled eggs, anchovies, and wonderfully fragrant fresh parsley and basil.

"Well, shoot," Tiffany was saying as they sat beneath the bougainvillea, out of earshot of the rest of the group. "That Hans sure was one crazy coot."

Tiffany struggled to suck a stray noodle between her lips, which were lacquered an alarming shade of coral. Clearly, Tiffany had grabbed her make-up case before fleeing her crumbling room. "Woo-ee," she said, slapping her knee. "This sure beats Chef Boyardee. Now, the steak, though"—as Wolf hovered hopefully by her side, she cut into her *bistecca* and a trickle of blood oozed out—"is a bit rare for my taste."

Rita sighed. It was for her too, but Luisa insisted that this was the only acceptable way to eat a steak made from the prized Chianina cattle of Tuscany.

Beside her, Running Bear shrugged and tucked into his steak with gusto. Tiffany had insisted on being interviewed with Running Bear, and Rita had no leverage to object.

"I like it," Running Bear said. "All it needs is some fry bread on the side."

"So tell me," Rita said, "exactly what you did, said, or heard last night."

"As we were getting into bed," Running Bear said, "we heard an argument between Alessandro and Giovanna."

"An argument!" Tiffany hooted. "I've heard bar brawls quieter than that. What a racket! And they were fighting 'til the cows came home."

Rita massaged her temples, feeling as though her head would explode if Tiffany hurled one more down-home saying her way. It would be a relief to speak Italian again.

"So that would have been what time exactly?"

Running Bear squinted and looked to Tiffany, as if she'd have the answer, but she shrugged.

"Oh," Tiffany said, "I just turned my hearing aid down and went to sleep, hon. That's after I realized I couldn't understand all the juicy bits. It turns out Italian isn't like French at all!" Tiffany smiled smugly. "I took two years of French in high school, so I can *parlez-vous* as snooty as the rest of them. Even that Diana. Deposed royalty, my ass."

"Tiffany," Running Bear said quietly, warning in his voice.

"Aren't you sweet?" Tiffany patted his hand. "Always trying to get me to shut my big trap. It's for my own good, I know."

Rita smiled ruefully. "My children," she said, "are always trying to get me to do things 'for my own good,' but I never listen."

"I don't either." Tiffany guffawed and winked. "And yes, detective lady, I get your hidden meaning. Running Bear is young enough to be my son."

Rita tried to look innocent and contrite, lest Tiffany clam up on her.

"Other than that," Tiffany said with a wide smile that suggested no offence was taken, "I heard nothing. But then again, I had my hearing aids turned down."

Rita turned to Running Bear. "Well, your young ears must work just fine. Did you hear anything?"

"Nope. Slept like a baby."

"And did either of you leave the room at any time?"

Running Bear said, "Not until I got up to take a walk just after daybreak."

"It's not much to go on, is it?" Tiffany clucked sympathetically. "A lover's spat neither of us could understand."

"No, it isn't," Rita agreed, waving them away and beckoning Monica towards her.

But Rita was lying, of course. Because Running Bear had just revealed more than he realized. He hadn't heard the splash. He hadn't heard the argument between Hans and Rose in the pool.

Which meant he hadn't been in his room shortly before Hans was killed.

Chapter Twenty

Rita was still pondering just what Running Bear's lies meant when Monica slid into the seat across from her just as Luisa plunked down two glasses of *vin santo* and two little plates of *cantucci.*

"*I dolci.* Fuel for your little *indagine*," Luisa said contemptuously.

Rita regarded the cook with a bemused smile. "Don't you want to know who killed your 'sainted employer'?"

Rita was not above throwing Luisa's words back at her.

"*Certo*—but I hardly think you'll be the one to get to the bottom of it."

Luisa spit on the ground as if to underscore her point and then stalked away.

"She's got a strong personality," Rita said to Monica. "Rather like your mother, wouldn't you say?"

"*Mia mamma?*" Monica looked confused, nervous, and something else—relieved, perhaps—all at the same time. "Oh, I wouldn't say they're the same at all. My mother's a strong personality, of course, but she's descended from nobility. She has every reason to be proud."

"And you, too," Rita said, dunking her *cantucci* in in the *vin santo* and bringing it to her lips. It was delicious—sweet, nutty, crunchy. It tasted as though the almonds had been shelled just yesterday.

"Me—too?"

"Well, if your mother's descended from royalty, you must be, too."

"Oh, no." Monica was almost whispering now, and Rita had to lean forward to hear her. "I'm adopted, you see."

Rita looked at Monica with renewed interest. Suddenly, so many things clicked into place.

"And Giovanna? She's adopted too?"

"Oh, no. She was—a surprise. A good surprise."

Rita got the sense that Monica forced herself to say that last bit. She had no doubt that Giovanna had been a good surprise for Diana, but for Monica, Rita rather thought the experience had been less about gaining a sister than about becoming an afterthought.

"My parents," Monica explained, "had trouble conceiving for many years, you see, so they adopted me from an orphanage in Sicily. The one run by the Sisters of Charity—you know, Mother Theresa's nuns."

Rita vaguely remembered hearing that Mother Theresa had an orphanage in Palermo, and that she had famously said, much to the embarrassment of the Italian government, that conditions in the city's poorer quarters rivaled those in India. Things had improved with the influx of development funds from the European Union, but Palermo must have been very poor when Monica was born.

"I'm very grateful to my adoptive parents," Monica added. "I want for nothing."

Except, Rita added silently, love, encouragement, and recognition.

"And your father—your adoptive father—is deceased. Is that right?"

Monica nodded.

"And even though they tried to conceive a child for years and couldn't, they were able to conceive Giovanna a few years after your adoption?"

Monica looked down and fiddled with her *cantucci*. "*Un miracolo*," she mumbled. "God works in mysterious ways." Monica's *cantucci* slipped through her fingers and fell in her wine. "Oh!" she exclaimed, flustered, frantically trying to extract her *cantucci* with a spoon. But it just kept sliding back down. The girl really was terrifically awkward, Rita thought, although in this case, she suspected there was more than a lack of coordination involved. Clearly, Monica suspected that her adoptive father was not Giovanna's biological father, but she would never admit it to Rita.

Changing tacks, Rita asked, "Did you see Running Bear last night?"

"Running Bear?" Monica finally fished the now soggy *cantucci* out of her wine. Her hands shook as she took a sip of wine, stalling for time. "I thought you were going to ask me about Hans. He's the one who's dead."

"*Bene*. Did you see Hans?"

Monica shook her head.

"And your mother? Was she with you all night?"

Monica's gaze darted nervously over to Diana, who was holding her wine glass high and seemed to be giving some kind of toast. Monica turned back to Rita and nodded meekly.

"And did you hear anything unusual from your cottage?"

"Anything, er...?"

"An argument, for instance."

"Oh..." Monica's voice trailed off and she shot a look at her sister and her intended. They were huddled together; Giovanna looked lost in a sea of grief. "A little argument between my sister and Alessandro. But everything's fine now."

Monica seemed to harbor no resentment towards her perfect, glamorous sister, the long-awaited biological child who could do no wrong.

"Did you hear anything else?"

"No."

Rita froze with her pen over her notepad. So Monica hadn't heard the splash either. Did that mean she'd been with Running Bear? Or with someone else entirely?

Monica flushed, realizing she'd given the wrong answer. "Uh, there were bird calls. Crickets, maybe a few trucks passing way over there on the road."

"Mmmmm." Rita made a big show of writing this down.

"And you didn't see Running Bear at all—not even through the window?"

"No." Monica tried to flash a smile at Rita, although it never reached her eyes. "I'm a sound sleeper, I guess."

More like a lousy liar, Rita thought. Had Monica's shy flirting with Running Bear led only to a tryst? Or had the two colluded in something far more dangerous?

Rita polished off a second plate of *cantucci* while grilling Padre Domenico, who obstinately—although very pleasantly—insisted he knew nothing that would have any bearing on the case.

"The only person I saw that night was my brother Alessandro," he said with a shrug, "who is staying with me."

"And you were both asleep the whole time?"

"No, he was with Giovanna first, arguing outside." He looked embarrassed. "I think most people heard that. And then, when he came in, we talked for about an hour. He was very upset. She'd called off the wedding, you see."

"She—why? He was the wronged party."

"Oh, you know"—he waved his hands dismissively—"emotions always run high before a wedding. I've counseled many brides through the bathroom door. I talked one groom off a ledge—literally. He was a construction worker and decided to sit on top of his latest construction site and 'get perspective.'" Padre Domenico chuckled. "He fell and broke his arm, I called the bride, and they exchanged vows in the hospital."

Rita laughed. "It took all four of his groomsmen to drag Sal out of the bathroom. He was shaking so hard I couldn't hold him still to slip the ring on."

"*Vedi?* Anyway, Giovanna thought that Alessandro wasn't respecting her professional independence. Would he expect her to always agree with him? Would he expect her to bring him coffee in bed, spend every Sunday making his favorite *ragú*, indulge his every whim?"

Rita was about to make a wisecrack that that's what Sal had expected too and, because it had been a different era, he'd largely gotten it. But perhaps that wasn't fair. She'd been fine with that identity—the best Italian-American cook in Acorn Hollow, and the fiercest, most devoted mamma bear—until she'd decided she wanted more, first as a reporter, then as a sleuth.

And Sal had supported her one hundred percent. She glanced at her husband, who was brushing *cantucci* crumbs off his lips, and winced. She was in the wrong. She'd hidden things from him and refused to admit it. And she would apologize as soon as she got through these interviews.

With a start, she realized that Padre Domenico was still speaking.

"So," he was saying, "I advised him to just let her cool off overnight and try to talk to her in the morning."

"And he accepted this advice?"

"He seemed to. We hugged, we prayed on it, and we both went to bed around one-fifteen. Other than being awakened by a splash and a little argument between your sister and Hans, I slept soundly." He winked at her. "I would have gone out to rescue Rose, but from what I could see from my window, it looked like she had the situation under control."

"And when did you wake up and go to the chapel?"

"Five-thirty. That's my usual routine—up at five-thirty for matins."

"And Olivia was there when you arrived?"

"Yes, she was there for...prayer. The only other person I passed was Luisa. She was coming out of the gatehouse, where she lives, and going to the kitchen to start breakfast."

Rita sighed. He wasn't giving her a lot to go on. So much for harboring a secret desire to be a sleuth.

"So did you know any of these people before coming here—other, that is, than your brothers and Giovanna?"

"Well, Olivia, my niece, of course, and Chiara, my sister-in-law."

"*Ex* sister-in-law," Rita corrected him, blushing and feeling as though he were accusing her sister of adultery.

But Padre Domenico just waved a hand dismissively. "She'll always be my sister-in-law. *Sempre*! Let's see...I met Monica and Diana at Alessandro and Giovanna's engagement party, and although I never had met Hans before this week, I did get a thank-you note from him once for sending him the best cook in Tuscany." He winked. "Well, until you came along."

"*Non ho capito*. How do you know Luisa?"

"I don't. I know her son, Vincenzo. He was an inmate at Regina Coeli."

"*Was*?"

"He was released last month after doing a five-year sentence as an accessory to murder. I assume he's now back in Testaccio, just outside of Rome, with his wife and children."

Rita felt a shiver go down her spine. "But he could be here...anywhere..."

And Vincenzo could be aware of the fact that, if Hans were to die, his mother would inherit Hans' estate.

Chapter Twenty-One

Rita had a brief interview with Alessandro and Giovanna but neither could shed much new light on Hans' death. Giovanna claimed to have gone right back to the cottage she shared with her mother and sister after her argument with Alessandro and to have gone straight to bed. She insisted that she never went to Alessandro's room to make amends and never went to confront Hans over his role in nearly ruining her wedding.

"So where did Hans," Rita said, "store the manuscript that he was going to send to *Archaeology Today*?"

Alessandro moved an inch or two farther from Giovanna, and Giovanna noticed. Eyeing her fiancé warily, she said softly, "On his laptop, of course, and a thumb drive he kept in his desk."

"And do you have a copy?"

"No—not of the final version."

"But you must know the main thrust of the article. I mean, you are the co-author, aren't you? So what was in the article?"

Giovanna colored deeply and shifted in her seat, but said nothing.

"*Dai, Giovanna!*" Rita snapped. "I'm interested in establishing a motive for murder, not some petty academic dispute. I'm not like I'm going to scoop you and send this to a rival journal." She sighed. "Just tell me what you and Hans dug up. I need to know where this artifact is, and whether it's gone missing."

Giovanna's expression turned sheepish. "It's not anything we dug up, at least in the archaeological sense. We found a portion of the Roman historian Tacitus' history of the Etruscans, which we can assume draws heavily on the Emperor Claudius's history of the Etruscans."

"Tacitus," Giovanna hastened to add, "frequently used Claudius' work as the basis for his own. And he claims that the Etruscans were a small tribe of expert bronze workers living in the southern foothills of the Dolomites, who then swept down into the fertile Po Valley, absorbing other more primitive tribes in the process, and eventually continued south to ancient Etruria."

Alessandro's jaw dropped. "But surely if something like that existed, it would be in the Laurentian, where Tacitus' other major works are stored, and every inch of that library has been scoured..."

Rita had a vague recollection of underlining the Laurentian Library—a masterpiece designed by Michelangelo to house the Medicis' priceless manuscripts—in her guidebook. With a sigh, she realized this was yet one more site she was going to miss.

Giovanna shook her head impatiently. “Not the Laurentian. The monastery of Yuste in Spain, to which the Holy Roman Emperor Charles V retired after abdicating the throne.”

A light began to gleam in Alessandro’s dark eyes. “And Charles sacked Rome when the Medici Clement VII was pope...”

“...who must have taken the manuscript from *his* family’s library to Rome....”

On and on they went, lost in their own esoteric scholarly world, seemingly oblivious to Rita and her *indagine*, as if a five-hundred-year-old theft were more important than a murder that had happened just that morning—and of one of their colleagues, to boot. Rita could not see what this really proved anyway. Tacitus may not have been a very faithful plagiarizer. Perhaps he embellished here and there; he was a Roman senator, after all, and politicians were never known for their honesty. And then there were the absolutely byzantine leaps of logics. They couldn’t prove that Clement took the manuscript to Rome, or that Charles stole it, or that he took it with him as a little light reading while basking in the Spanish sun. Rita wouldn’t have put it past Hans to forge the whole document.

“So just to be clear”—Rita cleared her throat nosily and looked pointedly at Alessandro—" you didn’t see or hear anyone or anything last night? That is, after you and Giovanna argued.”

Alessandro blushed. "I went back to my room and talked to my brother, Domenico."

Rita noticed he omitted the "*padre*" part.

"For spiritual guidance?"

"Brotherly advice."

"And your other brother, Paolo? Did you ask for his advice?"

"*Ho bu*–" Alessandro stopped abruptly and his eyes flitted to the loungers. Rita followed his gaze and realized, apparently to both of their surprise, that Paolo, Chiara, and Olivia had left. "No." His dark eyes flashed. "I didn't consult Paolo."

He and Giovanna abruptly sprang up and stalked away, back to the safety of the others.

But they had not fled quickly enough. Rita knew exactly what Alessandro had stopped himself from saying: "*Ho bussato.*" I knocked. In his hour of need, he had knocked on Paolo's door and no one had answered.

But even more significant was that he felt the need to hide this. Did he suspect that Paolo was behind Hans' death?

But Rita did not have a chance to ponder this, because at that exact moment, Luisa reached into her bra and brought out a folded sheet of paper. She brandished it in the air, not like a flag of surrender, but like a warning shot.

And then she announced that it was time for the reading of Hans' will.

****

Luisa began to read in a loud, solemn voice while Rose provided simultaneous translation for the Americans present. "I, Hans Clausnitzer, being of sound mind and body—"

"Oh," Diana muttered, "I very much doubt that."

Luisa pointedly ignored Diana and went on, stumbling over some of the longer words. Rita suspected that Luisa's education had been a casualty of Italy's wartime destruction and post-war poverty. But even so, Luisa insisted on reading the will herself, and her voice trembled with excitement. She held the paper, thin and yellow as onionskin, in both hands, devouring each word greedily with her eyes, no doubt hoping for riches beyond her wildest dreams—not only this estate, with olive groves and vineyards as far as the eye could see, but maybe his Audi, shined to a high gloss, a condo in a ritzy Swiss ski resort, or a flat in Munich.

Maybe money to help her errant son start a business, build a new life.

For a moment, Rita forgot how much she detested proud, haughty Luisa. She knew what it was like to have a wayward son. Although Rita's Vinnie was hardly *that* wayward.

"I leave the sum of twenty thousand euros to Luisa Molinaro, my devoted employee and the best chef in Tuscany." Looking genuinely touched, Luisa wiped away a tear. "I leave the contents of safe deposit box number 13-97443 at Deutschebank in Munich, Germany, to Tiffany Devereaux, to use at her discretion."

"Tiffany!" Giovanna exclaimed just as Sal burst out with "*ma perché?*"

Tiffany must have understood Sal's meaning, because she shrugged modestly and said, "It must be a little parting gift from Hans. Maybe some souvenirs from the digs I financed."

"Tiffany," Luisa continued, her eyes narrowing, "shall also inherit my home in Munich, including all art and furnishings therein, as well as my fifty-one percent stake in DeutscheChem."

There were gasps all around.

"Most of the company!" Diana exclaimed in English, presumably for Tiffany's benefit. "Why would Tiffany need more money?"

"It's not about the money, toots," Tiffany said. "At least, not for me."

Her tone of voice left no doubt that she thought Diana, on the other hand, was a gold digger.

"What is it about then?"

Tiffany just smiled enigmatically. "All will become clear," she said, "in time."

Luisa cleared her throat, and everyone turned back towards her. "I leave my villa, the gatehouse in front, and the front ten-acre plot to Luisa Molinaro."

There was a broad smile on Luisa's face, but it soon faded, and her hands shook. Looking up, she said, "There must be some mistake."

She uttered a little cry, and the paper fluttered out of her hands and fell to the ground. A gentle breeze picked it up, and the paper tumbled across the terrace towards the pool.

Just in time, right before it fell into the brilliantly turquoise waters, Sal snatched it. He held it at arm's length, pushed his reading glasses up his nose, and read,

"I leave the remainder of my estate to Giovanna Giambologna...."

Sal looked up, and Rita noticed that the telltale vein was throbbing above his left temple, and a pink flush was spreading from his ears to his cheeks. Something was wrong.

"My"—he paused and cleared his throat—"natural daughter."

Chapter Twenty-Two

The revelation came like a thunderclap announcing that a downpour was imminent. It was sudden and shocking, and it sent everyone scurrying away, as if to seek shelter from the storm. Giovanna bolted first, fleeing tearfully towards her little cottage and insisting she wanted to be alone.

Sal and Padre Domenico immediately hatched a plan to go rabbit hunting. "So that Luisa has the ingredients to make *pappardelle alla lepre.*" Padre Domenico winked and patted his round little belly. "Otherwise, the only meat we'll be eating will be Hans' prosciutto, which is excellent of course, but rather limiting."

Sal nodded along proudly. Rita could tell he was relishing his role as the manly hunter, the provider; he looked as proud as if he'd single-handedly brought down a wooly mammoth, even though he hadn't yet fired a shot.

"Don't shoot yourself in the foot, *caro,*" Rita admonished him, "you know, like that time with Calvino."

"A freak accident," he muttered, blushing and cutting her off. "It could happen to anyone. Look at Dick Cheney."

"And don't shoot each other, either," Tiffany shook a bejeweled, liver-spotted finger in their direction and laughed. "You know, in case one of you turns out to be the murderer."

Rita tried to laugh along, but it came our forced. Her husband was going into the woods, alone, with an armed man who was a suspect in a murder investigation. Padre Domenico wasn't a prime suspect, but still....

Sal grunted. "If you can't trust a man of the cloth, who can you trust?" He shot Rita a withering look. "I'll be back by five, with all my fingers and toes, plus half a dozen tasty rabbits."

Then he stalked off, leaving Rita once again unable to apologize.

Luisa and Monica set off on a truffle-hunting expedition in the company of Helga, Hans' prized truffle-hunting pig. Diana and Alessandro made their excuses, too, eager to join Paolo, Chiara, and Olivia—who had somehow slipped away even before the reading of the will—at the dig site. "A bronze statue!" Diana enthused, "It might be intact—it might even rival the Mars of Todi statue!"

Rose, Rita, and Running Bear decided to tag along with Diana and Alessandro—Rita because she hoped to find some additional clue at the site where Hans was found, Rose because she wanted to keep an eye on Paolo, and Running Bear because he'd apparently developed quite an interest in archaeology as Tiffany's personal assistant.

As they made their way down the dirt track, the conversation quickly turned to Diana's predicament.

"It was *un gran sbaglio*—a mistake," Diana said. She spoke a little too fast, a little too loudly, in a mix of Italian and, for Running Bear's sake, English. "A brief, torrid affair—totally meaningless—when I thought Giorgio was leaving me for another woman. My fears turned out to be totally baseless, of course, and I ended things with Hans. And then I was pregnant and it occurred to me it could have been Hans' child, but Giorgio was so pleased. *Felicissimo!* How could I tell him? And did it really matter anyway? Giorgio adored Giovanna—absolutely adored her, with a love I've never seen before—"

"You mean, he loved her," Running Bear said, "more than Monica."

He said this as a statement, not a question, with a quiet intensity bordering on anger.

"Oh, well, no—I mean, he loved his girls equally. Parents—good parents, that is—don't have favorites."

Oh, Rita thought, but they do. She had a soft spot for her boys, Marco in particular. He was the child that made her the envy of every mother in Acorn Hollow. He'd been valedictorian of his high school class and Volunteer of the Year at the senior center. (My, how the ladies had dolled up for his shift on Saturday afternoons!). His graduating class had voted him Nicest Boy, Most Likely to Succeed, Most Dreamed About, and even The Boy Your Mother Wants You to Marry. When Marco had graduated from high school, every hair on

Rita's head was still black, nary a gray root in sight. And while he was enough of a mamma's boy to take Rita's side in most matters, he was not so much of a mamma's boy as to still be living at home, expecting her to cater to his every whim.

Her daughter Gina was too complicated, too prickly—too much, frankly, like Rita—to be her favorite child, and Vinnie, her youngest, was just too much work.

They crested the top of the hill. The tombs came into view first, then the hill with the landslide, and the debris field at its base. The gleaming bronze finger pointing up to the heavens came into view first, then the grid of perfect squares that Paolo, Chiara, and Olivia had demarcated in the debris field with fallen olive branches. Chiara and Paolo assiduously scraped through each layer of earth with metal trowels that glinted in the hot sun. Their heads were close together and they frequently stopped to confer, exclaim over some little detail, or share a laugh.

"They're colleagues," Rose murmured through gritted teeth to no one in particular. "Purely professional colleagues."

But she did not look like she believed it at all.

Olivia sat a few feet away on a rock, her face shaded by a floppy sunhat. Occasionally, her parents shouted something to her and she jotted it down.

"So," Rose added grimly, "daddy's little girl is a budding archaeologist, too. It's a family affair."

As if sensing that she was being watched, Chiara suddenly looked up. She broke into a smile and waved, her tiny arms, hardly thicker than a *pici* noodle, tracing an arc through the cloudless sky.

"*Venite!*" she called. "*Vedete quello che abbiamo scoperto!*"

Her enthusiasm was palpable; her whole being seemed to reverberate with excitement. Gone was the melancholy, the reticence, the world-weary cynicism. Gone was the cigarette that seemed to be permanently dangling from her long, bony fingers.

"Rose," Chiara shouted, urging them on, "*vieni! Vieni!* You can help Paolo. I need to take a break from the heat."

Alessandro, Diana, Rita, Rose, and Running Bear were now just a few feet from them. Strewn across the ground were plastic Ziploc bags, each filled with a shard of pottery, a piece of jewelry, or some other ancient household item, each neatly labeled with a black Sharpie.

Chiara sighed happily and said in English, "I know it may not look like much to you, but this is incredible. Nearly every Etruscan site we've found is funerary, so our view of everyday Etruscan life and architecture is very limited. But this appears to be an ancient garbage dump, full of everyday objects."

Paolo's eyes shone. "Which means," he said, "this may be a real city, a residential quarter. The Etruscan Pompeii."

Chiara handed Rose her trowel. "You may as well get used to this," she said with a wink. "I see lots of digs in your future." She laughed and nodded in Paolo's direction. "She's got potential, this one. After all, she found the bronze."

Rita opened her mouth to object. The truth was that it was she who'd found the monumental figure, and her twin who'd found the corpse. But then Rita realized she was being selfish. There was no need for Rita to go down in the annals of archaeology as the discoverer of the "Etruscan Pompei," but attributing the find to Rose could very well secure her sister's future happiness with Paolo.

Chiara squeezed Rose's arm warmly and then sauntered away. When Chiara passed her daughter, she addressed her in a sharper tone of voice than Rita had heard her use before. "*Figlia*," she said in a low, but warning voice, "move closer to your papa and Rose. Get to know her—and be nice. She could be your stepmother someday, *ricordi?*"

"*Mamma...*"

"*Dai, figlia, dai!*"

Chiara helped Olivia to her feet, and Olivia hopped along while Chiara repositioned both daughter and chair next to Rose. She patted the chair, shot her daughter a warning glance, and helped Olivia into it. Then she slipped away without so much as a backward glance and headed into the cool, shady confines of a small limestone cave wedged between the Etruscan tomb in which Rita and Rose had found Hans and a second, smaller tomb.

Intrigued, Rita followed Chiara. "*Fa caldo*," Rita remarked, plopping down on a rock ledge beside Chiara and fanning herself.

Chiara shot Rita a wan smile. "You want heat? Come in July sometime. This is nothing."

Chiara gazed intently at the little tableau formed by her daughter, her ex-husband, and Rose, seemingly scrutinizing every interaction. Her expression was inscrutable; Rita could not tell if she was pleased, worried, or both.

"It was nice of you to help Rose out like that," Rita said, "but I don't think Olivia approves."

"Olivia will come around after…."

Chiara's voice trailed off. She reached into her purse, extracted the mysterious vial, and—before Rita could sneak a peek at the label—unscrewed the cap and popped a pill into her mouth. Then she unscrewed the cap of her water bottle and took a ladylike sip. "After the wedding," she finally said. "Rose and Paolo's, that is."

Rita was taken aback for a moment. She wondered if Chiara knew something that Rose didn't, and whether that's what ex-husbands really did: ask their ex-wives for their blessing to marry another.

As if reading her mind, Chiara said, "Oh, Paolo hasn't said anything to me, if that's what you're wondering. But he's the marrying kind. And Rose is good for him."

Fond as she was of her sister, Rita was not sure if this was entirely true. Rose wasn't inclined to be a stepmother, or to spend months a year at some dusty archaeological site. And then there was the considerable age difference.

"I didn't get to interview the three of you over dinner," Rita said. "You know, about Hans."

"Hans?" Chiara shrugged and lit a cigarette. "What's there to say? We weren't friends. We knew each other, of course. We ran into each other at conferences or"—she laughed sardonically—"perhaps, more accurately, we sparred with each other at conferences. That sort of thing. But our paths didn't cross beyond that. The same goes for Paolo. And Olivia—well, she'd never met him until this weekend."

As if on cue, Olivia rose awkwardly from her chair and hopped off across the sunbaked terrain. For a moment, Rita thought she was coming to join them, but then Olivia passed by their cool hideaway and kept going before disappearing from sight off behind Chiara's right shoulder.

"She's just using *i servizi*," Chiara said, although Rita knew full well there were no bathrooms for miles. Chiara shrugged. "She's accustomed to this. She's been accompanying us on digs since she was a baby."

Chiara blew a ring of smoke, and Rita watched as it floated through the recesses of the cozy little cave and towards the azure horizon. Chiara turned to Rita and smiled. "Now, I've watched enough of the Detective Montalbano series to know that your next question will be 'And where were you on the night of the murder?'"

Rita had to smile. She had not thought that she and sad, cynical, chain-smoking, size-zero Chiara would have a thing in common. But she, too, was a Montalbano fan!

"Well," Chiara said, "I'll tell you: in my cottage. Olivia and I went straight there after the party broke up and we had a long mother-and-daughter chat—you know the type, she has a crush on some boy in her Physics class, but he's dating her best friend—and then we both went to bed around three. And we were there all night until just a few minutes before the earthquake, when I woke up itching for a cigarette. So I went for a walk to smoke."

"And Olivia was still in bed when you left?"

Two little frown lines appeared in Chiara's forehead. She stubbed out her cigarette in a tiny portable ashtray. "She was just heading to chapel."

Out of the corner of her eye, Rita spotted Olivia walking back towards the excavation site. She frowned, then immediately plastered a smile on her face to hide it. Olivia had been walking—not hopping, but walking. Walking with only the slightest of limps. And also nervously patting the outside of her pocket as if something valuable were hidden within.

"*Che c'è?*" Chiara demanded, whipping around. But Olivia must have had a sixth sense about her mother, because by the time Chiara turned around, Olivia was hobbling something terrible.

Mother and daughter waved at each other, and Chiara turned back towards Rita. "Well?"

"Oh, I was just marveling how religious Olivia is. I mean, I practically had to use Chinese water torture on my children to get them out of bed for Mass on Sunday. In the end, Gina went mostly because there was a cute boy in the choir, and Vinnie because there was espresso and *bignoli* afterwards."

With its nearly all Italian congregation, St. Vincent's had upgraded from regular old coffee and doughnuts to fancy espresso served in Illy ceramic cups and Italian-style doughnuts. Rita did not have to mention Marco because, as her perfect mamma's boy, Marco was always dressed in a suit and tie, waiting for them at the bottom of the stairs, while the others filed past, bleary-eyed and grumpy in mismatched socks and wrinkled sweatpants. Marco had even been an altar boy.

"Oh." Chiara visibly relaxed. "Well, her uncle is a priest, after all. It runs in the family. And Olivia loves medieval art. She was probably making a study of the frescoes."

"Your daughter is quite the scholar. A budding archaeologist, an art history buff. And her English is excellent! She's a very intelligent girl. You must be so proud."

Chiara acknowledged the compliment with a nod and a little smile. Then she turned away from Rita, and a little gasp escaped her lips.

Rita turned to follow her gaze, to see what had so startled her companion. There, beneath the broiling Tuscan sun, kneeling in the red-brown dirt beside Rose was Paolo, and he was holding something that glinted in the sun. Could it be a ring?

Olivia, who was still fifty feet away or more, must have thought so too, because she uttered a loud cry. But then the cry—which had sounded more startled than scared—morphed into shrieks, then piercing screams, then convulsions. She was pointing at a snake and a hole in the ground. Rita would have bet anything that Olivia had dug the hole herself, and that the snake had been the precious contraband in her pocket.

Rita was about to ask Chiara if there were poisonous snakes in Tuscany, but it was too late. Chiara had already leapt up and was running to her daughter's side.

"Papa!" Olivia was screaming. "*Mamma! Mia gamba! Mia gamba!*"

She was clutching her leg, hurtling one bloodcurdling scream after another. Rita would have fallen for it too if she had not ever so briefly glimpsed Olivia's earlier malingering.

Rose was right. There was nothing this girl wouldn't stoop to. And Rita wondered if this included murder.

Olivia slung one arm around Paolo and the other around Chiara, and together they slowly lowered Olivia into a wheelbarrow and pushed her towards the villa. Rose trailed helplessly behind them.

Rita felt a pang of sympathy for her sister. She'd been foiled, once again, by the world's most manipulative teen.

Rita was about to leave herself when she noticed that, in her haste, Chiara had left her bag behind. Slinging it over her shoulder Rita started towards them but then stopped.

She had the bag—the elusive bag with the mysterious golden vial that might contain any number of interesting narcotics. Maybe even a bag that contained some incriminating evidence. Maybe even the murder weapon.

Very quickly, before she could change her mind, Rita made a big show of tripping on a rough patch of ground and artfully twisting her body so that the bag fell to the ground. She crouched down, pretended to stumble a bit, and let the contents of the bag spill out over the smooth limestone surface.

She found a pack of cigarettes, a lighter, a tiny portable ashtray, a silver business card holder—all that was no surprise.

She found a tube of lipstick in a deep crimson shade, a compact mirror, and a wallet containing a few euros, a credit card, and a photo of Chiara, Olivia, and Paolo in happier times.

And then she found the golden vial.

Rita turned the label towards the sunlight and squinted. Keytruda, she read.

The vial fell out of Rita's hand and onto the rock. Chiara wasn't just some depressed pill popper.

She was a seriously ill woman.

For Rita had encountered this medication once before: in the medicine cabinet of a dear friend who'd died, just three months later, of cervical cancer.

Chapter Twenty-Three

Rita took the long way back to the villa, stopping by the raised garden beds to pick plump, deep dark purple eggplants, sweet yellow onions, garlic bulbs with skins delicate as parchment, and vine-ripened plum tomatoes that glowed a fiery red in the hot afternoon sun.

She tried to occupy her thoughts with visions of what a glorious *caponata* she could make with these ingredients, and how exquisite it would taste accompanied by wafer-thin slices of prosciutto, dollops of honeyed ricotta, and a hunk of pecorino cheese, all washed down with a tart, fruity Brunello di Montalcino. But all she could think about was Chiara. *Poverina!* She was a divorced, soon-to-be empty nester embarking on a long, lonely battle with the cruelest of maladies. No wonder she looked so sad, so cynical. No wonder she'd taken up smoking again.

Under those circumstances, Rita would too.

But before Rita could ponder this any further, her musings were cut short by the sudden appearance of Padre Domenico and Sal. They were sweaty, sunburned, limping—and empty-handed.

"No rabbits?" she clucked sympathetically.

Padre Domenico shook his head. "It must be too hot. They'll probably be more active at dusk."

"Yeah," Sal said, "then they'll be practically jumping in our basket."

Rita shot him a dubious look, and her husband scowled. "And no," Sal said, "I did not shoot myself. Or him. We still each have all ten fingers and toes."

"In any case," Padre Domenico interjected with an air of determined cheerfulness, "it was good to get some fresh air and exercise, to get away from this gloomy atmosphere, all this"—he shuddered—"talk of murder."

Rita raised her eyebrows and looked at Padre Domenico quizzically. "I'm surprised to hear you say that, Padre. I distinctly recall you saying when we were in the orchard that you'd like to be one of those citizens who solves crimes."

Padre Domenico laughed uneasily. His eyes did not twinkle, and his jolly little belly did not shake. "Ah, well, it's one of those things that sounds good when it's all hypothetical, no? But when it's real, well...."

His voice trailed off, and he gave her a little shrug before walking off towards his room. Sal started after him, but Rita put a hand on his sweaty forearm. "Sal, I want to apol—"

"Save it, Rita." He brushed her hand off his arm, as if removing a pesky gnat. "I need a cold shower and a change of clothes. I'll see you at dinner."

And off he went.

With a sigh, Rita trudged to the kitchen. It was the oldest part of the villa and had sustained relatively little earthquake damage, save a long crack in the wall. Rita eyed it nervously, then rinsed her vegetables and set them on a cutting board. She was just about to start chopping when Monica and Luisa plodded in, laden down with baskets of truffles. Monica was covered in clumps of dirt, her hair was stuck to her forehead with sweat, and she smelled no better than her porcine companion, but she was grinning from ear to ear. "Look how many truffles we found, Rita! Oh, Running Bear will be so happy. He told me he loves truffles...." Monica blushed. "And I do, too. And, of course, you and Luisa are both such wonderful cooks. I'm sure you'll do wonders with these."

Luisa looked less pleased. "An average day at best," she sniffed. "Helga"—she shot the sow, who was hovering just outside the doorway, a contemptuous look—"was a lazy pig today." She wagged a fat, arthritic finger in Helga's direction. "Mark my words, Helga. If you continue to displease me, you could end up as tomorrow's pork chops. *Non ci credi?* Well, you should. Ursula stopped laying eggs and look what happened to her." Luisa licked her lips. "She will be gracing our *tavola* tonight as a very tasty *pollo al mattone*!"

Luisa stalked across the kitchen, grabbed a sack of flour, and dumped it unceremoniously on the counter next to Rita. "We will make tagliarini," she announced, in the manner a Medici might have addressed a lowly servant. It might have been Rita's imagination, but it seemed as though inheriting part of Hans' estate—even if it was less than she had dreamed—had made Luisa even more insufferable. "I will supervise. Rita will"—Luisa wrinkled her nose—"follow my instructions."

"I've made tagliarini before, you know."

"With a pasta maker?" Luisa scoffed. "That hardly counts. That's like saying you made gelato because you opened the freezer and popped the lid off the carton. Now, if you'll excuse me, I must go collect the eggs for the tagliarini. But you can manage to at least help Monica clean the truffles, no?"

And without waiting for an answer, Luisa swept out of the room. Rita took a truffle, which looked like a lumpy, bumpy black potato, and ran it under the cold tap. She gently brushed the dirt away until the truffle's characteristic skin—ebony and goose pimpled, almost resembling a giant blackberry—emerged. Then she patted it dry, set it aside, and began to work on the next one.

"Have you ever been truffle hunting?" Monica sighed with a dreamy look in her eye.

Rita shook her head.

"Well, you should," Monica said. "It's intoxicating! At first, you think there's nothing there. But then you find a copse of oak trees, and Helga starts sniffing, and there's just this earthy smell wafting up from the ground. Then Helga starts breathing hard, really digging her hooves in. The dirt clods start flying and then, just as Helga's about to devour this little black nugget, Luisa swoops in, holds her back, and I scoop up the truffle! And it's the perfect time of year to go—about the only time you can get the *scorzoni*—those are the black ones—*and* the white ones."

"It's like life," Rita said, "or love. Sometimes, you have to dig a little beneath the surface to find a diamond in the rough." Rita cast a sidewise glance at Monica. "Like Running Bear."

"Hmmmm? Oh!" Monica nicked the index finger of her right hand with the knife she was using to cut the black truffles into wafer-thin slices. A trickle of blood oozed onto the countertop, and Monica reached for a clean dishcloth and wrapped it around her finger. "I'm not sure," she said, eyes glued to the dishcloth, "what you mean."

"Well, he's *bellissimo, certo?* That much is certainly not hidden. But he's more than meets the eye. He's quite intelligent, I think, and sensitive. Much more than he lets on."

"He's not paid to be intelligent."

There was a surprising flash of anger in Monica's expression and her tone, but she quickly mastered it.

"Oh? And what is he paid to do?"

Rita could tell a sharp retort was on the tip of Monica's tongue. But she limited herself to winding the dishcloth ever more tightly around her finger. "I don't know," Monica replied, tight-lipped and unsmiling. "Be her personal assistant, I guess. Keep her schedule. Make sure her bills are paid. That sort of thing."

"Flatter her? Stroke her ego?"

"I really couldn't say."

Couldn't say or wouldn't say? Rita rather suspected Running Bear had confided quite a few details of his arrangement with his employer, but whatever they were, Monica wasn't sharing.

"You know what I find curious?" Rita said. "Neither you nor Running Bear heard the splash when my sister threw Hans into the pool at three a.m., despite the fact that you are both young and have excellent hearing. It makes me wonder if you were nowhere near your rooms or the pool...together."

Monica blushed a deep scarlet.

"It's none of my business," Rita said, "and I wouldn't need to make it anyone else's business, either. But if you weren't in your rooms, you might have seen something that could be useful to my investigation."

Monica glanced at Rita, then away, and bit her lip.

"Which I would keep in confidence," Rita said. "And perhaps you didn't come forward before because what you saw seemed so inconsequential that it could have no bearing on the murder. But I assure you that sometimes the smallest detail can be the key to the whole case."

When Monica still said nothing, Rita smiled and said, "And if you were together...well, you'd both have an alibi. Because not being in your room, not hearing the splash, and lying to me about it–that certainly seems suspicious."

Monica sighed and put down her knife. "We were together." She blushed at this admission. Rita held her breath, waiting for her to go on. When Monica looked up again, there was a flash of defiance in her dark eyes. "It was stupid, reckless, wonderful, magical. It meant everything at the time and yet in the harsh light of day nothing's changed. But to my surprise, I still don't regret it." Monica folded her arms over her chest. "I don't expect you to understand."

"I was young once."

"Young," Monica said, "but not invisible."

"You're not invisible to Running Bear."

Monica managed a tiny smile.

"And where," Rita asked, "were you and Running Bear...er, sitting?"

"On a blanket in the meadow, just beyond the far end of the vineyard."

In her mind's eye, Rita traversed the estate from the snug stone cottages to the sloping vineyards to the moonlit meadows. "So about a kilometer along the path to the ruins. To where Hans was killed."

Monica acknowledged this with a slight tilt of the head and a deep frown.

"And you didn't see or hear anyone?"

Monica colored deeply. "We were...rather preoccupied, *capisci*? I didn't think there'd be a quiz later; I certainly didn't think someone would be murdered." She cleared her throat. "But we did see Hans fly past in a fury. Running Bear said that wasn't all that unusual; when Hans got upset, he would often go off to the ruins to think."

"I didn't realize Running Bear knew Hans so well."

"Oh, well, they weren't close, not like that. But since Tiffany comes to the villa often and brings Running Bear along...." Monica trailed off. Rita could tell she didn't like thinking of all the time Running Bear spent with Tiffany in these romantic surroundings, in these compromising circumstances. "Running Bear's observant, that's all. He knew Hans' habits. But I doubt Hans knew Running Bear at all, or even noticed him."

"He was invisible, you could say. Like you feel."

Monica shrugged.

"And after that?"

"It's probably nothing," she said softly, "and I don't want to get anyone in trouble..."

"Monica," Rita said in her best starchy matron voice, "if this individual has done nothing wrong, then there's nothing to get in trouble over."

"I didn't see anyone," Monica insisted. Her eyes, the color of earthy black truffles, looked up at Rita, wide and pleading. "All I could see was a tiny bright orange light in the darkness."

"Like a burning cigarette?"

Monica hesitated. "Well...yes. And then I heard a man's voice speaking in Italian. He said, 'I can't believe you told her what happened between us.' She said, 'I had to.'"

"And then?"

"I couldn't hear much after that. But at the end I heard her say, 'Let her go. She needs to be alone.' And then they walked back towards their cottages."

"You're sure? Not towards the ruins?"

"I'm sure."

"And what time was it?"

"Half an hour after Hans passed by? An hour? I'm telling you, last night, it was as if time stood still, as if we were the only two people in the world."

Yes, Rita thought, but you weren't. And one of those other people was murdered–and another was doing the murdering.

Chapter Twenty-Four

Rita took one speckled egg in her hand and cracked it in the depression in the mound of flour. It stared at her like an eyeball, a lone, naked eyeball.

Why couldn't Monica have seen anything useful? But the cigarette ember was something, she supposed. An Italian-speaking smoker could only mean one person: Chiara.

But to whom had Chiara been speaking? Her former lover, presumably. The person with whom she'd had a clandestine relationship that had so upset another woman that this second woman had stalked off into the night.

He was a native Italian speaker. Of that much, Monica was sure. So that narrowed it down to Alessandro and Padre Domenico—Chiara's two former brothers-in-law, one of them a priest, the other engaged to be married. It was like a plot of an opera by Verdi.

She supposed that Chiara might have been drawn into an illicit affair with Alessandro or Padre Domenico by sheer loneliness, by the terror of facing death alone. Perhaps this was a way to laugh in the face of the Grim Reaper, to taunt him, to announce that she was still young, still nubile. But she could not imagine Padre Domenico breaking his vows, or Alessandro forsaking Giovanna. Perhaps Rita was wrong. Perhaps it had been a long time ago, before Alessandro had met Giovanna. Rita frowned and corrected herself: before Chiara had introduced Alessandro and Giovanna.

That's what Chiara had claimed, after all: that it was Chiara who had introduced them. Rita frowned. Why was Chiara always so eager to play matchmaker? First, she foisted Giovanna on Alessandro; now, she never wasted an opportunity to push Rose into Paolo's arms.

Rita sighed. Shocking and confounding as it all was, she could not fathom how Chiara's love affair could possibly be connected to Hans' murder, particularly since Monica insisted that Chiara and the mystery man had walked back towards the cottages, not the ruins. And, according to Monica, they did not appear to be chasing Hans—or even aware he'd passed by.

"*Basta*!" Luisa hissed beside her.

Startled, Rita looked up at Luisa, then down at the dough in her hands. She'd been so wrapped up in her thoughts that she had lost track of the fact she had stirred in the eggs and been kneading and turning, kneading and turning, for several minutes now. The dough had acquired a beautiful smooth texture and golden sheen. Luisa was right; it was perfect, but any more kneading and it would become tough.

Rita let go of the dough and set it aside to rest.

"*Dimmi*," she said, "when was Hans' new will signed?"

Luisa made a sour face. "Yesterday—five o'clock. Or at least that's what the paper says. Witnessed, supposedly, by Anna Maria Contadini and Roberto Capra." She wrinkled her nose. "They're village folk—friends of Hans who live in Volterra."

"A middle-aged couple?"

"It depends what you mean by middle-aged. Fifties, maybe. She still thinks she's young, dyes her hair blond, wears lots of make-up. But she's not fooling anyone. And he's potbellied and balding. Why?"

"Oh," Rita lied, "no reason."

What she meant was that there was no reason to tell Luisa that she'd seen Hans with just such a couple yesterday.

The will was genuine. Clearly, something had happened yesterday to make Hans change his will, to add Tiffany and to recognize Giovanna as his daughter.

But what?

And the bigger question was whether the murderer knew Hans' will had been changed.

An hour later, Rita was fluttering between the tables on the terrace. She piled on more and more antipasti—artichokes marinated in vinegar and olive oil; tomatoes that had been dried in the hot Tuscan sun and then doused in olive oil; the eggplant-rich *caponata* that Rita had prepared just that afternoon; a mound of prosciutto, shaved wafer-thin; a hunk of crumbly pecorino; a few generous dollops of ricotta drizzled with acacia honey; a ball of creamy burrata, its center runny like an egg yolk, dotted with fresh-cracked black pepper and a swirl of balsamic vinegar. Every single ingredient, right down to the honey and vinegar, had come from the estate or, as Luisa called it, "my estate, if that little hussy Giovanna doesn't steal it from me."

Rita refilled the water glasses with *acqua frizzante* for the Italians and *acqua senza gas* for the Americans, and she kept the red wine flowing for everyone.

But most of all, she listened.

"I keep thinking," Running Bear was saying to Tiffany, Alessandro, Giovanna, and Monica, "that I wish I had gotten to know Hans better."

The fivesome was huddled around a table meant for four; on the heels of the revelation of Giovanna's paternity, Diana had been exiled to a lonely table with Padre Domenico.

Rita put a giant disk of herb-flecked focaccia, hot and blistered from the wood-fired oven, down in the center of the table, as Running Bear suggested, "We should have a memorial service for Hans. To give those of us who didn't know him so well a chance to get to get a better sense of who he really was."

"I don't think any of us really knew him," Giovanna replied sullenly. "He forgot to mention he was my papa. A big thing to leave out, no?" Her fiancé and her sister each squeezed a hand, and Giovanna smiled gratefully at them.

"Well, maybe he himself didn't know until recently. I mean, the will was just signed yesterday, and Luisa claims the prior will made no mention of you."

Rita frowned, wondering just when and why Running Bear had spoken to Luisa. Clearly, she wasn't the only one poking around.

Running Bear smeared some ricotta on a piece of focaccia and topped it with prosciutto and artichokes. He took a bite and smiled. "Maybe we should do something a little more irreverent than a traditional memorial service."

Running Bear had calculated the gesture to look spontaneous, but Rita had the feeling that he'd planned this turn of conversation meticulously. But why?

"For example," Running Bear said, "when was Hans' birthday? Where was he born? What was his favorite band?"

The questions pulled Giovanna out of her silent melancholy. "January sixth—I remember that because he always said it was Three Kings' Day. Munich, Germany. And judging by what he was listening to during our excavations, I'd say U2—or Mozart, if Mozart counts as a band."

"Is there any particular symphony he liked? Maybe we could play it at the memorial service."

Giovanna frowned. "There's one unofficially called by the name of a planet. Saturn, maybe?"

"Jupiter," Rita interjected. "Also known as Symphony 41."

"And his favorite U2 song?" Running Bear asked.

" 'One.'" Giovanna sounded quite confident about this.

"See?" Tiffany chortled. "You knew him pretty well?" She thumped Running Bear on the back. "I'll take Hans Clausnitzer for five hundred, Alex."

Shaking her head in disbelief, Rita went back to the kitchen, where Luisa was shaving white truffles onto heaping plates of buttered tagliarini.

"Here–take the ones with white truffles first," Luisa said. "The black truffles need a bit more time. I've got to sauté them first in some olive oil and garlic to really release the flavor. They stand up to heat, unlike the white ones." She wagged a finger at Rita. "Be back in four minutes, on the dot," she warned her. "You do not want this pasta to get cold."

Luisa was unsmiling throughout this little speech; she sounded like a drill sergeant barking orders in the thick of battle.

Rita took the platters to the terrace, serving the Hans trivia table first, Diana-in-lonely-exile and her confessor next, and finally the table at which were seated Sal, Rose, Chiara, Olivia, and Paolo. The sixth chair was empty.

Rita marched back into the kitchen and retrieved the tagliarini with black truffles and then, half an hour later, their *secondo* for the evening–*pollo al mattone*, a chicken seared under the heavy weight of a brick (*mattone*) until the skin was crispy and the meat tender and achingly juicy. She spared a moment for a quick prayer for Ursula, the recalcitrant chicken that now adorned their plates, then sailed back onto the terrace.

As she hoisted the platter over Olivia's head and towards the center of the table, she deftly flicked a chicken leg off the tray and into Olivia's open leather bag.

"*Mamma mia*!" Rita shouted, quickly dropping the platter onto the table. "I'm so clumsy." She snatched a napkin off the table, crouched down, and began rooting through Olivia's bag. "*Poverina*—I've got your bag all dirty. There's a chicken leg down in here somewhere—now if I can just get it out."

"Rita," Olivia protested, "please let me—"

But Rita was having none of it. "*Non ti preocupare*, Olivia. I've almost got it." Rita frantically thumbed through the contents, located the chicken leg, and let it drop through her fingers again. Her fingers brushed against keys, a tampon, a slim leather wallet, and endless tubes of lipstick and mascara. "Slippery little thing. Oh, there!"

Rita's fingers closed around the small vial that had once contained white oleander but now—unbeknownst to Olivia—contained only water. Rita looked up and locked eyes with her sister. Her suspicions were confirmed: tonight was the night Olivia planned to poison her sister.

Extracting the chicken leg, Rita hoisted it in the air, victorious. "You know what my mother always said, 'The slipperier the chicken, the tastier the bird.'"

Sal grunted and folded his arms over his barrel chest. "Your mother never said that."

Rose laughed uneasily, and Rita knew the message had been received. "Oh, you know men," she said to the rest of the table. "They never listen to their mothers-in-law."

Rita plunked herself down in the empty chair and attacked the chicken with gusto. The meat was so tender, the skin so crispy, and the blend of rosemary, oregano, and garlic so exquisite, that she almost forgot she was on a mission.

But only a few moments later, Rose doubled over coughing. "Oh"—she gasped—"I'm—I'm—choking—I can't..."

Rose sounded as though she were about to hack up a lung, not just a chicken wing. She gasped for breath, wheezed, writhed in her chair, and then slumped to the ground. Rita was in awe—her twin was a truly astonishing actress.

Paolo, Sal, and Chiara all rushed over to assist Rose. Sal put his arms around his sister-in-law, pulled Rose to a standing position, and draped her torso over a chair. Then he made a fist.

"I saw a video once," he bellowed. "It's called the Himmler."

"I think you mean the Heimlich, *caro*." Rita winced. Given Sal's brute strength, Rose could very well come out of this charade with a broken rib. "Let someone else try it, someone not quite so strong. Chiara, perhaps."

Chiara put her slim arms around Rose's waist. She found the sternum and made a fist.

While the others were distracted, Rita crouched back down beneath the table. She was just in time to see a slim, graceful, young hand reach into Olivia's bag and pull out the vial. Rita leapt up, her face towards her sister.

"How's she doing?" Rita yelled, all while sneaking a glance at Olivia through a curtain of bushy black hair. To her surprise, Olivia was steadying her own water glass in her left hand. The girl squeezed three drops from the vial into her water glass, quickly screwed the lid on, and dropped the vial back in her bag.

Rita waited with bated breath for Olivia to switch water glasses with Rose, but it never happened.

A moment later, Rose made a big show of coughing up a tiny piece of chicken bone, and they all sat back down.

Olivia reached for her water glass and took a big gulp. Then Rose reached for her water glass, ready to spring into her even more dramatic second act. But before Rose could take a sip, Rita tapped her on the shoulder and asked to have a word with her in private.

As soon as they were out of earshot, Rose huffed, "This better be good, sis. I spent all afternoon practicing in front of the mirror—the eyes rolling back in their sockets, the twitching, then the sudden stillness. I was about to deliver an Oscar-worthy performance." Rose crossed her arms. "So? What is it?"

"It's Olivia." Rita looked over Rose's shoulder to the terrace and watched Olivia with a frown. She wondered how long it would take the girl to realize someone had swapped out the white oleander in her vial for a completely harmless substance.

"Yeah—Olivia. As in, the daddy's little sociopath who was going to poison me. I was going to pretend to get poisoned, and we'd nab her."

Rita shook her head. "But that's just it. She put the poison—or what she *thought* was poison—in her own water glass. And then she took a drink."

Rose just stared at her sister.

"She's not trying to harm you, Rose. She's trying to harm herself."

Chapter Twenty-Five

Her head still spinning from what she had just witnessed, Rita scurried back to the kitchen. She slipped Wolf some leftover *pollo al mattone* and then began to prepare *il dolce* from the ingredients at hand. She peeled and halved rosy-fleshed peaches, then grilled them over the embers of the wood-fired oven, caramelizing them with butter and coarse brown sugar. Then she plated the glistening golden-brown peaches and topped each one with a generous dollop of sweetened mascarpone, a sprinkling of slivered pistachios, and a dusting of cinnamon and cardamon. She garnished each plate with a little amaretti cookie and then piled the plates onto a silver tray, along with demitasses of espresso black as ink.

Rita slipped an extra three shots of espresso into her cup as well as her sister's; she did not intend for either of them to sleep tonight.

Rita carried the dessert course onto the terrace. She snuck a surreptitious glance at Olivia, who was wearing a deep frown. The teen lightly pressed her belly, as if trying to induce the abdominal pain she expected to feel. Her fingers then fluttered to her throat, as if hoping to detect an irregular heartbeat. She dropped her fingers to her lap, and her frown deepened. Then her eyes darted around the table, as if trying to divine who had switched her water glass and why.

Paolo, however, seemed oblivious to his daughter's distress. In a loud voice, he said, "We should sleep out here in the open. In case of more aftershocks."

Giovanna accepted a demitasse of espresso from Rita, took an appreciative sip, and made a face. "I rather think we're in greater danger from the murderer, don't you?"

Padre Domenico shook his head. "In my experience, most murderers only kill once. Once the person they want is dead, they have no need to kill again."

Rita settled into a chair and took her first bite of the dessert. The peaches were warm and spicy, meltingly tender, while the mascarpone was cool and refreshing, fluffy and sweet. The pistachios added the perfect crunch. Rita licked some mascarpone off her fork and merrily inserted herself into the morbid conversation. "Well, it depends on the motive," she said. "I mean, if the motive is revenge or jealousy for something one person did, then sure, it's a one-time thing. But if the motive is greed..."

"...then a newly wealthy woman like me," Giovanna said, finishing Rita's thought, "would be a target."

Giovanna wagged her chin in the direction of the kitchen, where Luisa was washing up the dishes and singing off key.

Chiara blew a smoke ring. "But then you'd hardly have anything to fear from Luisa, Giovanna. Your death wouldn't invalidate Hans' will. Your portion of the estate would just pass to your heir." She looked from Giovanna to Diana and Monica, then Alessandro. "Which, assuming you have no will, would vary depending on whether you were murdered before your wedding or afterwards."

Giovanna emitted a nervous laugh. She seemed not to have considered the impact of her nuptials on a motive.

"But," Chiara reassured her, "I'm sure none of them would murder you. No"—she stubbed out her cigarette—"I'm quite confident no one will be murdered tonight. In fact, once the authorities investigate, this whole 'murder' may turn out to be no more than an unfortunate accident."

Paolo frowned and nudged his ex-wife, who just patted his hand. Rita saw that Rose noticed this gesture of easy familiarity too and was not pleased.

"All I'm saying," Chiara clarified, "is try not to worry too much."

Diana took a sip of espresso and set it down on her saucer with a clatter. Clearly, she was rattled. "Even so," she said, "there's safety in numbers."

Luisa decided to sleep in her quarters in the guardhouse as usual, but the rest of them heeded Paolo's advice and dragged their mattresses out onto the terrace, Rita and Sal snagging a prime spot away from the bushes and the bugs, with Wolf curled up on the grass beside Rita. One by one, everyone fell asleep, first Olivia, wedged between her parents and hugging a ratty stuffed animal and, moments later, Chiara and Paolo. Then Padre Domenico, his hand resting on his rough wooden cross. Then Sal, who snored like a freight train. Then Tiffany, who was slathered in blue face cream topped with a bejeweled face mask.

Diana (who had mercifully decided to make an exception just this once and *not* sleep in the nude) drifted off to sleep next. Rita was disappointed to discover that Diana did not drool in her sleep or snore. Her mouth did not hang open, and not a hair was out of place. She was as glamourous asleep as awake.

Giovanna, who had wedged herself between her sister and her mother, drifted off next, followed by Monica. Alessandro tossed and turned for quite some time, but eventually he, too, succumbed.

An hour passed, then two. Rita lay awake, on high alert, listening for the slightest rustle, watching for a flash of movement. But all she heard was the hooting of owls, and all she saw were a few shooting stars. At last, just as the espresso was wearing off and her eyelids were growing heavy, she saw, out of the corner of her eye, Running Bear creeping from his mattress. Across the terrace, Diana was doing the same.

Were they simply answering the call of nature, or was something more sinister afoot?

Rita waited until they were both out of sight, then plumped up her comforter until it resembled her short, lumpy, bumpy shape. Catching her sister's eye, she motioned for her to go after Diana while Rita pursued Running Bear's whereabouts. The twins parted and then went their separate ways across the dew-soaked grass.

In the moonlight, Rita could just make out the path Running Bear had trampled through the grass, then the damp footprints he'd made on the dirt track towards the heart of the farm. She followed the footprints past the greenhouse, then alongside the hulking stone warehouse. The footprints stopped at the door.

Rita rolled a boulder quietly beneath a shutter and balanced on top. She eased open the shutter and peered over the sash.

At first, the blue light blinded and confused her. But then her eyes adjusted and she saw Running Bear hunched over Hans' laptop, typing furiously and shaking his head in frustration.

She would bet anything he was typing passwords—passwords that included "Munich," "Jupiter," "One," and every other bit of personal information Giovanna had unwittingly fed him.

Rita stepped back into the dirt, scratched out her own damp footprints with a stick, and hurried back to the terrace. Halfway there she met Rose.

"What's Diana doing?" Rita whispered.

"Ransacking Hans' living quarters. Probably looking for that manuscript he was going to send to *Archaeology Today*. You know, the one that he claimed would expose Diana as a fraud."

"That doesn't prove she's the murderer."

"What's Running Bear up to?"

"Trying to break into Hans' laptop."

"Which doesn't prove he's the murderer."

Rita shook her head. "I agree. Actually, my suspicions have gone in a completely different direction."

****

The next morning, Rita took a refreshing dip in the pool and then went to help Luisa with breakfast—thick, Italian-style hot chocolate served in big drinking bowls; *cornetti*, Italian-style croissants served hot from the wood-fired oven with whipped butter, homemade cherry preserves, and raspberry jam; homemade yogurt and muesli; a fig and chestnut torte (because Italians, Rita thought approvingly, embraced the concept of dessert for breakfast); and a goat cheese and porcini mushroom frittata for the Americans. The frittata mystified the Italians, who regarded eggs as strictly lunch and dinner fare.

The other guests wolfed down breakfast and then scurred off to the new dig site—the debris field at the base of the landslide—eager to unearth the secrets that still lay buried. So Rita finished her meal alone, fortifying herself with two jam-smeared *cornetti*, a big slice of fig and chestnut torte, and two big bowls of hot chocolate. Then she piled a wheelbarrow high with water bottles, a sunhat, a patio umbrella, and a lounge chair, and headed down the dirt track to the ruins. She had quite a lot of work before her, but she was determined to do it in comfort and in style. And if she looked like she was simply lounging—if she looked like just one more lazy American armchair archaeologist—well, it was all the better.

When she crested the first hill, she was greeted by a beehive of activity. Everyone but Luisa was there—even Sal—trowel in hand, eyes glued to the rich sepia-toned soil, impatient to find just what additional treasures it might yield.

"Oh, Rita!" Tiffany shouted, waving her over. "Set your tush down right here, hon. You are not going to believe it what we've found— tablets with the second literary inscription in Etruscan ever discovered!"

"Really?" Rita said. "What was the first?"

"The Zagreb mummy." Chiara laughed. "As strange as it sounds, the linen wrappings on an Egyptian mummy that was donated to a museum in Zagreb, Croatia. Everything else we have is just matter-of-fact inscriptions, like 'I gift this statue on the occasion of my son's wedding to so-and-so.' Not terribly interesting— unless you're a linguist like me."

"So what do the tablets say?"

"Hard to say exactly since we're still uncovering tablets and there are many words I can't decipher yet."

"But I thought you're a linguist."

"Yes," Chiara said, looking amused, "but it's not like the Etruscans left us a dictionary. We only know what certain words mean because there are many inscriptions written in both Etruscan and Latin. But if a new Etruscan word is found that isn't on a bilingual inscription...."

"Ah," Rita said, "so you too are a detective of sorts."

"I suppose you could say that." Chiara gestured towards the landslide and sighed. "I don't know if I should curse Mother Nature or thank her. On the one hand, we never would have found this if it weren't for the landslide. On the other hand, what we have is a giant jig-saw puzzle with all of the pieces mixed up. Normally, you would start from the top—which contains the most recent artifacts—and work your way down. But here everything is jumbled up. But some of what we're finding seems very, very old—much older than any Etruscan artifacts we've found so far. I can't be sure until we do radio carbon dating, of course, but I think this could be the oldest Etruscan site found yet."

"And it's in Italy," Rita said slowly, "not Anatolia." She could not understand why Chiara looked so excited. "Does that mean Hans was right? That the Etruscans really are of Italian origin?"

"Well, it's a possibility." Chiara shrugged her bony shoulders and shot Rita an impish smile. "But maybe they still came from Anatolia, but earlier than we thought. Really, there's nothing truly definitive in archaeology. You're always just one find away from changing your mind."

"And is everyone taking this well?"

"Oh, yes," Chiara said mildly. "Well, everyone except Diana."

Tiffany guffawed. "I'll say! She said she didn't want to be part of this 'charade'—this 'rape of history.' What a drama queen! She's pouting by the pool now, like a five-year-old after you've taken his favorite blocks away."

Chiara shot Rita a small, embarrassed smile, as if to say she agreed with Tiffany's assessment but wished it could have been expressed more diplomatically. Chiara seemed to feel only sympathy for her colleague, whose identity had become so thoroughly entwined with being the leading proponent of the Anatolian origin theory that she could not bear the thought of any evidence to the contrary.

But Tiffany did not notice this nonverbal exchange between Rita and Chiara at all. She was looking over at where Running Bear and Monica were digging side by side. "Cute, aren't they?"

Rita tried to hide her surprise but evidently failed because Tiffany took one look at Rita's stunned expression and burst out laughing. "I wasn't born yesterday, you know. Between three husbands and one lousy high school boyfriend with a car and not much else going for him, I've had eight kids and seven stepkids."

Rita's jaw dropped. She suddenly felt very deficient in the child-bearing department.

"I've got eyes on the back of my head," Tiffany said, "and I know when someone's sneaking around behind my back."

"And you don't...mind?"

Tiffany laughed. "Fair's fair. How do you think I went from a trailer park—and we didn't have no double-wide, that was *luxury*—to living like the Queen of Versailles?"

Rita wasn't sure how to answer that politely, so she kept her mouth shut.

"I admire ambition," Tiffany said, "and I nurture it. I like to think of my personal assistants as scholarship recipients. I pay them handsomely, I teach them the secrets of the rich and famous, and then I set them free."

"Now, Running Bear"—Tiffany cast a cool, appraising glance in his direction—"might be the most ambitious of all. He's got a real chip on his shoulder, too, which always comes in handy. You ever notice how lazy people all had nice childhoods—tennis and swim lessons, tea and cookies after school, bedtime stories, and actual beds to sleep in?"

Rita frowned. If you swapped lattes for tea, that pretty much described the childhood she had given her brood.

For a moment, Rita glimpsed the girl from the trailer park, shrewd and calculating, behind Tiffany's bejeweled, good-time girl façade. Rita noticed that Tiffany's ridiculous homespun expressions had faded away, and Tiffany's Dallas twang has morphed into something harsher. She wondered just who the woman before her really was. She wondered if Tiffany herself even knew.

"I can't imagine breaking in three husbands," Rita finally said. "I have enough trouble with one."

"The only people who say that haven't been hit upside the head for burning toast." Tiffany shrugged. "'Necessity is the mother of invention.' Some famous person once said that. But I say, 'necessity is the mother of *re*-invention. Whenever the going gets tough, I just latch onto a new man and—presto change-o!—I get a new personality, a new look, and a new name. It's much easier than any other way, trust me. And the parting gifts couldn't be better."

As if to prove it, Tiffany held up a diamond bracelet that sparkled in the sun. "My last husband says the four years he spent with me were the most fun ten million he ever spent."

A thought suddenly occurred to Rita. "And were you thinking of making Hans husband number four? Is that why he left you a substantial amount in his will?"

"Hardly." For once, Tiffany's perpetual mask of gaiety slipped. Tiffany looked almost angered by the suggestion, which seemed odd given that Hans fit the bill rather well: divorced, wealthy, good-looking, and worldly. "Hans' conscience got the better of him."

"What's that supposed to mean?"

"And spoil the fun? Not on your life, toots. You're the detective lady." She shot Rita a flinty-eyed smile. "So let's see what you can do."

Chapter Twenty-Six

Inadvertent though it was, Tiffany had given Rita an idea. She set her lounge chair down next to Monica and Running Bear, made a big show of hoisting her umbrella, and then took a big swig of water. Then she plopped down on the chair and chirped, "So, I see you're budding archaeologists, too!"

Neither of them looked thrilled to have her hovering nearby, able to overhear their sweet nothings.

"Oh," Monica murmured, pushing a clump of sweaty, mousy brown hair out of her eyes, "I have no training or talent at all. I'm just a worker bee; I tag along with my mother and sister, I dig where I'm told, and then let them know if I find anything. If you want to actually learn about archaeology, you really should shadow Chiara and Paolo, or perhaps Giovanna and Alessandro."

Rita knew that was Monica's way of dismissing her. Her dark eyes were clouded over, and frown lines formed as she worked. Monia had clearly not told Running Bear that she had confided in Rita about their tryst, and she was anxious for Rita not to reveal this, either.

"And what about you?" said Rita, turning to Running Bear and ignoring Monica's hint. "Is this a new hobby for you? Or have you been involved in any excavations in the Southwest? As interesting as the Etruscan ruins are, I would think it would be so much more rewarding to excavate a site where your ancestors actually lived. Somewhere like Mesa Verde—"

Running Bear cut her off with a severe look. "My people are Navajo. Mesa Verde was inhabited by ancestors of the Hopi and Tewa. And no, there's not much to excavate. The white man stole most of it, put it in museums, hoarded it in 'curiosity cabinets.' Human bones—curiosities. Playthings."

"The modern-day name for these people would be antiquities thieves."

"When the pyramids are ransacked, those responsible are called grave robbers. When Etruscan, Greek, or Roman ruins are pilfered, they're called antiquities thieves. And when our ancestors' tombs are desecrated? They're collectors."

Rita snuck a quick glance at Monica, who seemed to be holding her breath. She held her trowel in mid-air.

"The British have the Elgin marbles," Rita said. "The Germans have the Pergamon altar, the bust of Nefertiti."

"The Germans are still coming," he said, disgust creeping into his voice. "They love coming to our reservation, buying trinkets, sleeping in a tepee. They want to play cowboys and Indians."

Rita thought of her own mother's grave in the Acorn Hollow cemetery, of the oak that spread wide above it, of the rose bush that sprang over top of it. She shuddered to think of her mother's bones tossed in some museum case, poked and prodded by curators, squinted at by schoolchildren titillated by all things macabre. "I understand," she murmured.

Rita picked up her umbrella and lounge chair. "I think I'll take your suggestion, Monica, and go have a nice chat with Chiara and Paolo. Maybe get some insights I can share with the readers of the *Morris County Gazette*."

Taking her leave, Rita trudged across the uneven, sunbaked terrain. She had intended to make a beeline for Chiara, Olivia, Paolo, and Rose—my, but her sister was tenacious!—but she stopped when she caught a glimpse of Sal, sweaty and exhausted, lying face-up on the ground like a beached whale, his trowel still clasped in his hand.

Rita veered off her intended path and set her things down beside him.

"*Caro*," she murmured gently, looking down at his fluttering eyelids, the trickle of sweat gliding down his long nose to his fleshy lips, the stubble that was already threatening to become a full-blown beard, and the rise and fall of his barrel chest.

Sal was fast asleep.

It was perfect, really. He couldn't slip through her clutches by pleading the need to go rabbit hunting or dredging up an old theology lesson from a terrifying nun.

Right now, he was as vulnerable as a newborn baby.

His lips were twitching now, and she heard a faint noise wafting in her direction. Rita knelt in the dirt and leaned closer, straining to hear.

"Get son...out of house," she heard him mumble. "Sin...cerely, the Dude."

Rita jumped to her feet. Could it be? Could her oh-so-self-righteous husband actually be working on his column for the *Morris County Gazette* behind her back whilst complaining that *she* was working? Oh, the irony! The hypocrisy!

And to think that she was actually starting to believe she had ceded the moral high ground to her husband. Well, that was the last time she'd be tricked into thinking something as ludicrous—laughable, really—as all that!

She was about to rudely awaken him and give him a piece of her mind—a very big piece—when she stopped herself. Was this what she really wanted? Endless arguing, one battle after another with the end of the war nowhere in sight? Would she rather be right or happy?

Rita knelt back down and shook Sal gently. "Hey, Dude, I need some advice."

"Huh?" Sal's eyelids fluttered, as if he was about to awake, but they stayed shut. "Oh? Advice?"

"This is 'Worried Workaholic in Acorn Hollow,'" Rita said in a sudden fit of inspiration. Those who wrote in to The Dude always had some memorable pseudonym, the more alliterative the better. "It's about my husband, you see. He surprised me with a wonderful trip to Tuscany—one of my lifelong dreams—and instead of being grateful and focusing on us, I ended up plunging into a criminal investigation of antiquities trafficking."

"Hans," he muttered. "Can't...trust...those Huns...my dad says."

So Sal suspected Hans was involved as well.

"Now, I'm not saying I regret it exactly..."

She noticed a scowl on his face.

"...but I should have told him. Then I could have asked for his help and we could have spent time together instead of pushing him away."

Sal opened one bleary eye. Rita held her breath as he slowly opened another one. For a moment, they were glassy, unfocused. Then his eyes narrowed, and he propped himself up on one arm.

"So," Rita said, smiling at him and getting an encouraging half-smile in return, "what is The Dude's reply to 'Worried Workaholic in Acorn Hollow'?"

Sal put his hand under his chin and regarded her with those maple-syrup eyes that used to make her weak in the knees. He was quite a bit older and stockier than Rodin's model, but in her suddenly love-addled state, Rita decided he looked just like The Thinker. Only he was *her* thinker—and a very original one at that.

"Dear Worried," he began with just the right touch of gravitas, "if you're like most women of a certain age, you've spent decades fulfilling your hubby's and your kids' every wish. You've got a gazillion jobs: cook, cleaner, tutor, dog walker, party planner, chauffeur, therapist, and spy."

Rita coughed. She did not like the insinuation in the last one.

"Hey, do you want The Dude's advice or not?"

Rita tilted her head slightly to indicate he should go on.

"You're like James Bond," he said, "except your informants are in the funeral choir and quilting club, your gadgets are the vacuum cleaner and the toilet brush, and the only Russian in sight is the harmless geek in the high school chess club. But, as your adversaries soon learn, you're a force to be reckoned with—and never underestimated. If you're like my wife, you even solve murders!"

Rita smiled. That last bit would never make it into a column. The identity of The Dude was known only to Rita, their daughter Gina, and Sam, the editor of the *Morris County Gazette*, and Sal wanted to keep it that way.

"Now, when men get old...they just get old. They go bald, get paunchy, take up golf, and become the neighborhood crank who yells at kids to get off his lawn. Men retire and think 'great, I don't work anymore, but my wife still does. She cooks and cleans. I put my feet up.'"

While there was an element of truth in this, Rita thought he was perhaps being a bit harsh on his sex. In their case, at least, Sal was still working full-time, and he did sometimes serve as her sous chef. Plus, he'd been known to fold laundry while watching football.

"Now, you ladies on the other hand, suddenly get wind of the fact you've gotten a raw deal all this time. While your husband's been busy being lazy and going to pot, you suddenly take these crazy mom skills and put them to use saving the world. Your hubby feels kind of useless. He starts to worry. You're changing your hair color, your job. You're suddenly wearing hot pants and doing yoga and quoting Gloria Steinem. What's to stop you from waking up one day and deciding 'Hey, maybe I'll change my husband, too'?"

"Oh, Sal, I'm sor—"

"Hey, The Dude isn't done yet, okay? The editor bumped the 'Silver Lifestyles' column this week to give The Dude extra space. Because this is a very important issue facing the men of Acorn Hollow."

"And the women."

"Yeah—them, too. Anyways, 'Worried,' men are men and unless your husband's a total ogre or you decide to start waving the rainbow flag, I'm guessing you want to stay married."

Rita nodded, her eyes wet with unshed tears.

"I'm guessing he knows he can't get all of your attention anymore. He'd probably settle for fifty percent. But you gotta give him some. And if you're one of those hotshot career ladies, well, share that with him. He'd probably be flattered to be asked his advice. After all, he always yakked about his work around the kitchen table for all those years because that was what was important to him; that was part of his identity and he wanted to share that with the most important people in his life."

He paused and looked at her expectantly. "Well?"

"I think that's excellent advice, Dude." Rita moved closer and kissed him on the forehead. "You know, you remind me of my husband. Sometimes, I forget just how smart and perceptive he is"—she kissed the tip of his nose—"not to mention how devastatingly handsome."

She kissed him on the lips, and he kissed her back. Their foreheads touched; his was wet and sticky, but it didn't matter.

"I missed you, Sal."

"I missed you, Rita."

"Now, I'm going to take The Dude's excellent advice and ask my smart, sexy, perceptive husband for his thoughts on a particularly tricky matter."

She looked over to where Paolo, Chiara, and Olivia were huddled together, examining a pottery shard. Rose was just slightly further away, outside the immediate circle. Poor Rose–she would probably always be outside that little circle.

But before the question even formed on her lips, Sal had an answer at the ready.

"I think justice must be done," he said, "but compassionately, woman to woman, mother to mother. And there's no one better equipped than you, Rita."

Chapter Twenty-Seven

"I'm enjoying getting to know your sister," Chiara said as they entered the cave and took a seat on a low rocky ledge. "She's so witty. And so smart, so self-confident. I admire that in a woman."

Chiara shot Rita a quizzical look. "That is what you wanted to talk to me about, no?" Without waiting for an answer, she went on. "*Ma non devi preocuparti*...I've got everything under control. Paolo just needs one last little nudge, and I'm working on getting Olivia's blessing. Little cracks in her armor are starting to appear. Yesterday, she even laughed at one of Rose's jokes. And I've been telling her how good Rose will be for her father, especially after..."

In the dim light, Rita thought she saw tears in Chiara's gray eyes, hastily blinked back.

"....especially after you're gone?" Rita prodded her gently. "That's what you were going to say, isn't it, Chiara? That you're sick?"

"Is it that obvious?" Chiara let out a bitter laugh and then reached up to adjust her wig ever so slightly.

"No, you look splendid. In that skinny-as-a-string-bean kind of way, but that's the fashion these days."

Rita looked down at her own decidedly Rubenesque frame. She had often wished to magically change places with a thin woman while—because this was magic after all—still being able to eat all the tiramisu and gelato she wanted. And yet if a fairy godmother had appeared at that exact moment, she knew that the very last thing she would wish for was to change places with the miserable wisp of a woman before her.

"I found your pills and recognized the label. I snooped, I admit it. I'd say it's a bad habit, but it comes it handy as a reporter and a 'sleuth'"—she said this last word in English since it had no real Italian equivalent—"and, especially, as a mother."

"Oh, you don't have to tell me," Chiara replied ruefully. "Olivia never tells me anything. I have to read her diary, and the annoying thing is she writes it like Da Vinci did—backwards and right to left, so that I have to hold it up to the mirror to decode!"

"Being a mother is a terrible responsibility, isn't it? The bond between a mother and daughter can be so strong and yet so fragile. It's a love like no other but it can lead to madness, violence...even murder."

Chiara froze. She was as still as a statue, as immobile as the bronze finger protruding from the hillside. But her eyes, wide and dark as coal now in the dim recesses of the cave, and the slight flaring of her nostrils told Rita that Chiara had heard her and understood her perfectly.

"I see," Chiara said slowly, her eyes never leaving Rita. "It wasn't Rose you wished to discuss." Her hands flew to her bag. "Mind if I light a cigarette?"

Rita felt her throat constrict, her pulse quicken. She'd searched Chiara's bag and not found a firearm. But that didn't mean that Chiara hadn't placed one there later.

But, if their roles were reversed, she knew she'd want the comfort of an entire tray of tiramisu, so she felt that, as a mother, she could not deny Chiara's request.

"*Certo.*"

Rita watched Chiara reach into her bag, take out a lighter and a cigarette, and attempt to light it. Chiara's hands trembled so badly that it took her three tries.

Rita said, "I want to tell you a story about a love between mother and daughter that was so extreme, it drove each one to the unthinkable."

Chiara leaned back against the ledge and looked at Rita sulkily, the way Rita's kids had when they were about to get a lecture.

"The daughter, a lively young girl of sixteen—let's call her Olivia—is absolutely devoted to her parents who, a few years ago, inexplicably divorced. She continually schemes to get them together, but so far, all her schemes have come to naught. But when they all get an invitation to a wedding in Tuscany, she sees her chance. And her task has taken on new urgency because her mother is seriously ill. She wants her father to be by her mother's side during her treatment—maybe, if all goes poorly, her deathbed. But either way, she thinks her father's presence would be such a comfort to her mother. So she pulls out all the stops—maneuvering to get her dad's upstart girlfriend moved to another cottage, thinking up reasons her parents need to collaborate on their respective areas of research."

Chiara nodded ever so slightly.

"Then," Rita continued, "one night the girl overhears her father arrange to meet his girlfriend by the pool. She's crushed; she thought her plans were going so well! So she decides more extreme measures are called for. She alters her father's watch so that he will arrive at the rendezvous late. Then she slips a note under the door of another man—let's call him Hans—pretending to be her father's girlfriend and asking Hans to meet her at the pool. And then she hides in the vineyard to watch her plan play out."

Chiara frowned, stubbed out her cigarette in her portable ashtray, and lit another. Clearly, this part was news to her.

"Her plan," Rita said, "works to perfection. Her father arrives just as Hans is putting his hands all over her father's girlfriend. Her father storms off, confused, enraged, and disgusted. But before he leaves, he says something that shakes her to her very core. Her father says '*Altra volta? Non ci credo.*' "

Rita put extra emphasis on the last phrase.

" '*Altra volta?*' " she thinks. What does that mean? And then, the penny drops. The first time—the '*altra volta*'—that her father was cuckolded by Hans was with her mother. That's why they divorced—her mother had an affair with Hans. The girl is incensed. She rushes off to confront her mother who confirms this. Her mother takes all of the blame for the divorce. The daughter storms off into the night. She happens to see Hans walking off towards the ruins, so she follows him, intending to confront him about his role in the demise of her parents' marriage."

As she spoke, Rita could see it all in her mind's eye: Monica and Running Bear on the blanket, arriving just after Olivia has passed by, Paolo and Chiara chasing after their daughter. "Let her go," Chiara had said, referring to her daughter, never realizing her daughter had murder in her heart.

Rita went on. "The daughter finds Hans on the hillside behind the tomb, she and Hans argue and, in a fit of rage, she strikes him with a rock and kills him. Then, filled with remorse, she goes to her parents and tells them what she did. But instead of urging her to go to the authorities and confess, they rush to where Hans lies dead and, cleverly taking advantage of the earthquake, arrange his body under a fallen pillar to look as though he died in the earthquake. Sadly, while they might be renowned archaeologists, they are not forensic archaeologists, so they make a few mistakes. And, of course, the main problem is that Hans' body is discovered too soon—so that the time of death can be pinpointed to several hours before the earthquake."

Chiara looked chagrined, but neither confirmed nor denied it.

"The only thing I can't understand in all of this is, with all of the gorgeous men in Italy, why *Hans?*"

Chiara shot Rita a bemused look and took a drag of her cigarette. "Woman to woman? There never was an affair with Hans."

"Then why did Paolo think there was?"

"Because I told him."

"*Ma perché?*"

"Because he wouldn't divorce me when I got cancer the first time, or when I spiraled into depression and agoraphobia. Paolo was loyal—too loyal. He refused to leave my side, which not only kept him from his digs, but led to him being passed over for tenure. His social circle dwindled, invitations dried up. I was a recluse, Rita. A horrible wife."

"You were mentally ill," Rita said gently.

"I was doing a good enough job ruining my life. Why ruin his as well? So that's when I hatched a plan to set him free."

Rita thought back to their odd conversation at the pool. " 'If you love someone, set him free.'"

"*Esatto.* It was quite easy, really. Hans had slept with half the female archaeologists in Italy, *e le voci corrono, sai?* And he had openly flirted with me at several conferences. So, I just spread a rumor to the right people..."

"...and things took their course. You're a schemer, I see. Like mother, like daughter."

Suddenly, Chiara sat up straight and fixed Rita with a defiant look. "You're got one thing—one very big thing—wrong. Olivia didn't kill Hans. I did. I was the one hiding in the vineyards. I was *arrabbiatissima* with Hans for ruining my plan. I wanted Rose to end up with Paolo, to be a loving stepmother to Olivia after I'm gone—and Hans was in the way. So I followed him into the tomb, hit him with a rock, and left him there. Then, after the earthquake, I had the idea to go back and stage it as though he died in the earthquake."

Rita shook her head and sighed. "While I admire the maternal instinct to protect Olivia, that's just not true."

"No? Prove it."

"I can't, but what I can tell you is that you'd be signing your daughter's death warrant if you take the blame."

"*Come?*"

Chiara's thin wispy eyebrows furrowed into one long thin line.

"I watched your daughter put poison—or at least what she believed to be poison—into her water and drink it."

"Impossible. She would never—"

Rita held up a hand as a silencing gesture. "But she did. As an absolute last resort to bring you and Paolo together. She tried bringing you together through your work, but that failed. She tried throwing Rose into Hans' arms, but that failed. Then she tried pretending she was seriously injured in the earthquake when in fact she had, at most, a mild sprain, but still you persisted in foisting Rose on Paolo. So finally, she tried poison. She may not have wanted to die, but she was willing to risk it. She wanted to go into convulsions, so you would be brought together at her bedside."

"Or over her coffin," Chiara muttered, looking rattled. "That's madness." She let out a bitter laugh. "Like mother, like daughter, right?"

"So you see," Rita said, "if you confess to murdering Hans, Olivia will feel so guilty, she'll make a second suicide attempt. Only this time she may succeed."

Rita squeezed Chiara's bony little arm. "It might have been an accident. Let me talk to her, get her side of the story. Then we can decide how to present it to the carabinieri in the best possible light. She's a teen, she was provoked, the victim was a foreigner, and this is Italy. I imagine she'd only get a few years' sentence."

Chiara stared coldly at Rita. "I hope I'm six feet under by the time this comes to trial."

But Rita noticed that Chiara did not say no.

Chapter Twenty-Eight

Olivia's words tumbled over one another, as if she couldn't expunge her guilt fast enough, as if it was a blessed relief to confess to someone other than her priestly uncle—someone who might be suitably outraged rather than pastoral.

Rita frantically jotted down the girl's rambling confession, her frown deepening. When Olivia finally stopped to take a breath, Rita said, "Show me."

Olivia turned white as a sheet, but she meekly led Rita out of the cave, around the landslide and the excavations, and up and over the hillside. Olivia came to a halt midway down the other side, in front of an enormous boulder.

"I found him here," Olivia said.

"*Qui?*" Rita looked around in bewilderment. From her vantage point, she could not see the villa, the row of cottages, the Etruscan tombs, or even the site of the current frenzied excavations. She could not see a single sign of human habitation, in fact, other than a tiny, distant ribbon of country road and a single stone farmhouse on a far-off, windy ridge. "What would Hans be doing here in the middle of the night? He doesn't seem like a 'communing with nature' type."

"*Non lo so*—I wasn't exactly in the mood to ask him."

Rita frowned. Olivia seemed so sincere, and yet her story did not add up. It made no sense to find Hans here. It made no sense that she would have known to find him here.

"And why did you think he'd be here?"

"I didn't exactly. I thought he was going to the tombs to think or...I don't know. But when I got there, he wasn't there, but I could hear a metallic clanking sound accompanied by the faint sound of humming. That song from U2-'One.'"

Rita wondered whether Olivia had overheard the conversation between Running Bear and Giovanna about Hans' favorite things, and if Olivia had just invented this detail on the spot.

"So, he was—what?" Rita squared her shoulders and looked Olivia directly in the eye, which had the effect of causing the girl to squirm, but whether from guilt or embarrassment, Rita could not tell. "Just standing here looking right at you?"

"No, he was bent down partway, looking at the ground. At the rock, maybe. And when I came over the top of the hill, he seemed startled. He looked up, spun around, and leaned against the rock. Yes—like that."

Rita had leaned back against the boulder just as Hans had supposedly done. She had expected the rock to radiate heat after baking in the afternoon sun, but it was surprisingly cool. She reached out and ran her fingers over the surface. She had expected it to be hard, unyielding, gritty, and uneven, riven with bands of mineral deposits, but instead it was soft, almost like Styrofoam. A light in Rita's eyes began to glimmer.

"Where's the rock you used to bash in his head?"

Olivia bit her lip and looked around frantically, tearing welling up in her eyes. "*Non lo so. Non ricordo niente.*"

Rita slid on one of her opera gloves. She scanned the rocky terrain for a chunk of rock small enough to fit in Olivia's delicate little hand. There were perhaps a dozen candidates, she turned over each until, on her sixth try, she found one with a rust-colored stain.

"*Ecco la pietra*," Rita said grimly, and Olivia nodded.

Rita held it in her hand, felt its heft, and knew that it was heavy enough to kill a man.

"Now," she said, "pretend I'm Hans. I know you think you don't remember anything, but I'm quite sure you do. Where should I stand to be in the position he was in? *Qui?*"

"A little to the left?" Rita tried to interpret the vague, queasy nod, which seemed to be gently nudging Rita. "A little more? *Qui?*"

Olivia nodded vigorously. Her lips were pursed together so tightly, as if she feared opening them would unleash something terrible.

"*Bene*. Now come towards me, Olivia. Show me what you did."

Olivia hesitated for just a moment, then suddenly lunged at Rita. Just a millimeter from striking her, she stopped short.

"*Così?*" Rita murmured and when she got a nod of confirmation, sank deep into thought.

"And did you hit him again?"

"No."

"And then he was dead?"

Olivia nodded. "Or very nearly so. He wasn't moving at all."

"Did you check his pulse?"

Olivia looked at Rita as if she'd gone mad. "I fled. I couldn't get away fast enough."

Rita took the rest of Olivia's statement and then let her go. Olivia did not need to be told twice. She was off like a shot, tearfully stumbling up and over the hillside and then slipping out of sight.

Rita photographed the rock with which Olivia had administered the blow, then the boulder. After taking a furtive glance around and ascertaining that she was alone, Rita bumped the fake, hollow boulder with her ample hips and sent it rolling down the hillside. Just as she suspected, a blast of cool, musty air shot out of a shadowy aperture. Rita tucked a hand inside and met no resistance. She crouched down, took out a pocket flashlight, and shone it into the gloom. What she saw astonished her: a warren of tunnels branching out in every direction. One was wider than the rest, and so Rita shimmied through it, praying that her extra *cornetto* this morning wouldn't be the difference between making it out alive and meeting a slow, painful end.

Only a couple of yards in, her hands curled over something hard and thin, with a slightly curved, sloping surface. She brushed off a layer of dirt and swung her flashlight until it landed on something that glinted. Holding her breath, Rita burrowed past. Her clothes were filthy, there was grit in her teeth, and she felt as though she were kneeling on broken glass. But Rita felt a rush of adrenaline. "I am an Army Ranger slogging through the mud," she grunted, trying to give herself a pep talk, "a bloodhound on a scent, Helga on a truffle hunt."

Then she frowned. Perhaps an enormous sow was not the most flattering image to keep in mind. "I'm supposed to be on a relaxing honeymoon, lying by the pool. But what am I doing?" She blew a lock of bushy black hair out of her face. "Crawling on my belly like a slug."

The tunnel suddenly widened, and Rita felt her knees scrape something hard and solid. She looked down to see a heavily grooved gray slab under her feet, a high rock-hewn ceiling above her. "A *via cava*!" she exclaimed. She felt rather pleased with herself—how many Americans would have the foggiest idea what this was?—then slightly chagrined. If it hadn't been for her husband—the husband whose uber-romantic gesture she had spurned—she wouldn't have a clue, either.

Rita tried to remember what Sal had said. Something about mysterious underground passages, possibly used as a means of escape during warfare, a way to surreptitiously evade a siege. Or maybe the *vie cave* served a more ceremonial or spiritual purpose, a way to commune with the underworld.

She stood and walked along the passage, marveling at its construction and wondering just where it would lead. She walked on and on. Just as she was starting to get tired, a few wooden crates appeared and beyond it, several more. Rita took a deep breath, lifted up the lid of one, and gasped. Nestled within was a delicately carved alabaster sarcophagus.

She inspected the contents of a few more crates and found giant amphora, delicately-wrought gold jewelry, Roman coins, two enormous gold scepters, a pile of bronze coins, and, most astonishing of all, a breathtaking carving of two winged horses. At last, the *via cava* dead-ended at a stone lintel, above which was a small metal door. Rita tugged at the handle and peeked inside. Her view was obscured, but she didn't need to see to know where she was. The smell of aged oak and grape must was enough.

She was in the warehouse.

When she emerged into the sunshine, Rita went back to her room to retrieve her binoculars. Then she went for a long walk along the perimeter of Hans' dominions, stopping here and there to scan the horizon. What she *didn't* see was far more surprising than what she did.

She went to go find Sal.

"*Eccoti!*" she shouted when she finally had him in her sights. He had already given up on his budding career in archaeology—thrown in the trowel, literally—and was now floating blissfully in the pool, eyes closed, beer belly protruding, stubble glinting silver in the sun. Rita couldn't help noticing that he rather resembled a walrus. But he was her walrus, she reminded herself, and she was lucky to have him.

"Sal," she said, and his eyes flew open. "You're my knight in shining armor. Or, more accurately, my sidekick-slash-chauffeur on a Vespa." She clapped her hands peremptorily. "*Dai*! Out of the pool, Sal, and into the saddle. We need to pay a visit to the carabinieri in Volterra."

"But Running Bear said—"

"We're cut off." Rita nodded sagely. "Yes, I know that's what he said. But Running Bear lied about many things. Then again, almost everyone else did, too."

Rita hung on for dear life as they sped down the road, kicking up clouds of dust and sending a torrent of loose gravel raining down upon her ankles. She muttered a "Hail Mary" as Sal revved the engine and sailed, Thelma-and-Louise-style, over a three-foot-wide chasm in the earth. And as they careened up the winding road to the walled city, which was now cracked and buckled in several places, she swore that if she survived this white-knuckle ride, she would never criticize Sal's driving again.

So it was a relief when they sputtered through the city gate, and the cobblestones and pedestrians forced Sal to slow down.

The damage was not as bad as Rita had expected. Many facades were cracked, and a few walls had completely sheared off into the street, but most buildings were still standing. Clearly, fourteenth century construction was in some ways far superior to modern methods.

They screeched to a halt in front of a small storefront labeled 'carabinieri.'

"How's that for door-to-door service?"

Rita gave him an appreciative squeeze. "I'll tip you later." In a loud voice, Rita called out, "*Auita! Auita!*"

The lone guard stationed outside looked startled. Despite the submachine gun strapped across his chest, he had the sleepy, disoriented countenance of someone who'd just been jolted awake from a pleasant afternoon nap. He glanced over his shoulder, as if he expected her to be talking to someone else.

"There's been an *omicidio*!" Rita grabbed him by the lapels until they were eyeball to eyeball and the butt of his gun grazed her shoulder. She hastily moved back. "We need your help apprehending the murderer"—Rita regarded him doubtfully—"well, perhaps not *your* help, but that of your colleagues. Is the *commissario* on duty?"

The young recruit frowned. "He's left instructions not to be disturbed. He just got off a forty-eight-hour shift assisting in rescue efforts and he's finally asleep."

"What time does he come back on shift?"

"Nine tomorrow morning."

"*Bene*. Tell him to meet me at Villa Belvista at nine-fifteen tomorrow. Breakfast—and justice—will be served."

Rita left the carabinieri gaping at them, speechless, and then she hopped back on the Vespa, and she and Sal sped off towards the villa.

"I feel sorry for Paolo and Chiara," Sal shouted above the hum of the motor. True to its name, the scooter really did sound like a buzzing wasp. "Only one more night with their daughter."

"What?" Rita grasped Sal even tighter and shouted in his ear. "Oh, no, it's not Olivia. I was wrong."

He whipped around and demanded, "Well, then who is it?"

Ahead of them, a cherry-red Alfa Romeo braked for an oncoming tractor.

"Watch the road, Sal!" Rita shrieked as Sal swerved and narrowly missed a collision. When her heartbeat had returned to normal, she said simply, "I don't know."

"What do you mean you don't know? Then why did you call in the carabinieri?"

"Because they're the police. Because we're in a foreign country. Because it's the right thing to do." She checked her watch. "And because—hopefully—I'll have a breakthrough in the next fifteen hours."

Chapter Twenty-Nine

On the way back to the villa, they stopped at a high point on the road where Rita at last had three bars on her cell phone. She did a few quick but very illuminating Google searches and then, with her phone on speaker, put in a call to Commissario Zingaretti.

"*Pronto?*" he answered with a dashingly professional, almost curt, air. Then he must have checked his caller I.D. because he dropped into that meltingly tender tone and cooed, "Rita, I've been worried about you."

Rita almost dropped her phone into a ditch. But when she caught Sal glowering at her, she quickly recovered her composure and said in her most businesslike tone, "*Sto bene.*" She tried to sound dispassionate, clinical, as if she were a doctor giving an update on her patients. "Everyone's *bene*—well, except Hans. He's dead—murdered, in fact."

"*Ucciso?*" The alarm was evident in his voice. "*Oddio*—Rita, this has gone too far. I sincerely apologize for getting you involved. *Per piacere*, leave at once. I'll contact my colleagues in the homicide unit and send someone there *subito subito. Dove stai? Ti prendo*. Just let me know where you are."

"Oh, there's no need," Rita replied breezily. "I can't be in any danger because I don't actually know who the murderer is. Not yet anyway..."

"Now, Rita, don't go investigating," the *commissario* said in that thrillingly authoritative yet protective voice. "It's too dangerous, and I would never forgive myself..."

"Oh, relax. If I can handle myself in New York, surely I can handle myself in Italy." She patted Sal's hairy arm and winked at him. "Besides, I have my husband to protect me."

Sal's chest swelled with pride.

"So all you need to do, *commissario*, is be here by nine-fifteen tomorrow for breakfast. Come hungry—it will be a meal you won't soon forget. Because while I may not know the identity of the murderer—yet—I am ready to deliver the antiquities trafficker into your hands."

Before the *commissario* could say anything further, Rita stabbed the off button and hopped back on the Vespa. A bone-jarring fifteen minutes later, Sal let her off by the kitchen door just in time to see Luisa storm out.

"*Sciopero!*" Luisa declared, eyes blazing and fists clenched and jabbing the sky.

A strike? Italy continually had its share of strikes, Rita knew. But she associated striking with railway workers angling for a few extra holidays, bored college students itching for a return to the country's tumultuous sixties, and Southern migrants to Italy's prosperous North eager to show their coiffed overlords just who was boss. It was a combustible mix of protest, identity politics, and street theater. It was a way to stand up and say, "We're not like those dour, hard-working Swedes or capitalism-mad Americans. We're Italians, and we prize *la dolce vita* above all else."

But she did not associate strikes with older women in frumpy housedresses on beautiful Tuscan estates.

Rita's furrowed brow and look of complete and utter bewilderment seemed to infuriate Luisa even more.

"Giovanna thinks she's the boss of me? Thinks she's going to profit after sinking her little hooks into Signor Clausnitzer. Ha—we'll see about that! Let's see how well she does without me." Luisa spat on the ground. "She may be able to trick her mousy little sister into working for her, but not me. The next time I see her will be in court!"

Elbowing Rita out of the way, Luisa barreled past back to the gatehouse where she lived.

Rita sighed and stepped over the threshold. The kitchen was even warmer than the outside air; at a glance, she could see that the fire in the wood-fired oven was already flaming.

Wolf was lying on the floor near the refrigerator. He perked up at the sight of Rita.

Monica was standing at the counter, her back to Rita. Rita cleared her throat, and Monica spun around and greeted Rita with a slightly shaky "*buona sera*." Her gaze flicked nervously to the doorway, as if expecting Luisa to return at any moment.

"I don't think Luisa will be back," Rita said, and Monica sighed with relief. Rita came up beside Monica, who was arranging a goose pimpled, just-plucked chicken in a flat earthenware dish. Monica carefully tucked the legs under the thighs and spread the wings, and Rita wondered if Monica caught the irony—here she was spreading the chicken's wings and yet it seemed as though Monica's own were clipped. She was always at the beck and call of her mother and sister, always defined in relation to glamorous Diana and perfect, intelligent Giovanna. Always the bridesmaid, never the bride. What had she called herself? The worker bee.

"Giovanna wanted *pollo al mattone* again," Monica explained, filling the pan with olive oil until it was halfway up the side. "Not an unreasonable request, I would think. She is the bride and she does own the estate."

"Not according to Luisa. She thinks Hans might be mistaken. Maybe Giovanna isn't really his daughter."

"But she is." Monica said this with far more certainty than she made most statements. "Didn't Tiffany or Running Bear tell you?" Monica peered at Rita through her bangs. "When they searched the warehouse—you know, when we were looking for Hans—they found a DNA test in a drawer, saying that the two samples he sent in indicated a close blood relationship—a fifty percent match."

"No, they didn't mention it."

"Well, perhaps they forgot all about it after we found Hans' body. That was shocking enough to forget, well, just about anything."

Monica brushed the chicken with olive oil, then rubbed oregano, rosemary, thyme, garlic, salt, and pepper all over. The oil was sizzling now. Monica lifted the lid and deftly slid in the chicken, skin side up. Then she placed a metal round on top and weighted it down with a brick.

"You're quite the cook, I see," Rita said. "I have to admit, I'm surprised. I would have thought someone raised in such a wealthy family–someone raised in a castle–would never need to cook. That you'd have servants."

"Oh, we did have some. But papa and I always enjoyed cooking together. We'd shoo out the cooks when mamma and Giovanna were gone, give them a day off." She made a face. "We'd cook something simple and delicious, *la cucina povera*, as papa would say. Not like the fancy French food the cooks made. They were from the best cooking schools in Paris. Mamma always insisted on the best."

"You were close to your papa."

"Oh, yes, very." Monica blushed. "Maybe that's hard to believe–you know because I'm adopted."

"Not at all. One of my son's friends is like a son to me, and I've never even formally adopted him."

Monica smiled. "So you do understand. Papa and I were two of a kind."

"Two peas in a pod? That's what we say in English."

"*Esatto.*"

"And your sister and your mother?"

"Oh, they were two of a kind too. But not–what did you say?–peas in a pod. Something much more special."

"What? Two"–Rita groped for something rare and expensive–"pearls in an oyster?"

Monica nodded slightly, but Rita had the impression she had not hit on quite the right analogy.

"Two suns in the sky," Monica finally said.

"There's only room for one sun in the sky."

"In our universe perhaps. But in theirs..."

Monica removed the brick from the lid on the chicken. The skin was now crispy and brilliant golden hue. With an enormous set of tongs, Monica turned over the chicken, slid the lid back on, and then replaced the brick. "Papa always used to say, 'your mother is the sun, and I am her mirror. We all bask in her reflected glow.'"

"So he must have been crushed when he found out Giovanna wasn't his child."

"Oh, no, that wasn't like Papa at all. He hadn't a jealous or resentful bone in his body. And yet"—Monica took off the lid, squeezed in a lemon, and added in some white wine, causing the oil to spatter—"sometimes I'd catch him looking at Giovanna and then at me."

Monica bit her lip as if to stop herself from saying anything more.

"And?" Rita prompted.

"And I'd see how proud he was of her, but it always seemed that he was also thinking, 'Giovanna is perfect and beautiful and intelligent, but she isn't really mine, not the way Monica is."

Rita looked down at the gold watch that adorned Monica's wrist. The face looked masculine, not at all like something Monica would normally wear, but the band that it hung from looked far more feminine.

"Was that his?" Rita asked.

Monica nodded. "He left it to me in his will. It's the only time Giovanna's ever asked me for something and I said no. He wanted *me* to have it. It's a family heirloom that goes back to his great-grandfather, you see. It was his way of saying, 'you're mine, you are the keeper of my legacy.'"

Monica abruptly pointed at a pile of ripe golden pears and held up a bottle of wine. "What shall we do about *il dolce*? I'm thinking pears poached in red wine. *Sei d'accordo?*"

Chapter Thirty

By the time Rita took the poached pears out to the terrace, Luisa had already festooned all the entrances to the villa with large—and horribly misspelled—homemade signs warning that the villa was private property and that anyone entering would get an all-expenses paid trip to Regina Coeli Prison where, she hinted darkly, she "knew people."

It was not the most soothing backdrop for a meal.

"*Non ti preocupare, cara,*" Diana was saying to Giovanna. To Rita's surprise, mother and daughter were sitting at the same table, although Giovanna's crossed arms and frosty expression showed that Diana was not yet entirely back in Giovanna's good graces. "You're doing the right thing. You have to show her who's boss. And who needs a villa when you have a castle?"

"I don't have a castle," was Giovanna's testy reply. "*You* have a castle. One that needs five hundred thousand euros worth of repairs."

"But just think!" Diana exclaimed in her breathy, everything-is-marvelous screen siren voice. She flung her arms wide. "The income from this estate can pay for all that."

"It's my money, mamma, not yours."

"Well, yes, of course, but then..." Diana tilted her head and winked at her daughter, "if I hadn't dallied with Hans you wouldn't even be in a position to inherit now, would you?"

Giovanna scowled, while Alessandro took a bite of poached pear with crème fraiche and, feigning obliviousness to the bickering between mother and daughter, smiled gratefully at Rita. "*Delizioso*," he murmured. "*Grazie*."

Rita set down another plate of poached pears and took a seat at the table. "So," she said, looking at Giovanna as she took a bite, "you're giving up your career in archaeology?"

"What?" Giovanna looked confused. "Oh–because I'm getting married?"

"No, because you'll be far too busy running this estate. The cows need to be grazed. The pigs need to be fattened with acorns, then slaughtered, salted and cured into prosciutto. The goats need to be milked, the cheese needs to be aged, the pears need to be picked. The soil needs to be tilled, the cottages need to be booked....This estate won't manage itself."

"Oh, but that's where my sister comes in! She'll manage everything, like she always does. She's the best factotum anyone could ask for. She has a real gift–she knows what you need before the thought has even formed in your head. She's a mind reader, really. Very intuitive, very helpful."

Giovanna beamed at Rita. Rita smiled back, pleased to hear that long-suffering Monica was at least appreciated. Giovanna might be the sun around which everything revolved, but she did not take her mirror for granted.

Rita cast her gaze across the terrace. She saw that Paolo, Chiara, and Olivia were huddled together away from the group. Chiara and Paolo wore pinched, worried expressions and then each clasped one of Olivia's hands, like shipwreck victims grasping at a life raft. For all they knew, this was the last time they'd be together as a family. Olivia, however, was beaming; the impending loss of freedom, she apparently thought, was a sacrifice well worth it. Rita could tell from her expression that she was at peace.

Rose watched them, arms folded over her chest, from afar. Tiffany and Running Bear sat across from Rose. Rita noticed that, as usual, Tiffany had her blood-red talons resting possessively on his arm. She watched Running Bear look down at his arm—at Tiffany's fingernails on his arm. Then he looked towards the kitchen—where Monica, out of sight but clearly not out of mind, was cleaning up after serving a delicious meal. Then he swatted Tiffany's hand off him—quite rudely, Rita thought—stood abruptly, and began stalking across the terrace towards the kitchen, a determined look on his face.

Rita hurried after Running Bear, intercepting him halfway across the lawn. "Going to see Monica? To tell her how you feel?"

His mouth fell open. "How did you—?"

"Oh, a woman's intuition," she said modestly. "A mother's intuition. You've got that lovesick puppy look my son Marco had when he met Susan, who's now his wife."

She decided not to mention the fact that her twiggy, vegetarian Southern belle daughter-in-law was not exactly what she'd had in mind for her son. She rather suspected Running Bear's relatives might have a similar reaction to his Italian paramour.

He glanced back at Tiffany, and Rita's gaze followed his.

"Something tells me she'll understand," Rita said to him. "Tiffany's much more sympathetic than you would think. But you need to level with her."

He squared his shoulders. "I fully intend to. But I thought first, before I rock the boat, I should find out if..."

His voice cracked and then trailed off.

"If?" she prompted him.

"If...my feelings are returned."

Rita frowned. "But surely that night in the vineyard..."

He looked at her innocently, slightly confused. "What night?"

"Well, that night, I mean..." She stared at him, scrutinizing each line in his face. Could it be? Could he really have no idea what she was talking about?

Rita shook her head and smiled. "I'm sorry," she said. "I was mistaken. I was thinking of someone else." She patted him on the back and shot him a smile that she hoped looked encouraging rather than giddy.

She tried to still her pounding heart, quell the dizzying rush that was rising up inside her. She could not give away the fact that she now knew that the alibi Monica had given him was all a lie.

"Good luck," she said, clapping him on the back. "Or, as we say in Italian, '*in bocca al lupo*.'"

Chapter Thirty-One

Rita and Sal slept by the pool once again, though it seemed as though the aftershocks had abated. Rita slept fitfully, bolting off their mattress at the rooster's first crow. By the second, she had tossed on her robe, and by the third, she was stealing across the terrace, watching the sun break through the clouds which hung low over the eastern mountains, suffusing the earth with a warm buttery glow.

Before the cock crows three times...

Rita shuddered. Before the day was through, she would turn in the guilty party. It should have been a relief, and yet somehow it felt like a betrayal.

Rita swung open the gate to the walled little orchard and walked slowly, almost meditatively, along a row of pear trees. She reached up and felt the weight of the fruit in her hand, the smooth rounded curve as the flesh flared out beneath its long graceful neck, the golden skin that was just slightly rough, like fine-grained sandpaper, the flesh that yielded to her firm touch, leaving shallow dimples where her fingers had pressed.

As she dropped the fruit into her basket, she thought of all that it had taken to produce this one perfect pear. Farming was a true labor of love, a leap of faith, a belief—however misguided—that if you did everything right, if you nurtured your soil and your plants in just the right way, you might one day reap what you sowed.

It was not, she thought, all that different from parenting.

Rita picked two last pears and then trudged back to the kitchen, which was eerily silent; she'd told Monica to sleep in, to let Rita prepare breakfast that morning. What she hadn't told Monica, of course, was that there would be several additional guests from the law enforcement community.

Rita flung open the window. Cool, fresh air rushed in; birdsong floated in on the breeze. She threw together the flour, butter, and sugar for a shortcrust pastry dough, then rolled it out with Luisa's rolling pin. Next, she blended the eggs, sugar, butter, vanilla, and almond flour into a glorious pastry cream, the aroma of freshly shelled almonds wafting through the kitchen. Then she turned her attention to the pears, peeling and coring them, her knife slicing through flesh so soft it was like butter. She pinched the pastry crust into a tart pan, layered on the pastry cream, then fanned out the pear slices and topped it all with slivered almonds.

She tossed the tart in the wood-fired oven and then busied herself with the more pedestrian breakfast items—the jams and honeys, the brioche and *cornetti*, the enormous cauldron of steaming Italian-style hot chocolate.

The sun was now at a forty-five-degree angle; the heat of day began to set in. The farmyard grew quiet, the animals listless in the heat. She heard the crunch of tires on cobblestones. Rita whirled around to see a swarm of carabinieri parking their scooters and—her heart beat faster—Commissario Zingaretti coming towards the open doorway, a broad smile on his face.

"*Che donna meravigliosa!*" he cried, stepping over the threshold. Her kissed her on both cheeks by way of greeting, and Rita felt herself flush. "For breaking up a ring of notorious antiquities thieves," he declared, "you will have the gratitude of a nation. For unmasking a murderer, you will have the gratitude of my colleagues." He gestured towards the carabinieri outside. "But for a pear and almond tart that smells exactly like the one my *nonna*—may she rest in peace—used to make?" He wiggled his thick, dark eyebrows mischievously at Rita. "You will have *my* undying devotion."

"No one," Rita began as she paced the terrace, "is ever quite who they seem, but this group takes the art of dissembling to a whole new level."

Rita addressed the suspects and the carabinieri in the clear, well enunciated, standard Italian of TV announcers, the kind very few Italians spoke at home. She wanted to make sure everyone understood her perfectly, from the carabinieri, who had been recruited from all over Italy and spoke a variety of dialects, to the Americans, for whom Rose provided simultaneous translation.

"On this terrace," Rita said, "we appear to have one soon-to-be married couple, very much in love; one doting and very rich mother of the bride; one slightly mousy, not very bright sister of the bride—sorry, Monica—content to bask in her sister's reflected glow—"

Rita noticed that Running Bear clenched his fists tightly. He did not like Rita's characterization of his beloved. She also noticed that for once Tiffany's red talons were not resting on his arm; Monica's red, raw fingertips were resting there instead, and Tiffany, who was seated beside them, did not seem to mind in the least.

"—one crass, uncouth, nouveau riche socialite whose generous financial support of Hans' excavation secured her an invite to the society wedding of the year, and her personal assistant, seemingly hired more for his pool-boy physique than his secretarial skills—"

Now it was Monica's turn to look affronted on Running Bear's behalf.

"—two brothers of the groom, both extremely congenial, one a priest and the other an archaeologist; the latter's chain-smoking ex-wife, also a renowned archaeologist; their daughter, moody like any teenaged girl; and one devoted, fiercely loyal employee of Hans Clausnitzer, Luisa, the *second-best* cook in Tuscany."

Luisa scowled, raised her fist, and shook it in the air at Rita.

"And, of course," Rita said, "my twin sister Rose, girlfriend of the groom's archaeologist brother, and my husband and myself, who have no connection to the wedding whatsoever and are here on what was supposed to be a romantic second honeymoon." Rita looked at Sal and sighed. "*Mi dispiace, caro*—murder seems to follow me everywhere. And then there is the no small matter of who Hans appeared to be: a cultured, debonair

European man of impeccable taste, great wealth—never quite explained—and a towering, if somewhat controversial, professional reputation as the leading proponent of the theory that the ancient Etruscans originated right here on the Italian peninsula."

Rita shot a glance at Hans' empty chair, now occupied by Artemis, who was glaring at each one of them, as if they were all somehow responsible for Hans' death.

Rita savored a bite of tart and let all of that sink in for a moment. "But Hans was all of that and much more: a mentor to young Giovanna who, perhaps rebelling against her mother, embraced the Italian origin theory as well; a former lover to Diana; and, most importantly, Giovanna's biological father."

Diana did not look the slightest bit embarrassed by the mention of her dalliance. Instead, she shot a seductive glance at a pair of baby-faced carabinieri, who turned a deep scarlet and stared down at their boots. Diana grinned in satisfaction.

"But who," said Rita, "do we really have on this terrace? I'll tell you: the greedy, desperate mother of a convicted murderer; a girl willing to do absolutely anything to get her parents back together; a dying woman with nothing left to lose; a multilingual mastermind of one of the greatest corporate takeovers in history; a blackmailer; an antiquities thief and—oh, yes, Hans' killer."

Giovanna frowned and looked around wildly, as if she could not fathom that so much criminality could be concentrated in such a small group. "And these are all...different people?"

In response, Rita just smiled enigmatically. "To answer that question, let us reconstruct the last twenty-four hours of Hans' life. On Saturday morning, Hans wakes up in those ridiculous silk pajamas of his"—she thought of his cutting remarks about her dog pajamas and her cheeks burned with anger—"gets dressed, and comes down to breakfast. On the way to the terrace, he may have paused to look down on his dominions. He may have been pleased at his success in amassing such a rich, productive estate. He may have smiled thinking of the upcoming nuptials of his protégé Giovanna. Maybe he pictured walking her down the aisle in the chapel. Maybe he imagined telling her that he was, in fact, her biological father; maybe he agonized over the words he would use. Or maybe he was worried about something entirely different: how much his blackmailer would demand that day."

There was a chorus of gasps.

"Hans? Blackmailed?" Diana trilled. "Why, how absurd. The man was *German*, for goodness' sake. As boring as could be."

Luisa crossed her flabby arms over her chest. "Signor Clausnitzer was a saint," she insisted, "a saint, I tell you."

"We'll return to the subject of blackmail in a moment," Rita said. "In any case, whatever Hans Clausnitzer's thoughts, he went to breakfast and played the role of the proud, congenial host. When he gets wind that there's going to be a bake-off between me and his cook, whom his inflated ego believes to be the best cook in Tuscany, he's so confident that his cook will win that he wagers his beloved kouros statue"—Rita couldn't help from smiling at the memory of her victory—"which he loses. Then, after breakfast, Hans goes to his warehouse. A woman soon arrives. In excellent English, but with a slight Italian accent, she demands fifty thousand euros. And then Hans says to the blackmailer: 'You once wanted more from me than money.' And the woman replies, 'Look how that turned out,' and he says, 'Better than you realize.'"

"*Better than you realize*," Rita repeated slowly. "At the time I didn't understand what he meant, but in light of later events...."

Rita looked pointedly at Giovanna. "What positive thing—what secret—could come out of an affair? A child. A child that the blackmailer herself might not have known Hans fathered. Perhaps the blackmailer wondered, even suspected, but she didn't know for sure. Or maybe she did know, but she didn't know until that very moment that *he* knew...."

Diana laughed. She endeavored to make it light and airy, the tinkling little laugh of a bored socialite told a *bon mot*, but for once, her laugh had a bit of an edge. "And just what would I blackmail Hans over? That man was an open book. As I said, boring in the extreme. All work and no play."

"Then perhaps," Rita said, "you were blackmailing him over work."

"Don't be absurd. Our professional rivalry was well known. There was nothing hidden about it."

"Ah, but archaeology is only one of your jobs, isn't it? You're also a gallery owner in Switzerland. The kind of gallery owner who might come into contact with clients who are very rich, who prize discretion and privacy—and who may be a little unscrupulous. So you might be privy to a request to acquire priceless black-market antiquities, you might hear rumors about this illegal trade. You might even be asked by a client to authenticate something that came into his hands illegally, and then you might begin to suspect the provenance of these items. Which would give you the perfect opportunity to blackmail Hans, who values his professional reputation above all else and who, fortunately for you—the owner of a castle in need of five hundred thousand euros of repairs—is also fabulously wealthy."

Giovanna frowned. "But Hans would never do that. He would have wanted every last one of these treasures in a museum."

"Under normal circumstances," Rita said, "I might agree. But what if Hans was being blackmailed to traffic in antiquities?"

There was a chorus of gasps.

"There was a second blackmailer?" Alessandro exclaimed.

Rita nodded gravely. "But let us return to the identity of the second blackmailer later. So, where was I? Oh, yes, the warehouse. A second woman then arrives at the warehouse and speaks to Hans in German."

"German?" Giovanna repeated, dumbfounded. "There's no one here who speaks German."

"*Vedete?*" Diana smiled reassuringly at everyone and patted Giovanna's hand. "The murderer is not a wedding guest at all. It's some crazy German woman."

"Probably his ex-wife," Luisa growled. "A *strega* who never knew how good she had it—until he was gone."

Rita shook her head. "The carabinieri tell me his ex-wife has been in a spa in Baden-Baden this whole time. No, I'm actually quite sure that someone on this terrace—one of you—speaks German fluently."

Rita treated herself to a second *cornetti* smeared with apricot jam and freshly-churned butter so soft it resembled clotted cream before resuming her story. "Now, around six p.m. the night before he died, Hans went to Volterra to visit some friends, Anna Maria Contadini and Roberto Capra. But this was no mere social call; the purpose was to have them witness a new will—a new will with two important changes: one, leaving most of his estate to Giovanna, whom he had recently learned was his daughter through a DNA test; and two, leaving a substantial portion of his family's company to Tiffany."

"But why Tiffany?" Rose asked.

"Why Tiffany? Who was the woman speaking German with Hans in the warehouse? And who was the second blackmailer, and how did he or she come to possess information so compromising Hans was willing to pay for his silence? The three most perplexing questions in this case are all related, because Tiffany—like so many people connected to this case—is not at all who she seems to be. Tiffany presents herself as a thrice-married, low-class, crass, uneducated gold-digger. Thrice-married? Yes. From a poor background? Yes. But everything else you think you knew about Tiffany is wrong. In fact, Tiffany is cunning, brilliant, and multilingual. She plays the long game. She didn't get close to Hans because she was interested in archaeology, but because she wanted justice—justice for her aunt Elke."

Rita thought about the photo of the little moon-faced girl that Rose had found in Tiffany's luggage and shot them a grim, tight-lipped smile. "Elke, you see, was born in 1932 in Germany and had Down Syndrome—"

Sal's jaw dropped. "Tiffany's German? Tiffany *speaks* German?"

Rita nodded. "You yourself gave me the idea, *caro*. You pointed out that, at the banquet, Hans was speaking to Tiffany in German. You thought it was the wine talking—that Hans was so drunk he forgot Tiffany couldn't speak German. But what if...she could? What if she was the woman he was speaking to in German? What if there was some link between the two of them that went way back? And if that link was behind Hans suddenly changing his will to appoint Tiffany to his company's board of directors? And what if whatever Hans and Tiffany has agreed to was linked to his declaration of freedom at the banquet? What if he'd finally decided to come clean about something in his past or his family's past?"

Rita looked at Tiffany expectantly, waiting for her to confirm all of this. When she didn't, Rita said, "Does anyone know the source of Hans' wealth? Anyone besides Tiffany and Running Bear, that is?"

Eleven heads shook no. "Hans," she said slowly, "is the scion of the Von Bremerhaven fortune, the company that manufactured the poison gas the Nazis first used to murder handicapped children like Tiffany's aunt Elke, then millions of political prisoners, Gypsies, and Jews. So Tiffany resolved to get close to Hans to work on his conscience little by little until eventually he agreed to a public apology for the Von Bremerhaven's role in the Holocaust, appoint Tiffany to the board as an activist shareholder, and donate the firm's profits to charity. But the Von Bremerhaven's company also has a subsidiary, Hoffman-Engel, a mining conglomerate that invested heavily in the American Southwest. And this subsidiary cheated Running Bear's grandmother out of her mineral rights, leaving her destitute."

All eyes swiveled towards Running Bear.

"But Running Bear," Rita said, "is even more clever than his employer. He knew about the connection between Hans and the mining company, and between Hans and Tiffany. He knew Tiffany preferred personal assistants with, shall we say, athletic physiques, and he wormed his way into a position with Tiffany to get close to Hans. And then he hits the jackpot: through Tiffany he learns of Hans' family's dark and shameful past. But unlike Tiffany, he doesn't want to work on Hans' conscience; he wants revenge. Revenge for all the white people—Europeans, Germans in particular—who storm through his reservation as if it's a zoo, who traffic in the artifacts of his ancestors. Revenge for the fact that his grandfather, after being treated as a second-class citizen by the country that he so valiantly served as a Navajo Code Talker, was killed in a Nazi attack, dying before he could receive the recognition he deserved. And, most of all revenge, for the role of the Von Bremerhavens in cheating his grandmother out of the family's mineral rights, leaving them impoverished."

"That's a very good story," Running Bear sneered, "but you have no proof whatsoever."

"No? There is a shady antiquities dealer in Volterra who—once the carabinieri are done with him—will be willing to testify that you posed as an Arab or Indian middleman for black-market Etruscan antiquities. The carabinieri will find in your luggage the strip of cloth you used to fashion a turban. And I will testify that I saw you trying to break into Hans' laptop."

"So? Maybe I wanted to read his article for *Archaeology Today*. And that so-called middleman could be anyone," Running Bear scoffed. "Italians think all brown-skinned people look alike." He shook his head firmly, although the confidence in this gesture was not matched in his voice. "The charges will never stick."

Commissario Zingaretti reached out and snapped handcuffs on Running Bear. "We'll see about that," he said in English. Then he winked at Rita. "Signora Calabrese will make a very compelling witness."

Tiffany began to clap, slowly at first, then faster. "*Brava, Rita, brava.*" She spoke in Italian for the first time, shocking the Italians with her melodious intonation and pure, rounded vowels. "Oh, yes," she said modestly, "I speak Italian as well as German, Spanish, French, and Mandarin, too. Now, that last part about Running Bear, I didn't know." She shot Running Bear an admiring glance. "I see the student has become the master."

Then Tiffany lowered her voice and said, "But that still doesn't answer the question: who killed Hans?"

Chapter Thirty-Two

"Who killed Hans Clausnitzer? Well, to answer that, we have to continue the story." Rita helped herself to a second slice of tart and took a big gulp of hot chocolate. "At the banquet the night before Hans was murdered, Diana foretold his death."

"No more than anyone else's," Diana said tartly. "I said, 'he shall pass through the final red door when it is the gods' will.' That could be anytime at all."

"Is it just me, or does anyone else find the timing curious? You foretell his death and just like that"—Rita snapped her fingers—"almost immediately he dies."

"*Mia mamma*," Monica said tentatively, almost apologetically, "has a talent for divining the future. It's a gift, really."

"Our mamma doesn't do anything," her sister interjected. "She doesn't cause anything. Correlation isn't the same thing as causation—any scientist can tell you that."

Rita acknowledged their comments with a little smile. "I only hope that my children would leap to my defense like that. *Sei fortunata*, Diana, to have daughters like these." She raised her bowl of hot chocolate to

Diana in a sort of toast, and a little of the velvety dark brown liquid sloshed over the rim. "Now, where was I? Oh, yes—around eleven, Hans abruptly shuts off the music. As a result—and this becomes important later—everyone hears my sister Rose arranging to meet Paolo at two a.m."

She glanced over at Olivia, who colored; Paolo and Chiara each clutched one of her hands. Rose, however, looked completely unruffled and unconcerned.

"Then Hans," Rita continued, "gives a toast to Alessandro and Giovanna and drops a bombshell: he and Giovanna have proof—or so he claims—that the Etruscans originated on the Italian peninsula which, if true, would seriously damage the professional reputations of most of the other archaeologists present—Paolo, Chiara, Alessandro and, especially, the grande dame of the Anatolian origins thesis, Dr. Diana Rossi. The party breaks up and everyone goes back to their cottages, ostensibly to sleep, but really"—she raised her fork in the air and pointed at each of them in an accusatory manner—"to pursue their own hidden agendas. Very few of you actually slept that night. So, what were you all doing, and how did your paths cross Hans' that night? Alessandro and Giovanna quarreled; everyone seems to agree on that. Then Giovanna goes back to her cottage to sleep. For his part, Alessandro goes to see his brother, Padre Domenico, after his fight with Giovanna and then goes to knock on the door of the cottage in which his other brother Paolo is staying."

Alessandro opened his mouth as if to object, but then he frowned and abruptly shut it.

"You slipped up," Rita admonished him. "You started to say that you knocked on Paolo's door, but then you stopped yourself. Why? Because he wasn't in his cottage. So where was Paolo? Well, given that it was around two o'clock, he was probably on his way to an, er"—Rita searched for a polite word for it—"rendezvous with my sister which, as you will recall, everyone heard about at the banquet."

"Everyone but me," Luisa spat out. "I do not take part in such ungodly activities."

Ignoring Luisa's outburst, Rita said, "But what does he find when he gets to the pool? My sister in the arms of Hans—"

"—only because he dragged me into his arms," Rose insisted, glaring at her sister.

"And then," Rita said, "Paolo says a very interesting thing, '*Altra volta? Non ci credo.*'" Rita stopped and looked at each one in the eye. "Now, why would Paolo say '*altra volta*'—'again'—unless it had happened before? And that detail might not have mattered were it not for the fact that someone was listening: his daughter."

Olivia shrank back in her chair; all eyes were on her now. Chiara kept up her chain-smoking, grimly and methodically. She offered a cigarette to her ex-husband who accepted, as much to her surprise as to his own. Chiara then absentmindedly offered one to her daughter, too, before hastily snatching it back.

"So Olivia," Rita said, "hears this and thinks, 'who was my father with before Rose? Who did he break up with dramatically? Which one of his former paramours even knew Hans?' And she suddenly realizes the first woman to cheat on her father with Hans must have been...her own mother. So she storms off to confront her mother..."

In her mind's eye, Rita saw the tableau she had witnessed through the window of the cottage, which she'd mistaken for a tender heart-to-heart chat. How wrong she'd been!

"...and her mother lies to her and says, 'yes, it's all true—I had an affair with Hans.'"

Chiara looked up at Rita sharply. Paolo blinked, as if he'd just awoken from a dream. "Lies?" he repeated. "Did you say 'lies?'"

"Your wife—ex-wife, that is—never cheated on you with Hans. She never cheated on you at all. But since she'd lied to you all those years ago, she couldn't very well tell your daughter the truth now."

"But why lie?" Paolo cried.

"For your own good." Chiara blew a smoke ring and strove to sound casual, almost flippant, about her long-ago lie, but Rita noticed her fingers were shaking. "So you'd finally be free. So you'd have a better life without me."

"So you told me you had an affair..."

Paolo trailed off, unable to say the words out loud.

"...with the man," Chiara said, "you hated the most. And, for the record, Rose didn't succumb to Hans' charms either."

Chiara raised her water glass in Rose's direction as if giving a toast. Rose clearly had no idea how to react to an endorsement from a most unexpected quarter. She started to smile; then the smile turned to a frown.

"The scene in the pool was all our daughter's doing," Chiara said, pride briefly suffusing her features. But then she forced herself to compose them into a frown, turned to her daughter, and murmured in a disapproving voice, "Which was very naughty and for which she will be severely punished."

"But when Chiara tells her daughter that she had an affair with Hans," Rita said, "Olivia has no reason to believe her mother is lying. After all, plenty of people claim they're not having an affair when they clearly are, but who says they're having an affair when they're *not*? So Olivia goes in search of Hans, the man she holds responsible for the break-up of her parents' marriage. She finds him on the hillside. She confronts him; he denies the affair because, after all, it never happened, but she's enraged by what she perceives as his lies. So she snatches a rock and strikes him on the head."

Olivia had gone white as a sheet, as had her parents. A tear rolled down Chiara's cheek.

"This is all my fault," Chiara said in a hoarse whisper. She stood up and spun around to stare down a phalanx of carabinieri. She stabbed a finger to her chest. "My fault," she repeated, louder this time. "My lies drove my daughter to madness. I have failed as an academic, a mother, and as I wife. I screw up everything—absolutely everything. I couldn't even cover up a murder right."

Chiara's eyes were wild; she clutched at her wig and tore a clump of black hair before lunging at the carabinieri. They shrank back, terrified of the tiny woman before them. "Arrest me!" she exhorted them.

"Shackle me! Take me away. I'm a danger to my family. I'm a danger to everyone."

Paolo ran to her side and spoke in soothing, measured tones, as if comforting to a toddler. "*Tranquila, Chiara. Calmati...*"

His ex-wife turned towards him and caressed his stubbly cheek with one of her long, bony fingers. "You are too good for me, Paolo. You always were." In a calmer, steadier voice, she held out her wrists to the carabinieri. "*Per favore.*"

For a moment, the carabinieri were too stunned to react. But finally, a tall, burly policeman reached for his handcuffs.

Rita reached out and stopped him just as he was about to snap them around the petite woman's outstretched arms. "*Aspetti.* Just because Chiara thinks she covered up a murder committed by her daughter doesn't mean she actually did."

Chiara threw her hands up in the air. "What further proof do you need? I saw the corpse with my own eyes. I dragged the corpse with my own hands."

Rita was on the verge of asking her the obvious question: how had a cancer-riddled woman who weighed one hundred pounds soaking wet managed to drag a body by herself? But Rita already knew the answer: she hadn't. But she admired Chiara's single-minded focus on protecting her daughter and her ex-husband, and Rita figured Olivia would need at least one parent by her side.

Rita cocked her head. "You moved the body after the earthquake."

"*Sì, dopo il terremoto*," Chiara repeated. "I'm not sure what you're driving at."

"Simply that four hours elapsed between the time your daughter says she struck Hans and when you arrived at the scene."

Chiara took a long drag on her cigarette. "So?"

"So how do you know he died as a result of the blow administered by Olivia?"

"Well, she told me—"

"She told you—what? That she hit him in the head around three o'clock, he fell to the ground and was still, and she walked in circles for hours, half-convincing herself it was all a nightmare—a delusion. Then she went back to the site at nearly five o'clock and found her worst fears confirmed: he was dead."

"That's correct."

"That's what she told me, too, and that's what she told her uncle in the confessional."

Padre Domenico abruptly spit out a mouthful of hot chocolate, nearly choking.

Wagging a finger at the priest, Rita admonished him, "No sixteen-year-old girl gets up at five-thirty in the morning to pray unless she has something very heavy weighing on her conscience. And no one who wants to be Italy's answer to Father Brown suddenly lose interest in a murder that happened right under his nose unless he knew who the murderer was but, bound by his oath, could not reveal his or her identity."

Padre Domenico flushed and looked rather sheepish. "You *are* quite a good detective."

"Now," Rita went on, "Olivia said she struck Hans on his left temple, which is where a right-handed person would nearly always land a blow. And having eaten several meals with Olivia, I can say she is definitely right-handed."

Even as she said this, Rita was vividly remembering Olivia steadying her water glass with her left hand and squeezing the drops of poison with her right. But there was no need to mention that now.

Padre Domenico was staring intently at Rita now. "But the blood had pooled on the left side on Hans' body, meaning that after death he was lying on his left side, which is the position someone would likely be in if struck from the right..."

"...and a blow on the right side would be inflicted almost certainly by a left-handed person. And Hans had wounds on the right *and* left sides of his head."

Suddenly, every eye in the room was inspecting how their fellow suspects held their silverware or, in Chiara's and Paolo's case, smoked their cigarettes.

"Chiara's left-handed," Tiffany observed.

"True," Rita said, "but she would hardly kill Hans and let her daughter take the blame."

"Diana's left-handed too," Running Bear said, casting a pointed glances in the direction of Diana's left hand, which was raising a demitasse of espresso to her red-lacquered lips, "and she has any number of motives. She was upset that Hans wouldn't give in to her blackmail any longer. He was going to publish so-called proof that the Etruscans originated right here in Tuscany, blowing a hole in Diana's Anatolian origins thesis and harming her professional reputation. Maybe she even understood what he meant when he said that their affair had turned out better than he realized; maybe she knew that *he* knew that he was Giovanna's father and she feared he'd threaten her close relationship with Giovanna."

"And she did conveniently predict his death," Tiffany pointed out, "right before it happened." She switched to English. "All that 'red door of death' hooey. So that when he turned up deader than a doornail, these kooks"—she jerked a thumb at each of the archaeologists assembled—"would just shrug and say ' oh, well, I guess the gods smote him down. What's for breakfast?'"

Everyone swiveled to face Diana, who had lost none of her composure. She shrugged and smiled at them coquettishly. "It was the gods' will, as I said. Or someone carrying out the gods' will. But not me. I was lying naked in bed"—she smiled flirtatiously at a clutch of carabinieri—"asleep all night, completely unaware of all the bizarre goings-on."

All eyes turned back to Rita.

"Well," Rose snapped, tapping her foot impatiently, "was it Diana or not?"

Rita shook her head, but not firmly. "Not...directly. The person who administered the fatal blow was not a blackmailer, not an antiquities trafficker. Not even someone with an obvious motive to murder Hans. Someone so invisible that most of you never noticed this person was left-handed. Someone who was generally much more honest about his or her movements that night than the rest of you."

There was the satisfying click of handcuffs and then a collective gasp.

"Monica."

Chapter Thirty-Three

Rita had to raise her voice to be heard over the murmurs of disbelief. “Monica is left-handed,” she said. “I discovered that when I watched her prepare the truffles. Her account of her whereabouts the night of the murder had the virtue of being mostly true—which, as my children will attest from years of experience—is the best way to lie. Parts of your story are likely to be corroborated by the evidence, and you’re less likely to get tripped up by your lies. So what did Monica claim to have done that night? She claimed to have had a tryst with Running Bear in the vineyard, just a little off the path to the ruins where Hans’ body was found.”

A frown crossed Running Bear’s face.

“There was no such tryst, was there?” Rita said to Running Bear. “I could tell when I talked to you this morning. So Monica was alone, and she either lied to give herself an alibi or to give you one. Was she even in the vineyard at all? Yes. Because she shared a detail that was true—and whose significance she herself didn’t understand. She saw a small orange light like a burning cigarette and heard a woman and a man talking, both native Italian speakers. And she heard the woman clearly say, 'Let her go.' Now Monica told me she did not know the identities of these individuals, although she must have known I would guess it was Chiara."

Rose made a sour face. "And the man was Paolo?"

Rita nodded. "And the 'she' they referred to was Olivia, who had just found out that Hans—supposedly—was behind the break-up of her parents' marriage. Monica would only know about this conversation if she'd been in the vineyard around two-thirty, which places her near the scene of the murder."

Running Bear's eyes were blazing now. "Monica only lied to protect me, to give me an alibi," he shouted. "I was in the warehouse most of the night, trying to steal as many of the artifacts as I could...before Hans weaseled out of the arrangement. So Monica is left-handed and was in the vineyard. That proves nothing. And besides, why would Monica want Hans dead? She probably knew Hans least of all."

"The motive lies not," Rita said, "in how well she knew Hans, but in how well she knew each of you." Rita took a sip of hot chocolate. "On my first morning here, Padre Domenico said to me, 'If a crime is to occur here, it will be a crime of passion.' That prediction was nearly as close to the truth as Diana's supposed revelation from the gods. But it wasn't quite accurate. This crime was motivated not by passion, but by another type of love: agape."

Rita paused, the way she always did when lecturing her children, when she wanted them to arrive at her conclusion before she did. "Agape," Rita repeated, "which as all of you classicists surely know, is a self-sacrificing love that asks for nothing in return, the highest, purest form of love according to the ancient Greeks. Monica's love language, as my self-help-reading daughter would say, is obedience, to be the mirror to the 'two suns in her midst.'"

She shot a glance at Diana and Giovanna. Only Giovanna had the grace to blush.

Rita said, "Monica herself told me that she'd only said 'no' to her sister once: when she refused to give Giovanna their father's watch after his death."

Giovanna shifted uneasily in her chair. "I never asked Monica to kill Hans."

"No," Rita said slowly, "but did you need to? Did any of you need to?" She let that sink in for a moment. "Giovanna unwittingly gave me the key to the whole case when I asked her who would run the estate she'd just inherited and she replied that Monica 'would manage everything, just like she always does.' And then Giovanna said, 'She knows what you need before the thought has ever entered your head. She's very intuitive.'"

Giovanna hung her head.

"So what did Monica 'intuit' about the situation with Hans? Well, first of all, that her mother wanted him dead. Nothing could have been clearer than Diana literally saying 'the gods want him dead'—which, since Diana sees herself as the sun around which others revolve, almost a goddess like her namesake—essentially means, 'I want him dead.'

"So Monica realizes she must make a sacrifice—a human sacrifice, in Hans' case, and potentially a sacrifice of her own freedom—for the greater good. If Hans is dead, everyone will get their fairy-tale ending: her mother's professional reputation, as well as that of all the other archaeologists in the Anatolian origins camp, will stay intact, at least assuming her sister can be prevailed upon to squelch the offending article. The breach between Giovanna and Alessandro will be repaired. Giovanna will inherit Hans' estate, and turn the running of it over to Monica, her devoted factotum, who might even manage to convince Running Bear to stay and help her manage it. The income from the estate could help pay for the repairs on Diana's family castle. Long-suffering Luisa will even benefit, even if she gets less than she desires. Everyone will live happily ever after—well, everyone except Hans.

"So Monica goes down to the ruins, where she suspects she will find Hans. As if she needed another sign from the 'gods'"—Rita put 'gods' in air quotes and prayed not to be struck down that very moment—"Hans is already disoriented and weakened from the blow administered by Olivia. He's regained consciousness, but he's weak and bleeding. He pleads with her for help. In desperation, he lunges towards her, breaking the chain of the pocketwatch she had looped to her belt almost as a talisman, a good luck charm, a sign that her father is watching over her and granting his approval." Rita reached over and held up Monica's gold watch, which glinted in the sun. "No one wore a wristwatch in her grand-grandfather's day—only pocketwatches. But where's the chain? I'll tell you where one link of it is—clutched in Hans' curled hands, stiff with rigor mortis.

"Monica almost hesitates for a moment, but she convinces herself it's a mercy killing. After all, who knows what damage Olivia's earlier blow has inflicted? So she takes a shovel that's lying nearby, holds it in her left hand, hits him in the head—the right side of his head."

"Monica leaves him right where he falls, which is where Chiara finds him hours later, after the earthquake, before dragging him back into the tomb so it looks like he died in the earthquake."

For a moment, there was silence. Then Monica rose to her feet, dignified and poised despite being shackled. She was no longer meek or mousy. For the first time, there was a regal magnificence to her, backlit by the blazing sun, that reminded Rita of Diana. Monica touched the face of the watch that hung from her wrist by a gold band. Rita knew she was thinking of her father—that perhaps, to her warped way of thinking, he would be proud of her. She was the worker bee who'd sacrificed for the queen, the mirror who self-destructed before allowing the sun's image to be tarnished.

But at least one of the queen bees did not see it that way. Giovanna was staring at her sister as if she'd never really seen her before, tears streaming down her face. "Oh, Monica," she whispered, "what have you done?"

Then a sob burst forth from deep in Giovanna's throat. Her voice cracked, and when she spoke, it sounded like she had swallowed a million little shards of glass. "What have *we* done to *you*?"

Epilogue

"Well, I'd say everything has worked out just swell," Sal said as Giovanna and Alessandro swept past, illuminated by the strands of tiny white lights that stretched overhead. The bride was resplendent in an ivory-lace gown from Dolce and Gabbana, a crown of white roses in her hair; the groom was dashing in his tuxedo. Andrea Bocelli was belting out "O *Sole Mio*" from astride a white stallion while the guests quaffed *vin santo* and nibbled on slices of delicate *millefoglie* stuffed with pastry cream and topped with fresh raspberries and powdered sugar.

"Would you?" Rose grunted and crossed her arms over her elegantly beaded lavender sheath. From the neck down, Rose looked stunning, but the effect was ruined by her deep frown, furrowed brows, and lips so puckered she looked as though she'd been sucking on a lemon.

Chiara and Paolo twirled past them, only deepening Rose's fury. Chiara was nearly bald, save for a few odd clumps of hair, having tossed her chignon in the *rifiuti* with a cry of "No more pretense! No more lies!" But bald or not, Chiara had suddenly acquired a mesmerizing vitality. She danced song after song with her ex-husband, putting revelers half her age to shame. Rita suspected she was more alive than she'd ever been, even before the cancer.

"Yes," Sal said, pointedly ignoring his sister-in-law's sarcasm. "For one thing, I now have the ultimate bragging rights. I *used to* be married to the best cook and best detective in Acorn Hollow, but now I'm married to the best cook in all of Tuscany—and an internationally famous crime fighter! I mean, it's like being married to a cross between Wonderwoman and Giada di Laurentiis. Talk about a trophy wife! And Rita's even got the keys to the city. And free gelato for life."

Sal shot an admiring glance at the golden key that hung from Rita's neck. The mayor had presented her with it right before Andrea Bocelli burst onto the scene on his white horse. The owner of the local gelateria had been so moved by his brush with fame—Rita had slurped his *cioccolato fondente*, after all—that he had spontaneously offered her a lifetime supply of gelato as a token of appreciation.

"Thanks to my brilliant wife," Sal continued, "Hans' murderer is locked up, and a smuggling ring has been busted. Hans' will has been proven genuine, Giovanna will inherit the estate, Luisa and her wayward son have a great new gig managing it, and Diana will have enough to save her family's money pit of a castle. Tiffany is going to give Hans' millions to charity. Olivia will get a slap on the wrist and be out in no time—if she serves any time at all. Meanwhile, her parents will be spending the year making googly eyes at each other over cannoli at Vaccaro's in between Chiara being poked and prodded by mad scientists at Johns Hopkins and Paolo teaching trust fund babies how to use a trowel."

Rose looked confused, so Rita said, "Translation: Chiara's in a trial for an experimental cancer treatment—she's decided to live after all—and, thanks to Olivia, who apparently submitted an application for him without his knowledge, Paolo's got a new job as a visiting archaeology professor at Johns Hopkins."

Sal licked his lips, a dreamy look in his eye. Whenever they drove through Baltimore, they always veered off I-95 and made a beeline for Vaccaro's. Without a trace of irony, he murmured, "Gotta love Baltimore—the city of love."

Rose rolled her eyes and crossed her arms over her chest. "That's great, but what about me, huh? Where's my fairy-tale ending?"

"Oh, if I know you," Rita said, "you'll land on your feet—and in the path of an eligible bachelor. Two, in fact."

Rose eyed her sister suspiciously. "Two?"

"Two. Now, I wouldn't dream of meddling as you so uncharitably call it, because of course you hate that, but I just might have some interesting information...."

"Spill it."

"I have it on very good authority," Rita said primly (and by "good authority" she meant her son Vinnie), "that Annemarie Bonaducci sprained her ankle during Saturday's over-sixty pickleball tournament, which means she'll have to pull out of the Acorn Hollow Players' production of 'The Legend of Acorn Hollow.' Which means they are looking for a replacement to play Viviana Rossi, Joey Gambone's mistress."

Rose tried to look uninterested, but failed miserably. "Who's playing Joey?"

"A man really a bit like Paolo. Younger than you, of Italian heritage, very charming and cultured—honestly, too cultured for you though I'm sure you can rise to the occasion. An entrepreneur, a wealthy vineyard owner..."

Rose was practically salivating now. She knew just who Rita meant, and it was someone for whom she'd carried a torch for years. He'd always been attached, out of reach. But now that his fiancée was dead—murdered (with her killer nabbed by Rita, naturally)—Rose might finally have a chance with Morris County's most quasi-age-appropriate eligible bachelor.

"Orlando Rinaldi," Rose breathed, her eyes shining. "And who's eligible bachelor number two?"

Rita glanced over her sister's head, at the handsome middle-aged man coming towards them. His tuxedo was open at the neck, and his bowtie was rakishly undone. His five o'clock shadow glistened in the moonlight, and the chiseled contours of his lantern jaw were sharper than ever. Rita even thought she caught a glimpse of his six pack through his starched white shirt.

"Matteo," Rita said brightly, catching his eye and eliciting one of those spine-tingling grins. "Cousin of the famous Luca and every bit as handsome and charming—and much more single."

Earlier that day, during their poolside interview and photo shoot, Rita had discovered that Luca was every bit as charming as she had imagined but, regrettably, married.

Matteo came up beside an absolutely astonished Rose, kissed her hand, and said, "Your sister tells me you're a wonderful dancer. Shall we?"

Rose stood up and glanced from Matteo to her sister to Matteo again. "You know," she said, "I think I'm feeling better already."

Rita and Sal departed Villa Belvista the next morning. They travelled on to Rome, where they attended a papal audience in St. Peter's Square, ogled the Sistine Chapel, and descended into the catacombs. "So many nooks and crannies!" she enthused, prattling on about how this would be the perfect place to stash a modern-day murder victim, while their tour guide turned green.

They strolled down the Spanish Steps and past the Trevi Fountain, where, to Sal's disappointment, they did not spot anyone half so glamorous as Anita Ekberg. They gorged on gelato, Roman-style pizzas with crispy crusts, and heaping platefuls of *spaghetti alla carbonara*.

Then it was on to the shops of Milan (where, to Rita's shock and dismay, there was nothing sized for a woman of her Rubenesque proportions), the glass blowers of Murano, a moonlit gondola ride through the canals of Venice, and Florence.

On their last day, they toured the Uffizi. To Rita's secret dismay, the visitors were polite and orderly. They spoke in hushed tones, admiring the art with all the reverence it deserved. "Well," she sighed as she and Sal trudged towards the exit, "so much for your prediction about 'one crazed art lover bumping off another.' I didn't so much as foil a pickpocket."

"I saw someone take a photo with a flash. How's that for a crime?"

Rita laughed. "I guess that will have to do."

Sal gallantly took her arm and steered her out of the museum, down the steps, through the Piazza della Signoria and past its marble copy of David, and up elegant, cobblestoned Via dei Calzaiuoli to Piazza del Duomo. The setting sun cast a golden glow on the Duomo's medieval painted-lady façade, illuminating the rich greens and pinks; Brunelleschi's magnificent red dome glinted in the sunlight. A ray of light flitted between the austere stone buildings and shot through the center of the piazza, leaving the piazza's far recesses bathed deeply in shadow.

"There," Rita said, pointing across the piazza at a café. The tiny tables spilled out over the cobblestones; mustachioed businessmen in three-piece Armani suits drank Camparis, while elegant elderly woman sipped demitasses of espresso, watching the world go by. There were tourists, too, of course–Americans, fat, loud, and happy; serious-looking Germans, huddled over their guidebooks; and French tourists coiffed almost as elegantly as their Italian counterparts. "Wasn't that where we were supposed to meet?" Rita joked. "You know, after I witnessed a murder at the Uffizi and told the killer that it was his lucky day because I was on my second honeymoon and late for a date with, as you put it, my 'hot hubby'?"

"Yeah." Sal laughed. "I guess I owe you a coffee."

"And a tiramisu," Rita reminded him as they crossed the piazza. "Actually, make that two! These Italian portions are so tiny." Rita plopped down on a delicate wrought-iron chair that wobbled under her weight. "You know, Sal, in Acorn Hollow, I feel so Italian, but here, I feel awfully American."

"Really? So you're not going to ditch the *Morris County Gazette* to write for the *Corriere della Sera*? You're not going to leave the crime victims of the Hudson Valley in the lurch and try to worm your way into a spot on Commissario Zingaretti's art squad?"

She shook her head. "Nope." She leaned over the table and kissed him. "I guess home is where the heart is."

"With the kids?"

"With the kids." She winked. "And with you, Sal. Always with you."

Ripped from the Pages of Rita Calabrese's
"Top Secret" Recipe Book...

Blueberry Sour Cream Coffeecake

When you can't decide between blueberry muffins and coffeecake, choose this recipe! It's ideal as a mid-morning coffee break or paired with a frittata for brunch.

Cake:

8 tbsp. butter, plus more to grease the pan
1 cup packed brown sugar
2 eggs
2 cups all-purpose flour
1 tsp. baking soda
½ tsp. baking powder
½ tsp. cinnamon
½ tsp. salt
1 cup full-fat sour cream
1 tsp. pure vanilla extract
2 cups blueberries

Crumb topping:
½ cup packed brown sugar
½ cup flour
½ tsp. cinnamon
4 tbsp. butter, softened

Preheat the oven to 350 degrees Fahrenheit.

In a large bowl, cream the butter and sugar until light and fluffy. Add the eggs one at a time, beating after each addition. In a separate bowl, mix the flour, baking soda, baking powder, cinnamon, and salt until thoroughly combined.

Add the dry ingredients mixture to the large bowl with the butter/sugar/egg mixture in batches, alternating with the sour cream. Then add in the vanilla. Fold in the blueberries.

Pour the batter into a greased 13x9 inch glass baking dish.

Then, in a separate dish, combine the brown sugar, flour, and cinnamon for the crumb topping. Then cut in the butter with a pastry blender until it has the consistency of coarse crumbs. Sprinkle this topping onto the batter in the baking dish so that it covers the cake evenly.

Bake approximately 40 minutes until a toothpick comes out clean.

Serve with your favorite coffee beverage!

Farro Salad

I hate to admit it, but farro is one Italian ingredient with which I was not acquainted before my trip to Italy. It makes *pici* look like the new kid on the block—farro was cultivated in ancient Mesopotamia 20,000 years ago, and the Roman legions marched into battle with their bellies full of this high-protein, high-fiber grain. Maybe that's why they conquered most of the known world!

Sal may not be a fan of this whole grain, but I am. It reminds me of a slightly chewier, nuttier version of brown rice.

1 cup semi-pearled farro
1 medium cucumber
3 radishes
15 oz. can of chickpeas
¼ cup chopped parsley
1 tbsp. chopped chives
2 tbsp. chopped basil
1 tsp. chopped thyme
3 tbsp. extra virgin olive oil
2 tbsp. red wine vinegar
½ tsp. Dijon mustard
Sea salt, to taste
Fresh-cracked black pepper, to taste

Bring a pot of salted water to a boil. Add farro and cook 15-25 minutes until al dente. Drain farro and spread in a single layer on a sheet of waxed paper and let rest 20 minutes. (This avoids clumping and over-steaming.) While letting the farro rest, cut cucumber in half lengthwise and scoop out seeds. Then cut in half again so you have long quarter sections. Then cut into ¼" wide slices. Also halve radishes and then slice very thinly. Drain chickpeas. Coarsely chop parsley and basil; finely chop chives and thyme.

After farro has finished resting, pour into a very large bowl and add cucumbers, radishes, chickpeas, parsley, basil, chives, and thyme. Mix thoroughly to combine.

In a small bowl, combine olive oil, red wine vinegar, mustard, salt, and pepper. Pour over salad and mix to coat evenly.

Serve as a side to chicken or fish, or as the base of a grain bowl with roasted vegetables.

Pici with Tuscan Pesto

Pici goes way, way back. Some food historians say it "only" goes back to the fourteenth century, but others claim that the Etruscan "tomb of the leopards" features a 5th century B.C. fresco depicting a servant carrying a basket of *pici*. Today, *pici* is still very much a regional specialty. Rolled and elongated by hand, it varies in width from half the width of a finger to match-stick thin. If you can't find *pici*, substitute spaghetti.

This version comes with an unusual but delicious pesto. The anchovies give it a pleasant umami finish without imparting a fishy taste, while the eggs and cheese give it a rich, creamy texture.

2/3 cup fresh Italian parsley
1 1/3 cup fresh basil, plus a few extra leaves for garnish
12 anchovy filets
4 hard-boiled eggs
4 tbsp. olive oil
4 tbsp. grated Parmigiano Reggiano cheese
1 tbsp. minced garlic
Sea salt, to taste
Fresh-cracked black pepper, to taste
½ cup pasta water
8 oz. *pici* noodles
Butter for finishing, optional

In a food processor, finely chop and combine parsley, basil, anchovies, hard-boiled eggs, olive oil, cheese, and garlic. Add sea salt and fresh-cracked pepper to taste.

Boil *pici* noodles until al dente; reserve pasta water.

Thin pesto with pasta water, adding a little at a time, until you have a pasta sauce of the right consistency to easily toss with pasta.

In a sauté pan over medium heat, combine cooked *pici* noodles with pesto sauce and, if desired, a little butter, for 1-2 minutes until the noodles are evenly coated.

Plate and garnish with a couple of basil leaves.

Caponata

With its distinctive *agrodolce* (sweet-sour) flavor and origins in the 9th century Arab conquest of Sicily, this dish is often thought of as exclusively Sicilian. However, it is popular in Tuscany, Genoa, and other regions of Italy as well.

Sal's *nonna* made this with the traditional addition of celery, but I prefer it without. I've also switched from fried to roasted eggplant. But I've kept the olives, capers, and vinegar that give this dish its characteristic zing!

Serve with bruschetta as an appetizer; with marinated artichokes, roasted red peppers, and a selection of cheese and charcuterie on an *antipasti* platter; or as a *contorno* (side dish) to fish or chicken dishes.

1 large Italian eggplant
½ yellow onion, diced
1 ½ tsp. minced garlic
1 cup passata (tomato puree)
8 Sicilian green olives
1 tbsp. capers
1 tbsp. sugar
1 tsp. red wine vinegar
1 tsp. salt

Preheat oven to 400 degrees Fahrenheit. Cut eggplant lengthwise into quarters; then cut into roughly half-inch cubes. Spray 13x9 glass baking dish with cooking spray;

place eggplant cubes in dish and coat generously with olive oil. Roast for 20 minutes until fork tender.

Coat bottom of frying pan in olive oil and heat to medium heat. Combine roasted eggplant, chopped onions, garlic, passata, chopped olives, and capers. Evenly sprinkle salt and sugar over mixture and stir to combine. Add vinegar.

Serve warm or cold.

Grilled Peaches with Mascarpone

Make this recipe when peaches are in season. The contrast between the warm, soft-as-butter, syrupy-sweet peaches and the cool, creamy mascarpone is *meraviglioso*!

2 tbsp. butter
4 ripe yellow peaches
2 tbsp. brown sugar
½ tsp. cinnamon
4 tbsp. chopped pistachios
1/2 cup mascarpone
¼ cup honey

Peel, pit, and halve peaches. Combine brown sugar and cinnamon in a small bowl. Melt butter in frying pan. Place peach halves in frying pan and sprinkle with cinnamon sugar mixture. Cook 1-2 minutes, then turn and sprinkle the other side with cinnamon sugar.

In another small bowl, mix mascarpone and honey until thoroughly combined and shiny.

Plate peaches, spooning syrup from pan over them. Then top each peach with a large dollop of honeyed mascarpone. Sprinkle chopped pistachios on top.

Serve immediately.

Pear and Almond Tart

During the few short weeks when pears are in season, I make this indulgent tart every week. If you're stuck with unripe pears, you can poach them in sugar-water before using. Alternatively, you can use canned pears, although you must drain them well.

While my usual rule is that homemade ingredients are twice as good and should be used whenever possible, in this particular case I recommend using (gasp!) store-bought almond flour over your own ground almonds. Most food processors just can't grind almonds fine enough to avoid that gritty sand-between-your-teeth feeling.

For crust:

1/3 cup brown sugar
5 tbsp. butter, softened
¼ tsp. salt
2 tsp. vanilla extract
½ cup almond flour
1 cup all-purpose flour

For filling:
3 tbsp. butter, softened
¼ tsp. salt
2/3 cup brown sugar
2 tbsp. all-purpose flour
2 eggs
¾ cup almond flour
3 very ripe pears

For topping:
2 tbsp. butter, melted
2 tbsp. brown sugar
4 tbsp. sliced almonds

Preheat oven to 350 degrees Fahrenheit.

First make the crust. In a small bowl, cream butter and sugar; add vanilla and salt and mix to combine. Gradually add in almond and regular flour, stirring until a crumbly mixture forms.

Press the mixture into the bottom and up the sides of a round 9-inch tart pan; prick liberally with a fork. Place the tart pan in the freezer for 15 minutes, then bake until it's just beginning to brown on the edges, approximately 20 minutes. Remove from the oven.

While the crust is baking, make the filling. Beat together butter, salt, sugar, and flour. Beat in eggs, then almond flour. Spread the filling on the crust.

Peel, core, and quarter the pears. Then cut each quarter into thin lengthwise slices. Arrange pear slices in an overlapping circular pattern on top of the tart filling.

Brush the top of the tart with melted butter and then sprinkle on brown sugar and almond slices.

Bake 40-45 minutes until the top is a light golden brown.

Serve with whip cream or almond gelato if desired.

HISTORICAL NOTE

At the request of my friend Laurie Effron, I am including a historical note so that readers will not be left wondering whether the historical and archaeological references sprinkled through this book are founded in fact, or whether they are merely literary devices to manufacture intrigue and sow doubt where there is none.

Much is known about the Etruscans' customs, art, and technology, through a combination of archaeological finds and accounts by Roman chroniclers. The Romans, for example, were shocked by the Etruscans' custom of mixed-gender dining, remarking on how heavily the Etruscan women drank! The Romans were more than happy, however, to adopt the Etruscans' innovations in hygiene, including indoor plumbing and municipal sewage systems, and engineering, including the development of surveying instruments. The Romans may have borrowed gladiatorial games from their neighbors to the north. We know the Etruscans practiced divination using sheep livers, as Diana does in chapter thirteen, because archaeologists have found carefully labeled life-sized models that were clearly used as instructional materials for aspiring diviners. There is abundant evidence of their skill as expert bronze workers and alabaster carvers, from the bronze Mars of Todi statue to the countless gleaming white alabaster sarcophagi, typically of the deceased individual reclining as if at a banquet. I have seen several of these myself in the impressive Etruscan Museum in Volterra. We know a great deal about their funerary architecture and customs, since nearly every Etruscan site that has been discovered is a burial complex. Cerveteri and Tarquinia are two of the more impressive necropoli, and I encourage you to type these into your search engine to view some hauntingly beautiful images. The twin leopards and the red door of death described in chapter thirteen are from tombs in Tarquinia.

We have a fairly good idea of what the Etruscans ate, although no recipes survive so we do not know how they combined those foods. Chiara's description of the Etruscans' cuisine in chapter nine is accurate and gleaned from chemical analyses of Etruscan food vessels (amazingly, after twenty-five hundred years, scientists can still tell what was in them!), the Etruscans' own depictions of their banquets in frescoed tombs, and contemporaneous accounts of what the Romans ate (since they likely had access to all the same foods). Archaeologists Maureen Fant and Liz Bartman were skeptical that the tomb fresco in question actually shows *pici* pasta and believe that, at most, the Etruscans had a matzo-like cracker that they used to thicken soups, but some sources believe this to be *pici* and it suits my story, so I have included it.

The Etrsucans' origins, however, conveniently do remain shrouded in mystery. Many archaeologists believe the Etruscans are the descendants of the Villanovan culture that spread over what is roughly modern-day Tuscany (plus a small area around Bologna and the Veneto) from roughly 900 to 700 B.C. Evidence for the connection between the Villanovans and the Etruscans includes similarities in bronzework and pottery and, most intriguingly, a DNA study showing that a woman at a Villanovan burial site was related to a woman at a later Etruscan burial site. For me, however, that is hardly conclusive, as it would stand to reason that, even if the Etruscans migrated from Anatolia, they would mix with the local population. It also leaves open the possibility that the Villanovans migrated from Anatolia. I find the evidence for Anatolian origins—from the cattle DNA, to the histories written by the ancient Greeks, to the linguistic similarities to the Aegean islands—to be more persuasive. Everything Diana and Chiara explain to Rita about the Anatolian origins thesis is an accurate representation of modern scholarship on this issue (albeit one-sided, since they are partisans of this theory!).

Where the historical accuracy of my tale breaks down is, of course, when I stray into inventing evidence to support the Italian origins theory. While it is true that many sources refer to Emperor Claudius' history of the Etruscans, no one has ever located this; most likely, it has been lost to time. It is also true that Tacitus used Claudius' work as the source for many of his histories, two of which are stored at the Laurentian Library in Florence, but the story about the Holy Roman Emperor carting off Tacitus' copy to a Spanish monastery is pure fantasy. (Clement VII was a Medici, however; Charles V did sack Rome; and Charles V did end up retiring to a monastery in Spain!) Finally, as proof that truth can be stranger than fiction, the reference to the Zagreb mummy is actually true. A wealthy Croatian man on a nineteenth century "grand tour" brought a mummy back from Egypt, stored it in his attic for decades, and then, when he died, his heirs donated it to a museum in Zagreb. Years passed before someone said, "Hey, I wonder what this funny writing is on the linen bandages wrapped around the mummy?" And thus was discovered the only literary text written in Etruscan. (As to why an Egyptian embalmer was using an Etruscan manuscript for bandages, we can only assume that the ancient Egyptians also embraced the concept of "reduce, reuse, recycle.")

I hope you've enjoyed this little historical detour. If you are interested in learning more, I encourage you to visit the Etruscan collections at the Vatican Museum, Villa Giulia, or the Etruscan Museum in Volterra. Alternatively, watch one of the numerous YouTube videos that takes you inside an Etruscan tomb!

ABOUT THE AUTHOR

Maureen Klovers is the author of the Jeanne Pelletier mystery series set in Washington, D.C., as well as the memoir *In the Shadow of the Volcano: One Ex-Intelligence Official's Journey through Slums, Prisons, and Leper Colonies to the Heart of Latin America.* A confirmed Italophile, Maureen has studied Italian in Rome and enjoys testing Italian recipes (many of which make their way into Rita's cookbook!). She lives outside of Washington, D.C., with her husband, Kevin; her daughter, Kathleen; and their black Labrador Retriever, Nigel.

For more information on Maureen and her writing, or to schedule her for a book signing or book club event, please visit her Facebook author page.

AND IF YOU ENJOYED THIS BOOK...

Please post a review on amazon.com, goodreads.com, or your own blog! Thank you!

Made in the USA
Middletown, DE
11 April 2022

63653272R00189